Other People's Marriages

BOOKS BY KERRY FISHER

After the Lie
The Island Escape
The Silent Wife
The Secret Child
The Not So Perfect Mother
The Woman I Was Before
The Mother I Could Have Been
Another Woman's Child

KERRY FISHER AND PAT SOWA
Take My Hand

Kerry Fisher

Other People's Marriages

bookouture

Published by Bookouture in 2021

An imprint of Storyfire Ltd.
Carmelite House
50 Victoria Embankment
London EC4Y 0DZ

www.bookouture.com

ISBN: 978-1-80019-643-8
eBook ISBN: 978-1-80019-642-1

With thanks to the glorious women who knew me 'way back when' and whose friendships have carried me right through to today.

STEPH

5 MAY 2018

There's a special sort of melancholy that comes with big milestone birthdays. All that was, could have been and might now never be. The crippling clarity that if there's something you want to do, you'd better crack on because the sand is pouring through the egg timer at an alarming rate and now is still possible, but never is infinitely more likely.

And at my sixtieth birthday party with my husband of thirty-seven years, making a speech to a large gathering of my nearest and dearest, I could no longer silence the thought that had started as a low-level hum five years ago and was now reaching swarming bee proportions. If I said it out loud, the men in the room would clear their throats and mutter about needing a top-up. The women would fall into two categories: those for whom the big wide yonder without a husband bankrolling their handbags would be a wild west of peril and those who'd cheer and hop into the back of the pick-up truck in search of one final escapade.

I glanced at my closest friend, Teresa, who was standing next to me holding hands with her husband, Paul. They were both apparently fascinated by Mal's five hundred and fiftieth retelling of how his 'feisty' wife had come to his attention on New Year's Eve in Trafalgar Square in 1978. 'It has to be said that Steph's chat-up line was quite original: "Can you give me a leg-up so I can climb up here and take a photo?" I didn't realise that woman clinging to a monument, drunkenly waving her Kodak camera, would eventually become my wife.'

I remembered it clearly, despite the excess consumption of Oranjeboom lager that night. Mal had helped me up amidst much giggling and I'd hung on with one arm, snapping pictures of the Christmas trees and the crowds. He kept shouting at me to hold on tightly, but I'd felt invincible, daring and free, twenty years old, with life stretching ahead of me like a conveyor belt of adventures to choose from.

Thank God I hadn't known that forty years later, New Year's Eve would be a negotiation about who was bringing the cheeseboard and whether a cab at 12.30 a.m. was too late.

I imagined blurting out what I was thinking. Paul would furrow his brow as he often did when he wasn't sure whether I was joking. Teresa would most likely tell me I needed a good night's sleep or that it was the champagne talking and things would look different in the morning. Even after all these years of friendship, holding each other's heads above the surface through the rip tide of motherhood, I wasn't sure Teresa understood my inability to settle, to accept the status quo. Restlessness still stalked me and made me both reckless and brave. She'd just think my expectations were unreasonable, that I hadn't grown up.

Evie might have understood, despite her own baffling decisions. She'd be sixty next Thursday too. Evie. My gorgeous, glamorous friend. I still missed her.

I pulled my attention back to Mal, who was now making an overstretched analogy between my love of gardening and my alter ego as a Venus flytrap, snapping at anything that got too close.

Teresa nudged me. 'Aren't you making a speech?'

'Nah. I don't think people want loads of speeches, do they? More interested in eating and drinking.'

'They might not want them from anyone else, but the ones you make are hilarious. Highlight of my night.'

I loved Teresa for always finding me funny. Because I couldn't remember the last time I'd made my family laugh. I'd wanted to say a few words. I'd never bought into the idea that speeches were the domain of men, that brides should sit nicely with rosebuds woven into their hair while dads and husbands poked gentle fun at their ability to take out a lamp post while reversing. And for the last few decades I'd been resolute about it, had never questioned my right to stand up when and where I wanted, convinced that anything I had to say was just as valid as the blokes around me.

On my wedding day, my mother-in-law, Janet, had muttered about 'matrimonial tradition', but Mal had batted her off with 'Steph isn't your average wife, Mum'. That fact alone had led to her fascinator quivering with disapproval throughout the whole proceedings.

On my fortieth, I'd got quite carried away with my moment in the spotlight and started telling anecdotes about at least half of the people in the room. I'd still registered Evie's absence keenly, despite telling myself that I had so many other friends it didn't matter. But it did. I'd continued to nurture a hope that it wasn't too late, that we'd find our way back to each other somehow. I recalled surveying the room, all those faces turned towards me, with the realisation seeping in that some friends were great company, some were wonderful listeners but very few were friends of the deep heart, the ones whose lives you didn't just hear about but felt along with them. Evie was one of those. And as everyone clapped and did three cheers for me, I'd forced back the tears stinging my eyes.

Mal remarking on how quickly the last ten years had gone jolted me back to the present. Everyone laughed as he pointed to his lack of hair and said, 'The difference a decade makes.'

Teresa whispered, 'What you said at your fiftieth is even truer now. Look round the room.'

I smiled as I remembered making a joke that didn't go down too well about how my fortieth had been the kiss of death for at least half the couples at my party judging by all the new partners.

Mal told me the next morning that I'd been 'on the edge of rude'. I'd laughed. 'Can't wait to be sixty so I can fly over the clifftop of rude.' Honestly, if people couldn't take a joke, I'd save my Twiglets for someone who could.

Now, here I was, at my sixtieth, letting Mal do the talking for me. When I'd said I'd make a speech, he'd pulled a face. 'I don't think people want to listen to a lot of chat, do they? And you know what you're like when you've had a few drinks – a bit unwilling, shall we say, to relinquish the microphone…'

He'd turned to our son, Ben, for support, who'd said, 'Are speeches even necessary at a birthday party? People just want to get on with dancing and drinking, don't they? No offence, Mum, but they've probably heard all your stories before anyway.'

'No offence' was code for 'big bus of insulting observation coming through' disguised as gentle joshing in my family, but they managed to make me feel as though there'd be a collective eyeroll if I pinged my spoon on a glass. So I'd nodded and said, 'You're probably right, you thank everyone for coming then, Mal,' as though they'd relieved me of an onerous duty.

I tuned back in to Mal's words.

'I'd like to raise a toast to Steph, health – essential, of course…'

Teresa squeezed my hand and I felt the urge to cry.

'Wealth – not so much of that now Steph's retired and I'm the only breadwinner. Make the most of the champagne, everyone, we'll probably be bankrupt by the time she's seventy. I don't think the adjustment to being a kept woman is going to be as much of a challenge as I'd hoped.'

I felt the surge of fury that Mal was portraying me as a woman who'd piddled about for years contributing pin money to the family coffers and was now running amok with his credit card buying scented diffusers for the loo and witty little signs about my terrible cooking to hang around the kitchen. I had no doubt that all my guests would be surprised to know that over the years we'd kept entirely separate bank accounts and contributed equally to cover all our costs. Which hadn't changed since my retirement. If we really wanted to split hairs, it was my earning that had provided the lump sum for a deposit on a little flat we rented out in Redhill, which gave us a steady extra income.

I glanced around. If anyone else was outraged that Mal was claiming to be a long-suffering provider of fripperies for a lady who spent her time hoovering up chai almond lattes, they were disguising it well.

'And lastly, happiness – to us all!'

To the murmur of 'good health', I battled with my desire to spoil the evening by setting the record straight about our finances. Instead I pinned a smile on my face and sighed at the thought of how Mal's speech would inevitably form the basis of a huge row one day soon.

My daughter-in-law, Gemma, came up and interrupted that toxic train of thought. 'Are you having a good time?' she asked.

'Loving it.'

She clinked her glass against mine. 'To you. I can't believe how many friends you've got.'

'They're only here for the wine.'

'They love you. We all do.'

I tried not to dwell on the fact that the thing I loved most about my son was his wife. I'd decided long ago that whoever he married I was going to adore, but the daughter-in-law gods had not only smiled on me, but poured pots of molten gold in my direction. Gemma was smart, funny and, most importantly, skilled at handling my son. Despite thirty-six years of training with a mother who struggled to keep a thought to herself, Ben acted as though anything beyond a superficial exchange of which animals he'd treated at work was an intrusion. Even trying to pin him down to a family dinner was like trying to negotiate a date for the release of a hostage. Except, of course, when he needed childcare, then he had a lightning-fast memory for his diary.

Gemma put her head on one side. 'Are you all right?'

'Fine, just a bit hot.'

Burning hot, in fact, with the thought I'd been trying to deny for five years, to talk myself out of. As 'Brown-Eyed Girl' came on and everyone got up to dance, I had an image of all those heads swivelling, the eyebrows shooting up, the mouths dropping open. 'We were only at her sixtieth last week. Mal made a lovely toast to her. And now she's gone and left him!'

But leave him I would. If I lived for one more year or another thirty, it wasn't going to be to a backdrop of how the house insurance had gone up by nineteen pounds seventy and how he'd never really liked mushrooms every time I made a beef bourguignon. I wanted to feel like I was inhaling life in all its many colours, not sucking in just enough air through a Vicks-impregnated tissue. However I made it happen, my life would be totally different by the time my next birthday rolled around.

TERESA

January 1984

In a roomful of people, there's always one that everyone is drawn to. I never understood why, probably because I was never that person. My best guess was that the more someone bowled through life with a low-level challenge of 'like me, or don't like me, it's all the same as far as I'm concerned', the more those present were desperate for approval. I knew as soon as she walked into the fusty church hall for the mother and toddler coffee morning that all the other women would be dying to be her friend. She strode in, her long dark hair flying, swearing as the buggy wheels caught in the doorway. 'Morning! I'm Steph,' she said, waving to the circle of women. She nodded to the boy who was straining at the straps for release. 'This is Ben.'

As soon as he was freed, Ben immediately ran away from her to the toy garage, grabbing a couple of cars from the boy already there to a howl of protest. He lay with his cheek on the floor and started making loud revving noises. Steph glanced over briefly, shrugged and headed for the spare chair next to me. Despite the disapproving huff from the mother whose child had been dispossessed, she didn't feel obliged to referee over a toy Mini.

'What is it about having a baby that means you're stuck on hard plastic chairs for the rest of your life? Giving birth should be a free pass to sitting in goose down forever.' She turned to me and held out her hand. 'Steph.'

'I'm Teresa. Nice to meet you.'

'So how does it work here? Do the kids all disappear off and play while we drink coffee and moan about our husbands? Please tell me we don't have to take it in turns to play shops and pretend to eat plastic biscuits.'

I laughed. 'No, they have free play and we just chat. I think most of us use it as a way of getting out of the house on a rainy day, especially this time of the year.'

'So which one's your little one?'

'Ross, over there with the fuzzy-felt. He's just turned two.' I'd secretly hoped that bringing him here would equip him with an ease for making friends that I'd never mastered, but he showed no sign of wanting to join in with the other children, content in his own little world.

'Well done you for producing a child who can sit quietly and amuse himself. Ben was put on this earth to produce mayhem. Either that or I'm just a bad mother.'

'I should think every mother here thinks that at one time or another. I do, especially on the days I'm at work.'

Steph's eyes lit up. 'Oh thank goodness I'm not the only one who works. I always feel like a right old fraud at these things. This is the moment when I should say I'm here for all the benefits for Ben, but mainly it's to stop me going mad from being cooped up at home for the day. I've only come because I've got the next six Fridays off to use up my holiday from last year. What do you do?'

And with that, we launched into a discussion about my three days a week as a physiotherapist – 'Lucky you, bet you had all the tips of the trade to stop you wetting yourself for months after giving birth' – and her job working in the travel industry negotiating contracts with hotels abroad, which sounded unbelievably glamorous.

I immediately felt under pressure to make the slow process of easing life back into broken and injured limbs sound far more thrilling than it was, but she seemed genuinely interested: 'You must get to hear all sorts of stories from people while you're putting them through their paces. I suppose you can't tell me though. What a fascinating job.'

I nodded enigmatically but I'd never been any good at chit-chat, unlike some of my colleagues who knew everything about their patients except how to fix their torn rotator cuff. I preferred to work in silence, imagining in my mind's eye every ligament, every bit of cartilage under the skin. This woman with her leather trousers, bright orange blouse and serious shoulder pads would be my nightmare patient, diverting my energy to conversation. But before I could think of any amusing anecdotes, she leapt to her feet and said, 'I'll go and get us some coffee.'

I thanked her and watched her stride over to charm and chat to the helper who was guarding the refreshments as though some sleep-deprived mother might make off with more than her one allotted Club biscuit. Another woman joined her and soon they were laughing together and Steph put the coffees back down to gesticulate, hands flying about, both women a rapt audience. I'd given myself a pat on the back for managing a quick exchange of pleasantries with a couple of the quieter women after six weeks of coming here. Unlike Paul, I bet Steph's husband didn't pause on the threshold on his way to work, saying, 'Have a good time, you know you'll enjoy it when you get there. And Ross needs to get used to other children before he goes to school.'

The people I'd known at college like Steph, with a similar *joie de vivre* and sense of self, had inevitably drifted out of my reach, not lingering long enough to get to know me or for me to become confident enough to entertain them. It was incredible that I'd ever found a husband. Thankfully, a game of badminton and my expertise when Paul had twisted his ankle on court meant he'd seen some quality in me I'd yet to appreciate in myself.

Steph came whirling back over with her new friend. The other woman was tall with the sort of trousers that my mother would have said 'hung well' and a blouse that was just open enough to give a glimpse of a lacy black bra and the curve of decent-sized breasts. Breastfeeding had done for mine. Not much stuffing to begin with and now as desiccated as a dried-up riverbed in an August heatwave.

I dragged my attention away from her chest, briefly wondering if Paul also compared other women's breasts to my burst balloons.

'Teresa, this is Evie. She's one of those wonderful mothers who doesn't escape to work and puts me to shame. That's her little boy, Isaac, on the tractor.'

From anyone else, the comment could have sounded barbed or facetious, but Steph delivered it in a way that Evie just rolled her eyes and said, 'Wonderful? I don't think so. You probably enjoy your job more than I enjoyed mine in the underwear department of John Lewis. There's only so many times you can find an angle on lingerie for Valentine's Day that doesn't involve red knickers. And my husband doesn't want me to work so…' She pulled a face as though she was admitting an embarrassing truth.

Steph smiled. 'Your husband doesn't want you to work? And what do you want?'

My stomach tightened. I loved straight talking and straight asking in theory but found witnessing them excruciating. But Evie didn't snag herself on Steph's spikes. She shrugged good-naturedly. 'I haven't really given it much thought. I never really expected to go back to my job and I like being at home with Isaac.'

Steph shook her head. 'Hats off to you. I'm embarrassed by how liberated I feel when I have to go away on a work trip. In the office, they're all, "Do you want us to send someone else to Italy this time?" and I'm practically ordering the taxi to the airport before they've finished speaking.'

I was caught between admiration for Steph that she didn't worry about us judging her, feeling a bit sorry for Ben if she wasn't exaggerating and a weird sense of awkwardness, as though she was breaking the motherhood omertà by admitting what every mother must feel sometimes. At least I hoped they did. I didn't long to disappear to Italy for days on end, but there was no doubt that I loved sitting in the park over the road from work at lunchtime and having five minutes in my own head without having to answer 'Why?' or read about the truck that fell off the bridge again. I'd pretended to Paul I was fine about it, but every time I saw my colleague, Roger, lording it about in the senior physio position that I'd turned down because there was no option of working part-time, I felt a rush of jealousy. I'd inherited several of his patients, who told me that they had regained more function in a limb with me in four weeks than they had with him in months, which just rubbed salt in the wound.

Paul had hugged me and said, 'Your time will come when Ross is at school. It's not forever.' But sometimes when Roger was delegating the easy cases to me, rather than the ones that required an inventiveness, an experimental approach, I found myself wishing Ross's childhood away.

Before I could find the words to tread a neutral line between Steph's love of work and Evie's contentment at home, Linda, who ran the coffee morning, clapped her hands.

'Right, everyone ready for a little sing-song?'

Steph snorted. 'My singing should get all the babies screaming.'

Linda fluttered her hand dismissively. 'It's all about the joy of music. It's good for the soul. Right, if you'd like to call your children over, we'll give out some instruments.'

Ben wasn't having any of it. 'No. Not singing. Cars.'

Steph went over with a drum to tempt him, but he threw it on the floor and went back to hooking trailers onto lorries. She picked it up and sat back in her chair.

Linda stared at her expectantly. 'Steph, if you'd like to get – Ben, is it? – to sit down, we'll start with "Old Macdonald had a Farm".'

'He'll just start crying if I try to get between him and his lorries. Let's crack on without him,' she said, ignoring Linda's passive-aggressive raising of eyebrows. I already wanted to be Steph's new best friend. Perhaps her not giving a hoot about the opinions of an entire roomful of people would rub off on me. Maybe I'd stop jack-in-a-boxing Ross's jumper on and off twenty times a day in case anyone thought I was the sort of mother who didn't know how warm her son needed to be not to catch a cold.

Linda made sure everyone – without exception – had an instrument. 'No reason why the mummies shouldn't have some fun too.'

Next to me, I could feel Steph's eyes flickering with amusement. She whispered, 'If ever there was a good reason for going out to work...'

I ignored her but secretly I applauded her. Just yesterday I'd been justifying to my in-laws why I wanted to carry on with my physio work three days a week when Ross sneezed. The whole conversation stopped while my mother-in-law repeated 'Atishoo!' over and over again until I wanted to scream, 'The reason I like my job is because I have proper conversations with people who don't stop listening the second Ross sneezes or wets himself!'

'Come on, everyone, let's make some noise!' Linda shouted. 'Wonderful. Let's try "The Quartermaster's Store" next.' She was still trying to encourage Ben over.

Steph was growling away. 'For God's sake, there's plenty of time in life to toe the line. I mean, do you really have to start when you're two?'

She obviously hadn't grown up with a mother whose catchphrase was, 'What will that lady over there think when she sees you doing that?' I had though, so at twenty-nine, I was still worrying what 'that lady over there' might think, unlike Steph, who was belting out the song and hammering on the drum with such gusto that everyone in the room looked over. I stifled a giggle as Linda hovered between irritation that Steph wasn't taking it seriously and nodding approval that someone was prepared to join in properly.

I looked over to Evie, who had Isaac on her lap and was helping him hit the triangle with real pleasure on her face. I tried to hold on to the fact that socialising with other toddlers and thumping xylophones must be good for Ross's development, but a far greater part of me was wincing every time he put his fingers in his mouth. I kept surreptitiously wiping his hands with the wet flannel I kept in my bag in between singing 'He's Got the Whole World in His Hands' at a volume only someone with bionic hearing could pick up.

Thankfully, Linda drew the session to a close and said, 'Same time next week. If you could just give me a hand to tidy up the toys before you go...'

Evie and I immediately started picking things up and carrying them over to Linda, while Steph gingerly threw some building blocks into a crate. 'If you don't see me next week, it's because I've caught dysentery off the Stickle Bricks.'

We all walked out together and she nodded towards town. 'I live about five minutes down there. Do you fancy coming for a coffee at mine? And washing your hands? I reckon we'll have the antibodies to end all antibodies if we survive the septic tank of the church hall.'

I couldn't help but be drawn to Steph, her confidence in inviting us, two strangers, to her house. She obviously didn't weigh up all the pros and cons of looking desperate and needy, too pushy, too familiar, or any of the other hundred things that would have me saying goodbye at the corner instead of taking a risk and trying to make a friend. Nothing about Steph suggested she'd blush to the roots of her hair if we said, 'No thanks, another time though,' forever doomed never to have the courage to ask again.

I let Evie answer first, in case she didn't come and I had to maintain the conversation on my own for the next hour or so.

'I would have loved to, but my husband will be home for lunch soon.'

'Your husband comes home for lunch? Why don't you ring him from mine and tell him you won't be back?'

Evie vacillated. 'I could, I suppose.' She bent down and adjusted Isaac's hat. 'No, I'd better get back. He won't like it if we're not there.'

'Oh go on, live dangerously. Surely he can make his own cheese sandwich.'

'I'd feel a bit guilty about not turning up when he's expecting us.' I could tell Evie wanted to say yes but, like me, found it hard to be spontaneous. I hoped Steph would let her off the hook, not make her justify herself. 'Perhaps we could do it next week and I'll leave something out for him.'

Steph shook her head. 'For God's sake, never tell my husband what a good wife you are. He considers himself lucky if I don't use the last of the milk.'

Evie took her leave and walked down the road with Isaac, stopping to let him jump in the puddles.

Steph turned to me. I was expecting her to brush me off, to suggest we got together another time but she surprised me by saying, 'You're not going to force me to spend an afternoon trying to catch a shark on my magnetic fishing rod on my own, are you?'

I couldn't think of an excuse that wouldn't make me sound as though I was a 1940s housewife, and with Ross and Ben leaning over and talking toddler nonsense in their buggies, I nodded. I looked forward to telling Paul that I'd not only braved the church coffee morning but was potentially clutching the trophy of a new and interesting friend. The sort of woman my younger sister, Wendy, hung out with, that my mum would phone up and talk about her gadding about 'here, there and everywhere with those friends of hers, real live wires'. I couldn't ignore her disappointment that unlike my sister, I'd always been a bit of a loner. 'I mean Paul is a good man, but you need some friends and a bit of life of your own.' When I protested that I had a good job, she sniffed. 'You just need to let your hair down, Teresa. Stop being so serious.' As though I could wake up one morning, shake off my shyness and launch into a comedy routine for the postman. But she probably did have a point that, by the age of twenty-nine, I should have developed a bigger social circle rather than just clinging on to the few people who'd tolerated me through school and college. At the very least, I needed to find a few mums with kids the same age as Ross so he could learn alongside me. I didn't want him to spend his life feeling that everyone else had cracked the code to their place in the world but he'd scribbled his on the back of an envelope he'd lost before he'd memorised it.

As I dithered about, saying, 'I don't want to impose,' Steph waved me on. 'The boys can let off steam in the garden and we can eat biscuits while they're not watching. Let's go.'

I could hardly believe my luck that this vibrant and funny woman had sat next to me. She was just the sort of friend I needed in my life.

STEPH

7 May 2018

In the days following the party, I mooched around my house, staring at the gift bags that sat unopened on my dining table. I was clearly turning into an ungrateful mutt, but a scented candle and a few bath bombs weren't going to fix me. Just the thought of finding somewhere to put more crap made me want to sit in an armchair and eat peanut butter out of a jar. It was bad enough being stuck with the stuff I'd had a hand in choosing. I wasn't attached to any of it. The idea of walking out with Gladys, my black Labrador, free to start again in a quirky house with wooden floorboards and sloping ceilings rather than all these sofas Mal wouldn't let Gladys sleep on was liberating.

When we'd first met, I'd been the queen of rag rugs, beaded curtains and never knowingly passed up on a poppy print. Over time, Mal had convinced me that the gargoyles, the seashells, the ostrich feathers in jugs were tacky, that what the house needed was sharp edges, chrome, class. Somehow I'd let him convince me that my lovely salad bowl with the big cherries, my purple velvet cushions, my wicker hanging chair were aberrations of youth, things I'd grown out of now I was a proper middle-class adult.

Fake fur, feathers and sparkle were going to light up my next life, with some coloured glass lanterns, wind chimes and a few gnomes for good measure. I sealed my rebellion by rubbing in some hand cream and leaving big fat fingerprints on the chrome coffee pot Mal had bought me. I told him I didn't want one, but, as usual, Mal mistook what he liked for what I wanted. It wouldn't be travelling with me when I found my little cottage by the sea. I was going to take the Moroccan and Mediterranean to wherever I ended up, walls in orange, lime green, maybe the loo in turquoise. Mal would describe it as a 'child's splatter painting'. I couldn't wait. So much better than death by beige and mushroom.

I wandered out into the afternoon sunshine, with Gladys trotting behind me, marvelling that, for once, it wasn't raining on the bank holiday. I'd be sad to leave my garden. While I pulled up some weeds, I debated whether it was too petty to dig up my peony and take it with me, the garden equivalent of making off with the curtain poles.

My daughter-in-law, Gemma, letting herself in through the side gate with my two granddaughters, Dottie, three, and Nell, five, stopped me getting carried away with my plant pilfering. Right now, abandoning a few fuchsias was the least of my worries. I tried to imagine sitting down with Ben and Gemma and explaining that I was leaving Mal. I'd have to take the blame, of course, make sure I didn't badmouth Mal. But it would be worth it. Gemma would understand. With a stab of sorrow, I realised I didn't know how Ben would react. As always, I'd probably rely on Gemma to manage the fallout.

I bent down to scoop up Dottie and Nell. 'Hello, my darlings! Who's looking forward to a night with Grandma? Who wants to get the sandpit out?'

'Me! Me!' Dottie shouted, always the loudest, the most confident, despite being two years younger.

I unlocked the shed and dragged out the sandpit, which Mal insisted on putting away after every visit. The girls immediately started building a castle and Gemma and I took advantage of the five minutes of harmonious cooperation to catch up.

Mal wandered out, going over to the girls. 'You two troubles here again? Haven't you got your own home to go to?'

They laughed and Nell said, 'Yes, but we're staying with you, Granddad. Mummy is going away and Daddy is on call.'

Gemma glanced at me to check that it wasn't a problem.

I smiled reassuringly, wishing that for once Mal could rush out and say, 'How lovely to see you!'

He acknowledged Gemma, then turned to me. 'I suppose now it's nearly summer, you're going to be out here faffing about in the garden for hours on end.'

Mal was so good at delivering comments as though he was teasing, but over the years, I'd come to recognise the pattern of 'little jokes' that seemed innocuous but were basically a statement of disapproval.

Gemma was obviously much sharper than me and it hadn't taken her decades to cotton on. 'Think how much worse it could be, Mal. You could be spending a fortune on a gardener.'

His eyes flashed with annoyance. 'Barely see her for six months of the year. She's always in that greenhouse, singing to her tomatoes.'

'Can you imagine, though, what it would be like, if each time you went away for work or a conference, Steph was texting you every ten minutes because she was lonely and bored?' Gemma was so charming that even when she was sending someone to hell, she did it in such a way that they enjoyed the journey.

Mal acquiesced with a grunt that sounded like he was agreeing but left the listener in no doubt about how stupid he thought their opinion was. 'Talking of work, someone needs to crack on and keep the money rolling in.' He marched off back to the house.

Gemma raised her eyebrows. I loved her for sticking up for me, even though I was embarrassed that she felt the need to intervene on my behalf. Goodness knows what Gemma would think if I told her that I waited until Mal went out to scuttle off down to the garden centre. Instead of dithering about the perfect specimen for the shady corner by the fence, I'd do a quick smash and grab of anything I thought might survive. Not, as I told myself, because I needed to get on with other chores, but because I didn't want to have to justify to Mal why I needed to spend money on more plants. How could she understand that I'd let a man take control of me to such an extent that the height of my defiance was sneaking in a tray of pansies?

Gemma was smart enough to clock, however, that Mal resented anything that diverted my attention away from him, including her daughters. 'Thanks so much for having the girls. It was such bad luck that the childminder is on holiday this week. At least Nell's at school tomorrow. I'll get back as soon as I can. You know how these recruitment conferences run on.'

'I don't think it's just recruitment. Mal's technology conferences seem to go on forever. Though I'm surprised they expect you to travel there on a bank holiday,' I said.

Gemma glanced down. 'We have to be there for 8 a.m. tomorrow, so we all decided that we might as well go tonight and run through our presentation on HR trends. I hope the girls won't wear you out. Obviously Ben's around, but he's so tied up with work...'

I battled the surge of irritation that my son couldn't step up to the plate to look after his own kids. I'd vowed not to have that son. I'd been determined not to put another bloke into the world who thought he'd scaled the Eiger by putting on a wash or, God forbid, picking up some milk on the way home. Yet here we were. Gemma bringing the kids over to me because it would cause way too much disruption to Ben's daily routine. 'I'm sorry I didn't do a better job. I did try.'

Gemma laughed. 'He's got many other qualities.'

With a twinge of disloyalty, I thanked the universe for sending me this cheery, no-nonsense young woman who worked full-time, ran a home, was a brilliant mum and had chosen my son. She never seemed to mind the fact that Ben disappeared off on golfing weekends or stag dos with his friends but couldn't possibly defrost a lasagne and feed his family.

The first time the girls stayed with us while Gemma was away, Mal had said, 'Maybe she needs to have a career break until they go to school.'

He had soon climbed back into his box when I'd pointed out that Gemma earned nearly as much as Ben and carried the burden of all the domestic chores.

'He's bloody lucky to have her. He could have been married to someone who shopped for handbags all day. It's her salary that meant they could have the extension.'

Mal had nodded, but he still grumbled when he found the girls watching a DVD when he wanted to watch old episodes of *Morse* and looked as though his world was going to collapse if Dottie knocked over a glass of orange juice.

Gemma whispered to me, 'I think Nell's a bit anxious. She had a little cry about me going this morning. I hope she'll be okay.'

'Let's take them into the kitchen for a minute and I'll distract them with a biscuit while you disappear.'

We called the girls inside, where I went through the time-honoured routine of letting them choose which milkshake syrup they wanted and marvelling again at the power of the biscuit tin.

'I'd better get going, not quite sure how long it will take me to get to Gloucestershire. The traffic on the M4 is always so unpredictable,' Gemma said, pulling out her phone to check the time.

Dottie walked towards her clutching a lime milkshake. Before I managed to formulate the words, 'Sit down at the table', Dottie tripped over Gladys, who was lying in a strategic position in case Nell fumbled a biscuit or dropped a crumb in her direction. The whole glassful sloshed over Gemma.

'Your suit!'

Gemma had that look I recognised from when Ben was little and I thought I'd nailed everything I needed to do before leaving for an important meeting and then a last-minute drama meant I ended up rushing and arriving stressed and flustered.

I grabbed a cloth. 'Here.'

'I don't think I can resurrect this one without a dry clean. I'll smell like old yoghurt by tomorrow. I'll just nip out to the car. I packed another one, just in case…' With a calmness I would never have been able to summon in similar circumstances, she squeezed the tip of Dottie's nose. 'What did I say about wandering about with drinks?'

As Gemma headed outside, Dottie started crying and I gave her a hug. 'Never mind. Look, Gladys thinks it's her lucky day.' The dog was indeed slurping up the milkshake as though her ship had well and truly come in.

As I went to fetch the mop, Gemma's phone, balancing on the top of her handbag, beeped and, instinctively, I glanced down. A WhatsApp message flashed up.

Already at the hotel. Can't wait to see you (and be naughty!). Followed by a kiss-blowing emoji.

I stared at the sender. Gardener. Gardener? That didn't sound much like 'the leaf blower needs a service'. As far as I knew, Ben and Gemma didn't have a gardener. I felt my heart lurch, that unmistakeable chill that accompanies an ordinary day suddenly screeching off into unknown and unwanted territory.

I peered at the screen, trying to come up with an alternative explanation rather than the obvious one. My panic subsided as I realised that Gardener could be a surname rather than a code for someone else. Maybe it was a female colleague looking forward to escaping her own kids and letting her hair down with Gemma? I knew she liked a few drinks when she didn't have to get up at the crack of dawn.

Gemma came back in with her suitcase and snatched up her phone. She immediately asked, 'Do you mind if I pop upstairs and get changed?' Was she avoiding meeting my eye? Did she look guilty? I couldn't decide. She bent over Dottie, so I couldn't see her face. 'Try not to make any more mess for Grandma.'

Dottie giggled. 'Sorry, Mummy.'

Gemma swung her up into her arms and kissed the top of her head.

I stood, watching, my mind racing around, back to other times when Gemma had gone away for work. I sifted through my memory of her and Ben at my birthday party. No. Couldn't remember seeing them together, but then Gemma had spent most of the evening making sure the waitresses were keeping everyone topped up and the canapés rolling. I'd been so grateful to her for taking over so I could just relax and chat to everyone. I didn't remember anything odd. Could she really be having an affair? This woman who I'd come to regard as the daughter I'd never had? Who provided a communication bridge to my son, the man I loved dearly but never quite seemed to connect with. Without Gemma, I'd have no idea what was going on and would forever be reduced to begging for the bare bones of information about his life.

She disappeared upstairs to change. When she came back, I found myself studying her blouse, trying to work out whether she had some lacy camisole underneath. But what did that prove really? Maybe I'd turned into that old woman who was so dissatisfied with her own life that she saw deception and betrayal in everyone else's. But as much as I wanted to pretend there was no chance that Gemma would leave my son, take my granddaughters to live with another man, maybe cut me out of her life completely, every instinct was clustering around the fact that Ben took her for granted, we all did. And twenty-five years ahead of me, perhaps she'd decided not to play the game any more. Maybe this was just a fling, a sparkler in the dark sky of domestic drudgery that would burn itself out within weeks. My throat tightened with what it could mean for all of us if it turned out to be something more and Gemma cut loose.

She swung her handbag onto her shoulder. 'Right. I'd better go then. Got some emails to do before the rehearsal tonight.'

'Which hotel are you staying in again? I'd better write it down in case there's no mobile signal where you are.'

Gemma frowned. 'The staff are being put in two different hotels. Both are in Cheltenham. We haven't been told which one we're in yet. I'm just going straight to the presentation practice and then

I'll find out where I am. I'll text you when I know.' She paused as though she was about to say something else.

I thought I might cry or start screaming at her for being so stupid, but instead I said, 'Off you go. Have a good time.'

Anger coursed through me. Ben needed her. I needed her. I couldn't imagine a world without her, our conversations about Dottie and Nell, her phone calls to check how to cook a lamb shank, the wilted lavender she picked up at the garden centre and bought for me to resurrect. Tears blocked my throat. Ben did love her. I knew he did. Maybe he didn't show it in the way she needed. I'd have to have a word with him. But what could I say? 'When the name "Gardener" pings up on Gemma's phone, don't be fooled into thinking that it's a bloke coming to give a quote for trimming the laurel hedge'? Was I really going to blunder in sowing doubt about Gemma on the basis of one suspicious text?

As she cuddled the girls, I wanted to shout at her not to throw her life away on a dream, on a different man, who looked so tempting and fun and wonderful. I wanted to warn her that this new and sparkling version would eventually try to rein her in, change her, dampen down her spirit. He'd make sure that her exuberance, her joy, was tempered so that all her attention could focus on him.

I cleared my throat. 'We'll see you tomorrow evening.'

Gemma hugged me. 'Thank you. I don't know what I'd do without you.'

I waved her off. I was going to have to be vigilant. I couldn't let her leave my son. She'd been so good for him, made him less serious, more light-hearted. Kinder.

And as Dottie and Nell rushed over with a demand to get the tricycles out of the garage, the thought that had been hovering behind my shock shook itself free: I couldn't create a whole load of chaos of my own by walking out on Mal. Not if my son needed me to be a safe pair of hands steering his marriage carefully to shore.

EVIE

May 1988

Neil had been very lukewarm about us all celebrating Steph's and my thirtieth birthday with a picnic in the park watching a local band.

'Any band playing in our tinpot park is hardly going to be Simple Minds or U2.'

'Steph saw them play at one of her friends' birthdays and said they were brilliant. We just want to have a bit of a dance.'

Neil sneered. 'Steph probably still practises Michael Jackson's moonwalk in her bedroom.' He sighed. 'I had something a bit classier in mind. Dinner in London?'

I hated the way Neil always turned spending time with my friends into a competition. 'Why don't we do both? We could go up to London the next day, on Sunday. Or Friday if you want. Teresa's sister, Wendy, is coming down from Durham and the weather's been so lovely, we just thought it would be a nice opportunity to make the most of it. And it's ages since we've done anything like this. You used to love dancing with me.'

Finally, Neil acquiesced. 'I suppose it's your birthday, you get to choose.' He kissed me. 'You're not going to be off with your friends all night and leave me with Paul and Mal, are you?'

I pushed away the tightness in my stomach at the thought of having to sit out songs I loved to keep the peace. 'No, of course not. I will expect you to be up there with me showing them how it's done.'

Neil was placated, doing a little fancy footwork and singing Billy Joel's 'Uptown Girl' into my ear.

However, on the day, he was a bit snappy, quietly sandpapering the shine off the evening ahead, not helping me settle Isaac for the babysitter and still reading the paper at the kitchen table twenty minutes before we were leaving.

I didn't say anything, just carried on packing the picnic, pretending that everything was fine. 'What are you going to drink, red or white?'

Neil shrugged. 'You choose.'

I sighed and put in one of each and a bottle of champagne for good measure. Maybe if he had a drink, he might lighten up a bit. 'Right, are you ready? Steph and Teresa thought we should get there reasonably early.'

'I've still got to get changed.' He stomped upstairs. Fifteen minutes later, he came down, freshly aftershaved, in a blue shirt, and the tension in me eased as he picked up his coat and said, 'Let's rock and roll.'

I tried not to look like I was hurrying. Both Steph and Teresa were sticklers for timekeeping. 'I can't stand people who are late. So bloody rude, as though their time is more important than mine,' Steph said. Teresa liked what she called a 'wobble factor', though the chances of her forgetting anything and having to rush back or not checking the map properly before she went somewhere were negligible.

Neil was in the mood for smelling the roses, literally. He kept stopping to look at people's gardens, sniffing the wisteria. But as soon as we got to the park, my fear of being sandwiched into a tiny spot with Neil unable to stretch his legs out dissipated. Steph and Mal had claimed their pitch in a magnificent manner. With bunting hanging from four broom handles, and a mini-meadow of rugs, Steph was the epitome of 'doesn't do anything by halves'. She was barefoot in what looked like a red bridesmaid's dress, waving a bottle of champagne with joy flowing out of her.

'Happy birthday!' She threw her arms around me, then handed us plastic beakers of bubbly and waved us into her enclosure. 'Welcome to my castle!'

Teresa introduced us to Wendy and offered us some little ham and cheese tartlets – 'I made these in honour of your birthday, I hope they're all right. I'm not as good a cook as Steph.'

Paul squeezed her hand. 'They're delicious.'

Then the music started and before the first few bars had finished, Steph had jumped to her feet. 'Love this!'

We all turned to look at her. 'What is it?'

'Fairground Attraction! "Perfect". Come on, let's go down to the front and dance.'

Teresa shrank back against Paul. 'Not yet. Let's wait until someone else gets up. Wendy will come with you. She loves a good old boogie.'

But Wendy filled up her glass and said, 'Haven't had enough Dutch courage yet.'

'Evie?'

I pulled a face. 'I might just sing along here for a bit.'

Steph laughed. 'Cowards. Well, it's my birthday so I'm allowed to make a spectacle of myself.' And with that she was off, dancing right in front of the stage, singing her heart out and throwing herself about as though she was in her own living room with the curtains closed. The lead singer leant forwards and gave her a clap and, within minutes, a few more women were bopping about. She inserted herself into their circle, hands waving above her head, mirroring the woman opposite, joking with her as though they'd grown up together.

I tapped Mal. 'Are you going to join her?'

'Not me. I don't do dancing unless I'm very drunk. You go.'

I dithered between the desire to dance in the fading sunlight and the fear of making a fool of myself. I envied Steph, who didn't care at all, giggling as she got her timing wrong to 'Rockin' All Over the World' and clashed elbows with the stranger opposite.

Neil lost interest and started talking to Mal and Paul about the new sports centre opening up in town. I could see him getting irritated with Wendy chipping in with her tuppence-worth about how squash was a much better workout than swimming fifty lengths.

Eventually Steph returned, plonking herself down next to me, wiping her face with her hand. I couldn't relax because Wendy was trying to tell Neil how his whole exercise regime was flawed, which was blundering into dangerous territory, one of the many where he considered himself an expert.

Wendy nudged (nudged!) Neil – 'Dancing would be better for you than swimming.'

He ignored her.

She prodded him. 'Don't tell me you're one of those blokes who thinks women don't know anything about sport?'

He smiled. 'No, I'm one of those blokes who thinks *some* women don't know anything full stop,' he said to an open-mouthed Wendy, who immediately started canvassing Teresa and Paul's support.

I felt a flash of fear as I glanced over at Steph, who'd had plenty of run-ins with Neil on what she called 'the patriarchy' and wouldn't hesitate to join forces with Wendy. But today she just chuckled and swatted him.

'Give over. I'm not listening to that heresy on my birthday.' She leant towards Wendy. 'Don't take any notice. He's just winding you up. He knows Evie's brighter than he is.'

Thankfully, Neil took that as a joke and the rippling of animosity around the rugs smoothed out again. I loved Steph for her random and erroneous praise. She never looked down on me for being a housewife: 'Evie, you've got the hardest job of all. I'd go potty if I was at home with Ben all day.'

Steph swigged back her champagne, her eyes shining and delighted, as she topped up our drinks and unveiled her array of sandwiches. 'I've gone posh – smoked salmon with cream cheese and horseradish – or plain – cheese and pickle, ham and mustard.

For you, Evie, because I know it's your favourite, chicken mayonnaise and sweetcorn.'

I bit into the deliciousness that Steph handed me, touched by her ability to remember little details, the friendship equivalent of a love note left on the kitchen table. I never had to remind her that I took sugar in tea but not coffee. She even gave me a choice of mug to drink it out of. 'Nothing worse than tea out of the wrong mug.' She cared about things I'd never thought to have an opinion about, but everything about her added up to someone who was squeezing every last drop of joy out of life. And, unlike me, she didn't halt her search for pleasure or the next exciting activity just because Mal didn't find it convenient. 'He does what he wants to do. I'm a big believer in the fact that other people will fill the space that you don't reserve for yourself.' And, good as her word, the next week she'd be going on a familiarisation trip to some up-and-coming area in Portugal, and Teresa and I would trudge to school in the rain, watch Steph's mum pick up Ben and say, 'Lucky Steph.'

Neither of us ever discussed the growing view among the mums – that Steph going away too often was the cause of Ben's rowdiness and disruption in class. Me because I was ashamed of my envy of Steph's freedom and my eagerness to believe that there had to be a cost to it, and Teresa because she never had a bad word to say about anyone.

But tonight Steph was going to get her pound of flesh out of all of us. 'Right, it's our thirtieth birthday and we are dancing, Evie. Come on. Up you get. You can sit down at our sixtieth birthday party but not now.'

Neil seemed happy chatting, so I pulled Wendy and Teresa up, 'That's all of us, not just me.'

The wine was working its magic on Teresa as she stood reasonably willingly and allowed Steph to drag us to the front, where she danced wildly to Roy Orbison's 'You Got It'. I bopped about, avoiding looking over at Neil in case he wasn't talking to anyone, and concentrated on Teresa, who surprised me with her fluid rhythm.

Steph flung her arm round Teresa's shoulder and said, 'You're never sitting down again. Look at you go!'

After every song, Teresa paused as though she was about to head back to Paul, but Steph wasn't having any of it.

The lead singer noticed Steph preventing Teresa leaving and boomed over the mike, 'Come on, then, what song will keep her dancing?'

Quick as a flash, Steph shouted back, '"The Time of My Life".' And we spent the next few minutes twirling around, but thankfully not so shit-faced that we thought we could do the Patrick Swayze catch combo. Steph whispered to me, 'If I was single, I'd give it a shot with the lead singer.' Judging by the way he kept looking at her every time he sang, he was a black-shirted Johnny in his own mind, rather than a stocky bloke in a CND T-shirt relying solely on his charm and twinkly eyes.

I giggled, shocked, as Steph, for all her outspokenness and ease with the opposite sex, had never once given the impression that she was interested in anyone other than Mal.

The lead singer's eye for Steph wasn't lost on Wendy, who seemed to have entered into a competition to become top groupie, her movements getting more provocative and sensual by the minute. By the time the group launched into Marvin Gaye's 'Sexual Healing', Wendy's wiggling had come to Steph's notice and I couldn't look at her because I knew she'd make me laugh and I didn't want Teresa to think we were poking fun at her sister. To be fair, Wendy shared the same great sense of rhythm as Teresa, something that Steph lacked but made up for in enthusiasm.

The band played the opening bars of The Proclaimers' 'I'm Gonna Be (500 Miles)'. Wendy shook her head and said, 'I can't dance to this' and went back to our pitch. Before we knew it, the three of us were all promising to walk five hundred miles and fall down at each other's doors. I threw my head back, carried along with the wine, the sheer life-giving energy of singing at top volume under the stars with the two best friends I'd ever had in my life.

I had a little flashback to the me of a decade ago, the twenty-year-old who went clubbing, who ran up experimental outfits on my grandmother's sewing machine, who dreamt of sharing a flat in London with girls who'd grown up there, soaking up their knowledge about the history, the hidden corners, the trendy bars and quirky restaurants. Of becoming a fashion photographer. It was a long way from working in the lingerie section of a department store, but I had hope. And my gran's words – 'Someone's got to make it. Why not you?' But, of course, I hadn't met Neil then, hadn't expected that love would derail my dreams, when he carried in the advertising for our new collection of thermal vests and asked me out among the big granny knickers. I chided myself. Not derail. Reshape.

I sang louder, trying to recapture that heady feeling I used to have, that life stretched ahead with endless possibilities there for the taking, that decisions could be reversed, picked over, put right.

Spontaneously, as the song finished, we hugged each other, with Steph saying over and over again, 'I love my birthday. I love you two. We'll be friends when we're sixty, we will.'

And we nodded, though my mind couldn't compute a time when Isaac could be older than eighteen, a man rather than a six-year-old child who depended on me, let alone one who'd be thirty-six when I was sixty.

We staggered back to the blankets, collapsing onto the cushions.

'Where is everyone?' Steph asked Paul.

'Neil went to the loo and Mal and Wendy went to get chips from the burger van.'

'Typical Mal. Wouldn't matter what I put in a picnic, he can't resist a chip.'

Teresa leant back against Paul, who was lying gazing up at the sky. He sat up. 'Can I get a dance? They're playing our wedding song.'

She rose, her hand in his, Paul staring down at her and mouthing the words to 'Up Where We Belong' as though he was stepping right back to that day when they agreed to the adventure that was marriage. That odd envy I often experienced around my two best friends, a creeping sort of jealousy that made me ashamed of myself, surged up. Teresa and Paul seemed so uncomplicated, so straightforward in wanting what was best for each other, what was best for Ross, with none of the push-pull I felt: that being a good mother to Isaac immediately left a gap in being a good wife to Neil. Steph and Mal weren't lovey-dovey, but Steph's life was so rich. If anyone asked me, 'What've you been up to this week?' the most exciting thing might be the weather being good enough to hang the sheets on the line. Steph's week might have involved a flight to Mediterranean climes, an evening in London schmoozing with the great and good of the travel industry or a showdown with her boss, but all of it would be rolled up into a story to entertain us. And Mal never seemed to bat an eyelid, accepted Steph coming in after midnight, sometimes being out three nights on the trot. Neil did the Spanish inquisition if he came home at 5.30 p.m. and found the house empty.

I rolled towards Steph. 'What do you love the most – being a mother or a wife?'

She shuffled up onto her elbow and rested her chin on her hands. 'The truth? Now I know what marriage and motherhood entail, I wish I'd got married at thirty-three, not twenty-three. I thought we were really cool getting hitched young, having Ben almost straight away, while we had energy and drive. I thought we'd come out the other end in our mid-forties and still have all that life ahead.' She cast her hand around, picked up a glass and drained the dregs. 'To be honest—'

I saw Mal, Neil and Wendy approaching out of the corner of my eye. 'Sshhh, the others are coming back.'

Steph knelt and started picking up the rubbish. In a whisper, almost to herself, she said, 'I miss my old self. I miss being free.

Being selfish. Spending time, as long as I want, doing what I want, without feeling under pressure to leave, to stop enjoying myself because someone else needs me.'

I leant my head on her shoulder. 'So do I.'

Steph stuffed the remains of a sandwich into her mouth and said, 'The next fifty years are looking a bit long.'

Then just as quickly as that melancholy settled, we started laughing and laughing with little bits of bread flying out of Steph's mouth until Neil became irritable because we couldn't explain what was funny.

For once, I didn't care. With fifty years of marriage ahead, there was plenty of time to deal with his moods.

STEPH

10 May 2018

I always thought about Evie on my birthday. I tried not to. But we'd taken the fact that we shared a birthday on 10 May as a sign that we were meant to be friends. And just about every one of the eleven years we'd practically lived in each other's pockets, I'd invited her and Neil, with Teresa and Paul, and cooked up a storm. Evie would always bring me the perfect present – the pendant made out of an old sixpence, the gargoyle for my garden, the candle holder made from a reclaimed railway sleeper. I was never bothered about presents, but even I couldn't ignore the warm buzz of feeling that Evie really understood me. And now it was twenty-three years since I'd last seen her, that disastrous weekend in Norfolk that we'd planned as a birthday celebration, looked forward to and finished our friendship over.

Despite telling Mal I didn't want any fuss, that I'd had my sixtieth birthday party at the weekend and that was enough, the fact he didn't immediately look up from his computer when I walked into the kitchen made me consider cracking him over the head with the wooden chopping board. He was leaving for a work trip at eleven, so he only had to play the doting husband role for three hours. After I'd crashed about a bit emptying the dishwasher, he tore himself away from the screen.

'Tea for the birthday girl?'

'That would be lovely,' I said, wondering how despite having next to no expectations, even they weren't met.

Mal picked the wrong mug out of the cupboard.

'Could you make it in one of the red mugs, please?' I asked, refraining from adding, 'The only ones I have ever drunk tea out of in the last ten years.'

Only birthday etiquette, which forbade even the most disengaged husband snapping at me, allowed me to escape the 'it all tastes the same when you drink it' comment.

He handed me a pile of cards. 'Happy birthday.'

I flicked through them. Ben's addressed and, no doubt, bought by Gemma. Nell's painstaking 'grandma'. Teresa's careful script. My brain searched for Mum's whiskery writing, the Mrs with a full stop after it, before I remembered. But the writing on the turquoise envelope eclipsed that quick surge of loss. Evie's elegant calligraphy. A surge of adrenaline shot through me, straddling the line between fear and excitement. I turned it over. Nothing on the back. It was definitely a card though. I'd open it later when Mal wasn't buzzing about thinking he'd won husband of the year award for making tea in the right mug and producing a piece of toast with the butter covering a single square inch in the centre.

I ate it to keep the peace, staring at Evie's writing. It was definitely hers. No one could upgrade the outcome of a Bic biro like Evie. Why now? Was twenty-three years long enough to forgive me? Was it too long for me to forgive her? Had Teresa said something to her? Whenever I'd casually tried to winkle the tiniest piece of information out of Teresa about Evie, she'd acted as though Evie was in the witness protection programme. 'She doesn't want me to talk to you about her.'

I both admired Teresa for being able to keep a secret and could have shaken her out of frustration. But that was Teresa all over. She was like one of those money boxes that you had to smash open to retrieve the cash. I and, most probably, Evie were posting all our secrets into her, safe in the knowledge that she wasn't steaming into town, grabbing the first passing acquaintance and saying, 'Have you heard?' Which was great when I wanted to tell her about my shameful mothering moments and that time just after my fiftieth birthday when I hadn't behaved as well as I could have done. However, her tight-lippedness was utterly maddening when I had my scissors in the slot trying to manoeuvre out a little pointer on whether Evie was just letting the dust settle or actively torching the bridges that led back to me.

I wandered out to the garden with the card. What if I opened it and found an inane 'Happy birthday, Love Evie' to drive me insane speculating on how I should respond? Or, even worse, read something that would rip the plaster off the resentment and sorrow that had brewed for two decades? I'd learnt to live alongside this vintage wound, but it wouldn't take much to resurrect it into a far more present sadness.

I took a moment to admire my oriental poppies, toying with the idea of throwing the card away. Evie belonged to another life now. The one where I had all the answers. I'd been arrogant enough to think I knew everything in my thirties, but at sixty my certainty about my wisdom had shrivelled year by year. I ripped at the envelope, my heart beating as though I'd finally find out whether my sense of loss had lain unrequited all this time.

Dear Stephie,

Twenty-three years. And here we are. Sixty! Sixty! How did that happen? I didn't want to let another decade go past without getting in touch. So much to say but not sure if it's too late for you to hear it.

I've moved. I don't know if Teresa told you. I live in Whitstable now. On my own.

I don't know what else to write except I've missed you every day and I'd rather die making a fool of myself in front of someone who never wants to hear my name again than wondering whether we could have made up for lost time and had a right old laugh for however long we've got left. I'm aiming to live to a hundred.

How did we get to be mothers of boys who are thirty-six? Hope Ben is well and happy. And you and Mal are too.

Love Evie

PS Ring me on 07700 900267 if you want to take a gamble on the right old laugh.

I put my head in my hands, competing thoughts crashing through my mind. How long had Evie been living on her own? What had happened to Neil? And why hadn't Teresa broken her weird friendship vow of silence and filled me in? Over the years, often with the help of wine, I'd revisited again and again what had happened that day. Teresa would just sigh and say it was water under the bridge, but if I found out that Evie had been divorced for fifteen years and I'd been scratching about in my hairshirt for all of that time, I was going to be properly bent out of shape.

Teresa's name flashed up on my mobile. I tried to gather all the wisdom I'd gained in sixty years and not sound pissed off with her before I knew the facts. One thing I had learnt was that there was always plenty of time to be pissed off with people.

'Happy birthday! How does it feel to enter into your seventh decade?'

'Jesus, that's a cheery thought. Better than not moving into it, I suppose.'

'Did Mal surprise you?'

'In a good way, do you mean?'

Teresa tutted. But then she was the woman who was actually sorry for her husband when he had a cold rather than hissing unsympathetically under her breath about how women just soldier on and 'how lovely it must be to be able to do your dying duck in peace'.

I laughed. 'He remembered it was my birthday after about half an hour. I think he wore himself out asking me to book the caterers for the party.'

Teresa said, 'Poor Mal. He was very generous.'

There was no point in saying that I hadn't wanted caterers. I would have preferred to do it myself, rather than accept Mal's strict budget and forgo the asparagus wrapped in Parma ham in favour of a crappy cocktail sausage. That aside, I enjoyed experimenting. Preparing a feast for forty people was all part of the anticipation and fun. Mal had shaken his head. 'Don't be silly. It will be far too stressful. You want to be able to enjoy yourself.' I'd tried not to hear, 'I don't want to have to break off my conversation to top up people's glasses or have to give you a hand offering the canapés around.' Or 'If I pay a caterer, that means we can keep it down to six bites each and it stops you buying way too much food and splashing out on quails' eggs and smoked salmon and pomegranate molasses you'll only use once.'

If I said that out loud, Teresa, well, anybody, would just think I was spoilt and mean-spirited. And perhaps I was. But, somehow, what I wanted was always dressed up as me not knowing what was good for me and Mal stepping in to rescue me as though I was a sixty-year-old damsel dangling out of a castle window.

I changed the subject, deliberately making my voice light and cheery. 'Guess who sent me a birthday card? Actually, you won't guess. Evie.'

'Really? What did she say?' Teresa sounded a mixture of indignant and, without seeing her face, it was hard to tell, but if I was trotting down to Ladbroke's, I would have said 'annoyed'.

'Just that she was living on her own, she'd moved, times had changed and would I like to meet up?'

'Why would she get in touch now?' Teresa was definitely not in the 'you could get over your twenty-three-year blip with a coffee and a fat slice of chocolate cake' camp.

'You tell me. Have you seen her recently?' The straightforwardness of that question made me feel as though I was asking her when she last had sex with Paul.

'Last week. She didn't say she was going to contact you.'

It was tempting to reply that perhaps she didn't need Teresa's permission, but given that I was only on a fifty per cent hit rate of keeping my oldest friends, I said, 'Has she left Neil?'

'Yeah, a few years ago now.'

'And you didn't feel inclined to tell me?' I was struggling not to sound accusatory.

'I didn't think it was up to me. You had enough on your plate anyway. I thought you'd kind of moved on. Are you going to see her?'

'I haven't decided yet.' But, of course, I knew that the thing that had always got me into trouble, my curiosity, my inability to leave well alone, would be my undoing.

'Don't you think it would be better to let sleeping dogs lie after all these years?' It was less of a question and more of a statement.

'I don't know. It would be closure, if nothing else.'

Teresa did a funny little snort. 'Maybe. I'm not sure you could fix the friendship now though after so long.'

I wanted to be the judge of that. 'I might like to try. If it's a total disaster, we'll never speak to each other again. I've already proved I can survive that.'

At the time when we fell out, Teresa had been very keen for me to let the heat subside before I contacted Evie. But, of course, I'd rushed in, impatient, unable to understand that other people weren't like me – quick to flare but swift to forgive – and made things worse.

'Is it worth it at this stage of your life?'

'I'm not planning to drop dead in the next six months!' It was incredible how tempting it was to fall out with the friend who had stood by me over the one who hadn't.

'I didn't mean that. I meant you'd have to invest so much energy in it and I don't want to see you get hurt.'

I tried to push away the sensation that Teresa didn't want me to be friendly with Evie again. Initially I had hoped that she'd broker the peace between us, but she'd resolutely adopted a stance as the Switzerland of friendship disputes. Now, I was beginning to feel that she hadn't just remained neutral but instead had blocked off any paths home. I'd always assumed that Evie was the one who had been absolutely determined not to have any contact with me. I didn't want to believe my closest friend had been drip-feeding a 'You know what Steph is like, very black and white. I don't think you'll get the result you want', but I was disappointed that Teresa wasn't more 'Woo! Maybe we can all have a re-bonding weekend away!' But, to be fair, 'Woo!' wasn't really Teresa's USP. That had been more Evie. Teresa was better at the showing up with chicken soup, coming to my mum's funeral, making sure I didn't make a spectacle of myself when I'd celebrated the first signs of summer with more rosé than a menopausal woman could handle with elegance.

Thankfully, these days I was a bit more adept at letting my thoughts marinate rather than heaping everything straight onto the barbecue of accusation and watching the flames take hold. 'We'll see. Anyway, got some birthday laundry to do before Ben and Gemma come over for lunch.'

Teresa laughed, too enthusiastically, as though she was relieved to change the topic. 'Hasn't Mal given you the day off?'

'He's not even going to be here for most of it. "Unavoidable computer system installation", apparently. Perhaps you could send Paul round? I've got some duvet covers that need ironing.' It had always been a standing joke that he did all the ironing in their house. Although I paraded Paul as the gold-star standard of 'men who don't expect women to do all the boring chores', I still felt a quiver of something between disdain and incredulity when I walked into Teresa's kitchen and he was pressing tea towels. Shirts, blouses, linen trousers were a tick in the shared domestic drudgery box. Tea towels, underpants, handkerchiefs all strayed into deeply unattractive ironing territory.

We steered ourselves back onto neutral ground and Teresa rang off promising to come over for a drink the following week. I didn't pin her down to a day as there was only room in my head for one thought: Evie had left Neil. She'd actually done what I never thought she'd do. I wondered what the final catalyst was for that after all those years of sticking her head in the sand.

I watched a brimstone butterfly flit between the first sweet peas of the season. It probably had no idea that it would be dead within the year.

We all could be. I dialled Evie's number.

That voice. That deep tone, always sounding as though she was about to give in to a throaty chuckle. I expected to feel defensive, prickly, riddled with doubts about whether this was the right thing to do. But, instead, instinctive joy surged through me as her voice triggered a hundred happy memories.

I was laughing as I spoke. 'Happy birthday, stranger. Shall I sing?'

EVIE

Norfolk, 5 May 1995

As Neil carried the big box of wine out to the car, full of bottles of Taittinger and Amarone that we couldn't afford, I wished Steph had thought to consult with me first about what we might do for our thirty-seventh birthdays. Instead she'd bulldozed in with the idea of renting a house in Norfolk as an early celebration over the first May bank holiday in front of Neil – 'We've got to have a trial run for the big four-O in three years' time!'

Neil had immediately hitched himself to the party steam train. For me, that meant a weekend of doing a delicate balancing act between my alpha husband and full-on friend, not to mention Mal, who was capable of turning the tension up a notch or two himself. That was before we added Neil's lukewarm interest in Teresa and Paul to the mix: 'They're a bit beige, aren't they? You'd be hard-pressed to find an opinion between them.' And as every year went past, it became harder to persuade our three teenage sons to tolerate each other. They'd rubbed along all right over the years, but, at thirteen, were starting to assume that any offspring of their parents' friends were inevitably top-notch losers.

At the last minute, Teresa had insisted on bringing her sister, Wendy, because she was alone for the bank holiday while her husband-to-be was on his stag do. 'She gets nervous on her own overnight.'

Steph had caught my eye at that. She had very little patience with women who depended on men for anything and had failed to disguise her irritation. 'Surely she's got someone else she could stay with for a few nights? There's not really room for her as well.'

As usual, I'd been the peacemaker. 'The boys can all share and she could have the little box room.'

Steph had huffed and puffed, but when Teresa had started to say that she wouldn't come until the Saturday afternoon, Steph had acquiesced. As soon as Teresa was out of earshot, she said, 'Let's hope Wendy never has a family. Can you imagine how drippy her kid would be with a mother who won't stay in her own house by herself?'

I'd just laughed and said, 'It won't make any difference to us and I don't want Teresa to miss out on Friday night.'

So many competing dynamics and personalities, I felt weary thinking about it. However, the Friday of our long weekend had started in the promising way that had tricked me so many times in the past. Neil was all 'You take your time getting ready, make sure you've got everything you need. I'll wake up Isaac and go and fill up the car. On the road by twelve-thirty? Make the most of the weekend?'

I smiled at him. 'Sounds perfect.' I flicked away the thought that Neil's desire to be at the house the second we were allowed to check in was related to ensuring we had one of the two rooms with an en suite. Steph had shrugged and said we'd work it out when we got there, but the bathroom situation was stressing me out because we'd all paid the same and, in Neil's eyes, that meant that one of the others should have the rubbish room.

Unusually, though, we managed to get out of the house without Neil having a go at Isaac for 'sitting on his Nintendo and watching everyone else do all the work'. Isaac was also doing a reasonable job of pretending he was looking forward to the weekend, which saved us from Neil's diatribe about how he'd have loved an all-expenses-paid few days by the beach at his age. Plus a reminder that Isaac had been abroad nine times already and that Neil's first trip abroad was on a coach to Salou when he was twenty-five, just before he met me.

When we got to the house, sitting on a narrow lane just back from the beach, the gates to the drive were locked. Neil immediately started shouting, 'I'm blocking the road, get the gates open.' I couldn't recall Steph sending me the code for the padlock and started scrabbling about in the paperwork. He then turned on Isaac. 'Don't just sit there looking gormless. Help your mum get the padlock off!'

We both leapt out, with me still rootling in my handbag, when another car hooted at us to move out of the way. Isaac and I did what we always did and stood paralysed with indecision, not able to guess which course of action would inflame Neil more. On this occasion, it was not knowing whether to shut the car doors and let him drive off or try to open the gates before the man behind leant on his horn again. It could just have easily been not knowing whether to complain about bad service 'and show a bit of backbone' or to overlook it and 'not spoil every single evening by bellyaching about something'.

I ended up running over to the driver and apologising profusely, explaining that we'd just arrived. It did the trick and he smiled and said, 'Take your time.' With disproportionate relief, I spotted the combination in the corner of the booking form. I fumbled with the lock, stress making me all fingers and thumbs, and, eventually, Neil screeched into the drive, skidding on the gravel and giving the finger to the car behind. I avoided catching the driver's eye as he went past.

I made my way through to the back garden and found the key to the front door in the meter cupboard and let us in, feeling the tension roll off me. After a quick scoot around the farmhouse kitchen and the glorious oak-beamed sitting room, we ran upstairs. The second sitting room had a huge balcony with a view over the dunes and the beach beyond. My heart lifted. Steph had picked a winner. And as she would say, 'We deserve it! We've done thirteen years of bringing up kids, not to mention nearly fifteen of marriage. We're probably on borrowed time as far as persuading all the boys to come away with us, so we should celebrate our birthday in style.'

I quickly surveyed the rooms. We'd have to draw lots for them – everyone would want the big one at the front with the en suite and the panorama.

Isaac was all smiles. 'This is really cool. Can I go for a swim?'

'It's only the beginning of May. The water will still be really cold.'

'It'll be fine once I'm in.'

'Are you sure? Don't you want to wait for the other lads?' I didn't dare say out loud that I didn't like the idea of my boy, at thirteen, going into the sea on his own, even though he was a strong swimmer. Isaac would scowl as though I was the most pathetic mother on the planet and Neil would launch into a story about cycling twenty miles to the beach with just his friends and a bottle of pop from the age of ten.

Isaac shook his head. 'They can come down when they get here. There's a bodyboard on the patio. I'm going to give that a go.' Before I could object, he'd changed into his swim shorts and vaulted over the back wall, striding towards the dunes with an athleticism and enthusiasm for life that made my heart simultaneously sing and ache, the words, 'Don't go too deep' fading on my lips.

I didn't have long to ponder how my youthful living for the moment had morphed into a knot in my stomach about who'd be bagging the bidet and the balcony. Tyres crunched on the gravel and Steph came staggering in, carrying her ridiculously heavy Le Creuset pot, with a massive bag of potatoes balancing on top.

'Steph! Can't believe you brought that with you.'

'I can't cook in anything else.'

Neil came in behind her. 'Really?'

I sent up a quick prayer that Neil and Steph weren't going to bicker over every last thing, but, luckily, she was distracted looking around and contented herself with, 'If I'm in charge of the cooking, I can't be doing with some useless old saucepan with a thin bottom that everything sticks to.'

I stepped forward. 'Here, give that to me. Do you need help with anything else?'

Before Steph could answer, Ben appeared, empty-handed apart from a beach towel.

'See you're knocking yourself out carrying stuff in, Ben,' Neil said.

Steph frowned. 'He just wanted to have a quick look round, see if Isaac was here yet.'

Ben didn't acknowledge Neil.

I jumped in before Neil decided he would use the weekend to promote the parenting basics he felt Steph and Mal neglected. 'Hello, Ben. How are you? Lovely to see you again. Isaac's out bodyboarding if you want to go down to the beach.'

Neil poked in. 'Well, you'd better give your mum and dad a hand first.'

Steph waved Ben outside. 'We can manage. Go and make the most of the sunshine. It's forecast to rain tomorrow.'

Neil wasn't giving up. 'Surely you're not going to carry his suitcase in for him?'

That little burst of anxiety was flaring, but Steph was a good friend. She knew how to play Neil. She nudged his arm. 'Don't you remember being young? Wanting to dash into the sea as soon as you saw it? Come on, you're not that ancient. I bet you were a real lad about town in your teens.'

Just like that, the prickles of Neil's ego were smoothed and Ben went on his way, with Mal and Steph lugging in all their belongings.

Teresa and Paul arrived with Ross, followed by Wendy, who was already complaining about the house being in the middle of nowhere. Teresa kept casting irritable glances in her direction and had all the air of someone who saw the weekend as something to endure rather than enjoy.

I wanted to get the bedroom debate over and done with and was relieved when Steph said, 'Let's sort out where we're sleeping.'

Ross sensibly left that task to the grown-ups and disappeared off to the beach. Everyone was making the right noises of 'I don't mind where we are', but Paul was looking fidgety – Teresa had let slip that they thought the farmhouse was on the expensive side – and Neil would just assume that he was entitled to the best.

Steph made it easy. She turned to Teresa. 'As it's Evie's birthday, shall we let her have the big room at the front, then you and Paul take the other one with the en suite and Mal and I will have the little double? Wendy, you'll have to have the box room and the boys can all sleep on the pull-outs in the sitting room.'

Teresa nodded enthusiastically, looking thrilled that the decision had been reached without any awkwardness, though Wendy had the air of someone whose expectations went way beyond 'box room'.

Paul said, 'I'm not sure that's fair, it's your birthday too, Steph. We don't mind,' though his whole demeanour had relaxed.

But Steph was always about the good time, and as long as she could sit outdoors with wine and her favourite Cambozola cheese, I'd have struggled to think of anything material that really bothered her.

I suspected Steph thought that Paul was a bit soft – 'Goes along with anything' – but I found him a welcome breath of easy-goingness next to Mal and Neil, who often got caught in a competitive car conversation – 'I'm looking at buying a BMW/Mercedes/Audi' – where they both made out it wasn't about the money, as though tens of thousands of pounds were of no concern. They then went on to outdo each other on nerdy details, throwing out statements about torque, turbo lag and power-to-weight ratio, desperately hoping that the other would admit defeat and ask for clarification.

Mal didn't look as though he thought his share of the cottage rental was delivering, but Steph didn't placate him the way I did Neil. If it had just been me, I'd have argued that it wasn't fair on her but instead managed a feeble 'Are you sure?'

She winked at me. 'I'm going to be last to bed and first to rise... look at that lovely sea. I'm going in every single morning.'

Neil looked appalled. 'The water will be pretty chilly. I doubt even the boys will have braved it in the end.'

'Bracing, Neil, bracing. In fact, I'm going to have a quick dip now before the drinking commences.'

She disappeared into her room and, with great aplomb, whirled out in a bright green one-piece that was straining at the seams. She strode on through, grabbing a towel from a beach bag as she went.

'Big bus coming through. Service to all wives to make your husbands appreciate your lovely pert backsides and boobs. Come and join me, guys. Work up an appetite for my lamb casserole, which, though I say it myself, is the absolute business.'

Neil was staring at Steph with undisguised horror. I only had to suggest getting fish and chips for dinner for him to frown and say, 'Better not. It gets so hard to keep the pounds off as you get older.' I didn't dare look to see who was clocking Neil's 'Don't fancy yours much' distaste.

I watched from the terrace as Steph marched across to the dunes, stopping to stroke a cockapoo, chatting with its owner, who was clearly admiring her for braving the chilly sea. I was desperate to check that Isaac wasn't drifting halfway to Skegness by now. 'Do you want to go for a swim?' I asked Neil, knowing he wouldn't but might not sulk if I included him in the invitation.

He opened the fridge. 'You go. Me and Mal can sit and have a beer outside. You coming, Paul?'

Teresa agreed to join me – 'I might just paddle' – though we couldn't persuade Wendy. 'I don't do cold water. Just pools in the Mediterranean in August.'

Teresa and I changed into our swimsuits and went off to find the others. As we swished through the long grass, I felt a glorious sense of freedom, a bit like when my dad took me fishing as a kid and we'd just sit on the riverbank, watching the odd vole ripple the surface.

The sea was a long way out, but the boys and Steph had found a creek to swim in. Seeing Isaac diving and messing about with the others, sculling around on his board, made me think the weekend might be less of a drag for him than I'd dared hope.

In the meantime, Teresa and I stood on the water's edge, razor clams and stones digging into our feet as Steph shouted encouragement. 'You'll love it when you're in!'

Before I'd even made it to waist height, the boys raced over on their bodyboards to splash me, while I screamed, gasping for breath as the cold water washed over me. Eventually, Ben warning me not to tread on a dead crab he'd seen did the trick. Lifting my feet off the seabed seemed the lesser of two evils.

Within minutes, we were taking it in turns to share the boards, with the boys letting us hitch a ride, then upending us. After a while we all forgot to be cold and I felt daring and young and grateful for Steph, who always pushed me to do things I would never have done without her. And also for Teresa, who quietly went along with most of Steph's ideas, making me feel as though I wasn't the only one outside my comfort zone.

I stood for a moment, watching our boys, who'd had a lot of weekends away with each other, with varying degrees of success. It was incredible how the patterns established in toddlerhood still dominated today. Ben was taking charge as always, shouting instructions to Isaac about how he should hold his board to become more aerodynamic. To Ben's frustration, Isaac completely ignored him. Ross had already paddled away from them and was amusing himself in his own little world. I think it was a disappointment none of us voiced that they hadn't established their own close friendships with each other, but for this weekend at least, I hoped they'd manage to muddle along.

Teresa said, 'Funny to think that in five years' time, they'll be off to uni and we'll be able to go away whenever we want.'

'Can't wait,' Steph said. 'And half the time I'm going to leave Mal at home too. I'm not spending every holiday being dragged round museums and bloody churches while he bores the pants off me about how you can tell this church dates from such and such an era because it's got a round tower, yakety-yak. Nope. I will be taking me, and you two, to where the mojitos are calling my name. Corfu has got some fantastic beaches where we could properly chill out.'

'Sounds wonderful,' I said, already putting 'having the conversation with Neil about going to Corfu with Steph' onto my dread list.

Teresa said, 'Count me in. I'm hoping to get more of a full-time position at the clinic, so I might have a bit more money by then.'

Steph waved her hand. 'We'll sort something out. I'll probably be able to get a deal through work.'

I wished I could be more like her. Marching through life with this certainty that everything would come good in the end without worrying myself into a frazzle about the right thing to do or say. If I opened the door to the postman without my mascara on, I felt as though he'd be talking to my neighbours about me.

As we walked back up the beach, I said, 'Don't say anything about Corfu to Neil yet. You know what he's like.'

Steph sighed. 'Can't be left at home for a few days on his own? Damn good job he didn't marry me. I've been away for about a third of my married life. Only done about ten of the fifteen years. Goodness knows how Mal would have put up with me if I hadn't travelled so much.'

I shushed her as we climbed over the stile and approached the house.

She laughed at me and shouted up to the men on the balcony. 'Just telling Evie that our marriage has only survived because I've travelled so much.'

Mal raised his beer and said, 'I'll drink to that.'

As we climbed the spiral staircase that led to the terrace from outside, Neil caught my eye, a look of warning, reminding me not to let Steph's lack of filter contaminate me. He couldn't stand it when I talked about our marriage in public. On the odd occasion I let slip something to Steph or Teresa, even something so innocuous as 'Neil would be really cross if I cut my hair short', I felt a surge of panic in case they brought it up in front of him at a later date. Steph never worried a jot about what she said, which made her a funny and entertaining friend but a tripwire for my marital harmony.

Fortunately, the boys came bundling back, trailing into the house with wet sandy feet, demanding food and shouting about setting up the video recorder. Ben's voice carried up to us above the other two, with no small amount of swearing. I'd have been hopping up to tell Isaac off if I'd heard so much as a 'bloody', but Steph continued to talk against a backdrop of bad language as though she had selective hearing.

Eventually, Neil jumped to his feet and bellowed down the stairs, 'That's enough with the language, boys.' He turned to Steph and said, 'Honestly, you can't believe how these lads speak now. I'd have got such a clip round the ear if my parents had overheard me swearing.' Wendy was agreeing with him in the way that I might have done before I realised that child-rearing wasn't quite the simplistic 'manners in, manners out' that I'd envisaged before I had my own son.

I was pretty sure Steph hadn't missed the fact that Neil was criticising Ben and I wouldn't have put it past her to call Wendy out on her apparent parenting expertise, but she just said, 'I know, terrible, the youth of today.' She nudged Mal – 'Go in and help them sort out the telly' – and within minutes, Mal and Neil were competing over who could be the one to get it working.

Paul laughed. 'Think I'll stay out here with my beer. I'm not going to add value there. And two alpha males are enough for one small technological challenge.'

Steph disappeared inside and returned with a bottle of champagne and a tray of little salmon canapés on ryebread. 'Got given the fizz by work. Thought we'd have a little sip now before we go and have an explore of the village.'

We sat there, sharing the Pol Roger and talking about the kids and other trips away when they were little – 'Do you remember that time Ross slipped over on a rotting fish on the beach in Suffolk?' – and we laughed about how Paul had saved us all having to breathe in rancid cod for the whole weekend by stripping off and wading into the sea with him, even though it was October.

I raised my glass and said, 'Just in case I forget to say it later, you two, and your lovely husbands, have been the best addition to my life in the last thirty-seven years. Here's to you.'

Eventually, the sound of dinosaurs roaring across the landscape in *Jurassic Park* drifted out onto the terrace and Neil and Mal returned, joking about Steph giving them a task so she could keep the champagne for herself. I relaxed into the good-natured banter, one of those rare moments when I felt as though I was where I was meant to be in the world, doing what I was supposed to be doing, the distant alarms of my twin worries – something bad happening to Isaac and Neil losing it – muted.

Finally, Steph got to her feet. 'Before I peak too early, I want to go and have a look at the architectural salvage yard at the end of the village. There was a gorgeous gargoyle in the window. I love a bit of ugly.'

Neil nodded towards Mal. 'Hope you're not talking about your husband.'

Steph smiled tolerantly as though the joke was exactly what she'd expected from Neil.

He carried on. 'You're not taking Evie and Teresa with you, are you? We don't want to get home tomorrow to an empty bank account, do we, Paul? I know what you girls are like when you get together.'

Wendy giggled and said, 'Glenn has taken my credit card off me this weekend. He said the wedding was already putting us in a big enough debt without me being let loose on my own.'

Steph's disgusted expression made me itch to fetch my camera. I could do a whole compendium of the emotions that rippled across her face.

Steph leant forward and said, 'Good job I earn my own money and it's my bank account I'm emptying then. It's 1995, Neil. Not long until we tip into a brand-new century. Time to let go of Neil the Victorian and get with the whole Girl Power.'

Neil did that thin-lipped grimace that he did when someone had got the better of him. I'd already worked out that the noise travelled through the floorboards of the house. I hoped Neil wouldn't start foghorning about 'that old bra-burner' when we got to bed.

Thankfully, Wendy declined to join us on our foray to the village. 'Top up my tan for the big day.' I hoped Teresa didn't hear Steph mutter, 'Hope she burns her nose' as she walked downstairs.

Once out of the house, we all seemed to shake off our little irritations, liberated from family demands and relishing the change of scenery, a far cry from Surrey. We laughed and chatted as we meandered the mile and a half to Great Sedgeham. I breathed in the bitter tang of sea air and the scent of the wild hedgerows, alive with birdsong.

We pottered around the village, ambling in and out of the little shops selling driftwood sculptures and paintings of the sea in all of its many moods. Steph bought a vintage chamber pot – 'My spider plant will look lovely in that' – and a miniature oil painting that captured the big open Norfolk skies – 'I'm going to feel the wind on my face and freedom in my heart every time I look at that.'

We had coffee and Norfolk cider cake in the courtyard of the church, the late spring sun warming our pale arms, and started to relax into our holiday. We were an unlikely trio: Teresa, angular and alert as though she was always waiting for something unexpected to rush into the periphery of her vision. Steph, the total opposite, bowling through life as though she could change a tyre and still provide a tray of home-made cinnamon buns for the school bake sale without breaking a sweat. Me, I didn't want to think about what I'd become. Instead, I thanked my lucky stars that a church toddler group had made our paths intersect.

When we finally made our way back to the farmhouse, I couldn't help noticing I was the only one to seek out my husband immediately. I pretended it was because we were more in love than the other couples – 'Did you miss me?' – but really I wanted reassurance that I wasn't going to spend the rest of the day fluttering about teasing him out of a sulk. But, thankfully, Paul, Mal and Wendy had proved distraction enough and Neil was in a boozy good humour when we arrived.

The sunny afternoon melted into a mellow evening, which Paul and Teresa sensibly curtailed at a decent hour by reminding us that we were going on a birdwatching jaunt at the crack of sparrows the next morning.

Mal picked up the wine bottle. 'I, my friends, will need a surfeit of red wine to numb my brain to the boredom of tomorrow morning's search for the lesser spotted seagull, so I'm staying up for another little tipple. Anyone else joining me?'

I glanced at Steph to see if she was taking offence, but she just laughed and said, 'Don't come then. You'll be sorry when we see some super-rare bird that everyone will be talking about for years.'

I would have liked to stay up for another drink but knew that Neil would be expecting first-night-of-holiday sex. In any case, he was also approaching the tipping point of the evening, when rather than a witty raconteur, hitting the sweet spot with political observations and anecdotes about life in advertising, he was becoming a belligerent drunk. I took his hand, yawned and steered him off to bed, leaving Steph pouring herself a whisky and shouting, 'Lightweights! I'll still be up before the rest of you!' and Wendy holding her glass out for a top-up – 'As they say in France, "*un pour la route*"' – sounding like Del Boy from *Only Fools and Horses*. I could only imagine Steph's face. She had an inbuilt hatred of anyone butchering a foreign language.

Before I could worry about what Steph was thinking, I had to stop Neil moaning about the early start in the morning at the top of his voice. 'What person comes away on a weekend and makes everyone get up at 5.30 a.m.? Why does she get to dictate what we do?'

I didn't dare shush him as I knew he'd just raise his voice even more, so I started to take my clothes off to distract him. I spoke loudly enough that he wouldn't accuse me of whispering and turn nasty. 'But we do loads of things we wouldn't normally do because of her. They often turn out to be a really good laugh. I think we'll have a nice time. Even Isaac's quite keen on the idea.' I hated that beseeching note in my voice, that plea not to turn the weekend into a battleground. I just wanted to be a normal family, three people who could go away with friends for a weekend without me bending and stretching and smoothing to keep Neil sunny side up.

Thankfully, Neil's desire for sex triumphed over his grumpiness with Steph, and the next morning he was surprisingly conciliatory, swinging his legs out of bed with a mild, 'The things I do for you.'

I kissed his back, relieved that, for once, Neil was falling in line. I knew I would have ended up staying behind myself in case he was bored, or we were longer than we thought we'd be, or the others wanted to stop off for a bacon butty. Or, in fact, any number of scenarios that meant Neil would kick up a fuss because he'd 'been left twiddling his thumbs' and everyone would think I'd married an irrational loser.

Today, at least, I didn't have to face up to that.

TERESA

Norfolk, 6 May 1995

It was hard to believe anyone had slept through the boys thundering about getting ready for our birdwatching expedition, but there was no sign of Wendy. I knew I shouldn't care what the others thought, but as a late-addition guest, I wanted her to be super-enthusiastic as a payback for them allowing her to come.

I knocked gently at her door, then pushed it open.

Wendy greeted me with a grunt and snuggled further down into her bed, saying, 'I'll look at the sparrows in the garden.'

'Come on, it'll be fun. You'll be glad when you've done it.'

Wendy pulled the duvet higher. 'I've hardly had any sleep. I couldn't stop worrying about what Glenn was getting up to, what his mates had organised for him. I didn't drop off till about three. You go. I'll see you later.'

I could hear all the others in the sitting room, the smell of coffee wafting through, everyone joking about mistaking a seagull for an albatross. Steph's voice rang out. 'Where are Teresa and Wendy?'

I banged Wendy's door in a way that would have left her in no doubt that she'd annoyed me. Although by the time I'd walked across the landing to join the others, I was already relieved that I wouldn't have to see the look on Steph's face if we came across a rotting seal or rabbit skull, which would no doubt have sent Wendy off into a screeching fit.

'Sorry, Wendy's not coming.' I lowered my voice. 'Think she had a bit of a sleepless night stressing about what Glenn was doing on his stag do.'

Steph rolled her eyes. 'That doesn't bode well if she already doesn't trust him before they get married…'

I immediately felt defensive. 'It's not so much him, but his friends. They were teasing her about getting strippers in and it really got to her.'

Thankfully, the early hour stopped Steph treating us to her diatribe on how she never worried about Mal leaving her because if he didn't appreciate what he had, it was so much better that she found out before she wasted her life on the wrong man. 'Wendy can help Mal cook breakfast. He wouldn't get his lazy backside out of bed either. Think the red wine took its toll, though, of course, he was dressing it up as exhaustion from working too hard.'

Steph shrugged. 'Anyway, their loss. We'll all be experts on gannets and terns and they'll still only be able to spot a starling.'

I hoped her nonchalance wasn't relief because she didn't like my sister, but I suspected it was. Steph could be very unforgiving about women who didn't march through life with her purpose and confidence. It was still a mystery why she'd chosen me as a friend.

Steph swung her rucksack onto her shoulder. 'Right, let's go.'

We all trooped out behind her and once we were under the big open sky that Steph loved so much, all the petty concerns fogging my head faded away. After some initial groaning about 'having to get up for stupid birds', the boys were competing over who would see the most, the rarest, the best. Ross's words drifted back to me as he ran along the top of the dunes. 'Ben won't see any birds because he's too noisy. He'll frighten them all off.'

'I'll see the most because I'm the lightest and they won't hear me coming,' Isaac said.

Steph had handed everyone five different bird identification cards with twenty pounds for the winner, which had done a great job of motivating the teenagers. Not for the first time, I was in awe of Steph's ability to make everything so much fun, to go that extra mile to get everyone involved.

And in the dawn light, the world transformed into a magical place. As we walked along the boardwalk on the top of the dunes, we were rewarded with the sight of sandwich terns silhouetted against the brightening sky, hovering and diving for fish offshore. The white and black avocets were wading about in the mud and the boys were doing comedy quiet, creeping along, shushing each other so loudly that they startled the rabbits nibbling away in the morning light.

While the adults were becoming quietly competitive over who had correctly identified a spoonbill searching for fish in the shallows – Paul waving one of his cards in triumph: 'They're quite rare!' – the boys ran down to the edge of the creek, threw off their trainers and started paddling and squawking about the cold. Despite the early hour, I recognised it as a freeze-frame moment, the simple unadulterated pleasure of an adventure. Steph was responsible for so many of those.

Over the years she'd always elevated my off-the-cuff remarks about what would be a 'good laugh', what might be a nice thing to do 'one day' to an event in the diary, organised with home-made flapjacks and a flask of coffee or a bottle of fizz and some smoked salmon mousse that melted in your mouth. When we first met, Evie and I had been taken aback by Steph's assumption that our three families could go away and have fun together. Paul was a bit wary initially, nervous of spending our limited funds on a weekend with people we didn't know very well. But in the time-honoured tradition of reaching a man through his stomach, Steph had pulled off a feat of cordon bleu catering the first time she'd invited us over and been so warm and friendly that Paul had gone along with every plan thereafter.

Within minutes, all of us, apart from Neil, had followed the boys into the water, trousers rolled up to our knees, feet red from the cold. Eventually, after stone skimming and competitive shell collecting, we settled ourselves in a hollow in the dunes, looking out over the deserted beach, with the coarse grasses blowing around us. I was openly smug that the little egret snatching up shrimps with its long black bill was one of my cards.

Steph opened her rucksack and pulled out some banana bread, flapjacks and the trademark flask. 'Mal and Wendy don't know what they're missing.'

Through a mouthful of flapjack, Steph asked, 'Why is Wendy marrying Glenn if she's got herself in such a state about his stag do? Doesn't sound like love's young dream if she's already having sleepless nights.'

Steph's ability to voice what everyone else didn't dare say was admirable, but sometimes I wished she had mastered the 'discreet word in the recipient's ear'. In the end, Wendy was my sister and I didn't want to discuss her in front of the whole group. I sieved sand through my fingers. 'She'd probably be like it with anyone. She's a worrier.'

I felt a rush of love for Paul as he interrupted Steph's not-so-subtle criticism of Wendy by calling our attention to a majestic marsh harrier that was gliding and circling in the sky.

By seven-thirty, Ross was complaining that his trainers were soaking and Ben had shoved his cards at Steph, saying, 'You gave me all the hard ones.' We decided to get moving before the joy of the morning descended into a bad-tempered sugar slump.

With that sense of satisfaction that comes from being up early and grounding yourself in nature, we walked back along the boardwalk, with the boys sprinting off to explore in the dunes. Paul stopped every now and again to take pictures. He made me stand against a backdrop of sea-buckthorn, even though he knew I hated posing for photos. 'This scenery is gorgeous.'

I smiled. 'Shame about the wife.'

Paul laid his camera down and put his arms round me. 'To me, you will always be gorgeous.' Although his tone was jokey, there was a softness, a warmth in his face that still made me feel as though he was the only person in the world who really understood me. He bent his head and kissed me, his lips cold and salty. I wished I could have been one of those women who gave in to the moment, but instead thoughts of not holding the others up, or making a spectacle of myself, crowded in. I pulled away, just as Neil was turning round and shouting, 'Get a room!' which was a bit rich even by his standards as the creaking of the bed in the room next door hadn't left us in any doubt about how he and Evie had topped off last night.

But before we could catch them up, Ben came steaming up behind us, running past shouting. 'Evie! Evie! Isaac has cut his hand.'

Evie turned round and ran towards us.

Ben was panting. 'We went to see what was in the air-raid shelter and there was some broken glass.'

Neil charged off, with Ben leading the way and the rest of us stumbling as fast as we could over the dunes, down through the gorse and blackberry bushes to a half-buried concrete bunker. Isaac was propped up, white-faced with Ross kneeling next to him, his whole body sagging with relief as he saw us approach. I wanted to hug him to me but Neil started firing off questions about what had happened. As Neil inspected Isaac's hand, Ross averted his eyes. I had some sympathy with him, as my own stomach was starting to churn at the sight of the blood dripping onto the moss.

Steph wasn't fazed at all and got right up close. 'Would you let me take a look?'

Not for the first time since we'd become friends, I was in awe of the way she handled any difficult situation. She pulled some kitchen roll out of her rucksack. 'This needs cleaning to get the dirt out of it as quickly as we can. I think the best thing is to wash it in the salt water if you can bear it. I don't think it needs stitches, though it is quite nasty.' Neil, for once, nodded in agreement, as though he was grateful that someone knew what to do.

She carried on. 'A plaster would be good to protect it and help stop the bleeding until we can clean it up properly at the farmhouse. Evie, you're the fastest. Do you want to run home – there are some plasters in my suitcase, in the outside pocket – while I take Isaac back to the creek? Bring a towel. And a bottle of water. There's some in the fridge.'

Neil waved her away. 'Go on then!'

As Evie shot off, glancing anxiously at Isaac, Paul sat down beside the boys. He leant into Ross's shoulder. Ross relaxed against him. His teen swagger disappeared as Paul spoke in that reassuring, calm way that he had. 'It's going to be fine, we'll soon get Isaac sorted.'

Neil started having a go about why they went into the air-raid shelter in the first place.

Ben said, 'Dunno, just wanted to explore inside.'

Neil was having none of it. He was scuffing the sandy ground with his walking boots, appearing far less worried about Isaac's hand than telling them all off. 'You didn't think that it might be dangerous? You were lucky not to hurt yourself on some dirty old needles. Talk about idiotic! What do you use for brains?'

Steph helped Isaac to his feet. He was moaning quietly and trying not to cry as she shepherded him back towards the beach.

Ben's face clouded over and Ross stared at the floor. Neil reminded me of one of my old English teachers who used to stand over me saying, 'Teresa, do you actually know what a sentence is? I mean, do you? Because it doesn't feel to me like you do,' when I already wanted to sob because I'd got the worst mark in the class again. Goodness knows how Ross and Ben felt because my heart was fluttering about with panic and I couldn't think how to stop Neil getting more and more irate.

Thankfully, Paul was made of sterner stuff and said if he was thirteen, he would have wanted to explore too. 'It's just bad luck, Neil. All these little things are life lessons, learning to look before you leap and all that. They were just being curious.'

Neil swore under his breath and hurried off to catch up Steph and Isaac.

As soon as he'd gone, Ben scowled and said, 'He's the idiot, not us. We didn't do it on purpose. It was just an accident. Dickhead.'

It wasn't often I agreed with Ben, but on this occasion, he'd hit the nail on the head.

EVIE

Norfolk, 6 May 1995

My feet were thudding on the boardwalk as I sped along. I rushed in through the back door and dashed upstairs. Despite my haste, I paused outside Mal and Steph's room, wondering whether to go in and try to find the plasters without waking Mal or to knock loudly and announce my entry. There was something slightly too intimate about being in a bedroom with someone else's husband.

I was just about to knock and shout to Mal through the door when I heard voices inside. Wendy's giggle, that rather squeaky high-pitched noise that I'd caught Steph imitating to herself when she'd been fetching more wine out of the kitchen the night before.

Mal's low voice. 'Last-chance saloon. In two weeks' time you'll be a married woman.'

I couldn't make out Wendy's reply, just 'early' and a teasing tone.

But Mal's words carried. 'They'll be gone for ages. Steph said to get the sausages in the oven for 9.30. It's not even eight o'clock yet. Once Steph gets on one of her route marches, she'll have them sitting there until they've ticked off every last seagull.'

A squeal of laughter followed by silence, then a groan and some low murmuring I couldn't make out. Despite being in a hurry to get back to Isaac, I couldn't pluck up the nerve to burst through the door in case my first thoughts proved to be correct.

I ran back down to the kitchen, flinging open all the cupboards to see what I could find and coming up trumps with a first-aid kit.

Clearly no one staying at the farmhouse had had an emergency recently as everything was pristine. I grabbed a pair of scissors and a clean towel, picked up a bottle of water and raced out again, banging the door behind me as a pathetic protest.

I questioned what I'd heard as I headed back to the others, the maternal urge to reach Isaac as soon as possible driving me forwards. Why would Wendy be in Mal's bedroom? I couldn't think of a single explanation other than the straightforward one. Teresa's sister! Too feeble to stay in the house on her own overnight but not so fragile that she couldn't get up to no good with Steph's husband. Surely she hadn't been having sex with him? I just didn't understand women who would do that. What was that even about? Come away for a weekend, cosy up to someone else's husband and take the chance to have one last fling before getting married, thereby putting a whole family in jeopardy?

I wasn't sure whether it was the shock of what I thought I'd heard or the hard work of running up the sandy dunes that was making me breathless, but I slowed my pace as soon as I saw them up ahead. Steph had her arm around Isaac. I took comfort in the fact that Neil was sitting down on the bank of the creek. If there had been a real emergency, he would have been pacing about and shouting. Teresa and Paul were standing next to each other holding hands. There was a quiet togetherness about them that I envied, however much Neil slated Paul for 'being under the cosh'. I didn't think Paul was henpecked. On the contrary, he seemed to relish his role as a family man. He never seemed to be keeping a tally in his head of how often Teresa had been out with her friends, her trips to Durham to visit her parents and how that translated into reciprocal 'get out of jail free cards' for him.

I clattered across the shingle, my mind racing with concern for Isaac and fury at Wendy. As I jumped across a pool of water, a thought struck me. Mal. Why was I directing all the blame at Wendy? He had definitely been the one pushing the agenda.

Whenever Steph talked about this sort of thing, she'd throw her hands in the air and say, 'Why is it always the woman who gets the blame? Like the men are helpless saps powerless to resist?'

With a sickening lurch, I realised that I couldn't mention anything to Steph. I couldn't be the one to blow their family apart. I didn't want to know what I knew.

I reached Isaac. 'How are you, love? Has it stopped bleeding?'

Isaac nodded. 'Nearly.'

Neil said, 'He didn't like putting it in the salt water much, but he's been very brave.'

My heart ached as I saw Isaac positively glow with the unexpected praise from his father. I felt a burst of hope that when it came to real drama concerning his son, Neil would direct his energy where it was needed rather than rage about finding someone to blame.

Steph produced another bit of flapjack. 'As hero of the day, you get the last piece, while I find exactly the right thing in this kit to make it better.' She turned to me. 'Well done for bringing this. Much better than the silly little plasters in my suitcase. Are you happy for me to put on the bandage? Or would you like to do it?'

'I suddenly remembered I'd glimpsed something when I was looking for the teapot so I didn't need to disturb Mal after all. If you don't mind, I think you'll do a better job. I never did get my Brownie first-aider badge.'

I sat down with my arm around Isaac, while Steph unravelled the gauze. Bewilderment pounded round my head. Would I want to be told? I sieved through the fragments of conversation when we'd talked about infidelity in that rather smug way of wives who thought it was something that happened to other people. To women who'd chosen feckless husbands, who hadn't spotted that something was wrong, who hadn't known how to keep their husbands interested. Or perhaps that was just me. Now I concentrated my mind on it, Steph had always been very pragmatic. 'Frankly, if Mal gets his leg over at a conference and it doesn't mean anything, I hope he's smart enough that I never find out. I mean, honestly, what's the point of having to get divorced over a drunken fumble in a three-star hotel with a rubbery fried egg for breakfast?'

I didn't know whether I was clutching on to that because I was a coward, but what good would come from telling Steph? It wasn't like Mal was going to have an ongoing relationship with Wendy. She'd be married to the poor, unsuspecting Glenn in a fortnight. All that nonsense about his stag do and how she couldn't sleep for worrying about what he'd get up to. Maybe Mal was her pre-emptive strike.

I watched while Steph disinfected Isaac's hand.

I glanced up at Neil. He smiled. 'You were fast there and back. All that jogging has come in handy.'

And just like Isaac, I had that sense of conquering hero, derived from engineering a rare bit of praise from Neil.

I wouldn't want to know if Neil had had a one-off sex session. The idea of standing over our sideboard, bartering over who took the thistle-shaped whisky glasses over the Waterford water tumblers made me feel sick. And Isaac. He worshipped his dad. Maybe he'd even want to live with him. Surely it would be the same for Steph. She had a huge work project coming up, which involved her travelling backwards and forwards to Italy over the next few months. I knew she found it tricky enough making sure Ben was looked after when she was away as it was. She wouldn't thank me if she couldn't rely on Mal at least some of the time.

I glanced over to where Paul and Teresa were distracting Ben and Ross by skimming stones. Ross was biting his lip in concentration, listening to Paul and cheering when he managed more than one skip. Ben had already got bored and was chucking in the heaviest stones he could find. I heard Paul say lightly at first, then with a bit more irritation, 'Hey, Ben, buddy, if you want to splash, throw them over there so we don't end up soaked.' Ben carried on, just on the edge of defiance, until the others walked back towards us.

He was a handful and I was pretty sure that wouldn't be improved by shuttling between two homes if Steph and Mal split up.

Teresa knelt down beside me. 'Are you okay?'

'I'm fine. I mean, it's a pain and I'm sorry it's spoilt the morning, but I think he'll be fine.' I sniffed. 'When that little baby pops into the world, we really have no idea that endless heart-stopping moments will dictate the pattern of the rest of our lives, do we?'

'No, we really don't. Wendy makes me laugh when she says she's not going to let her kids go to McDonald's or play video games. I used to think that, but now I'm so grateful for the peace, I've found my principles don't seem quite as important any more.'

'Does Wendy definitely want kids?' I asked.

'I think so. She's always been brilliant around Ross. When he was little, she'd dress up and play make-believe battles. Much more fun than me. I always used to feel such an idiot pretending to be a baddie and leaping out from behind the sofa. She'll have to get used to fewer lie-ins though.'

I felt my throat vibrate with the effort of not blurting out what I'd heard. Maybe I should tell Teresa so she could have a straight talk with Wendy about whether she should be getting married at all. Selfishly, I didn't want to be the keeper of this great big secret that could cause havoc not only in Steph's life but would also ruffle our cosy little friendship group. It was unlikely that Neil would want to go away for our weekends if Paul was his only male company: 'I mean, he's a bit knitting and nut roast, isn't he?'

Steph held Isaac's hand aloft. 'The champion will live to fight another day. Super brave boy. Just stay sitting down for a bit to let the shock subside, then we'll get going.' After about fifteen minutes, she jumped to her feet. 'If we take it slowly, you should be okay to walk back now. Let's hope Wendy and Mal have got themselves out of bed and are, at this very moment, putting the finishing touches to Norfolk's finest sausages, eggs and bacon.'

I wanted to hold her back, to find some other must-see crustacean, rare butterfly or one-eyed goose that would slow down our arrival home. But Steph had a timetable in her head and was intent on gathering us all up.

'First one home gets double tomato ketchup and an extra sausage.' She leant down to Isaac. 'Yours is guaranteed, for being such a trooper.'

The other two boys tore off, with Ben quickly outpacing Ross, who dropped back to walk with Paul. Ben was like Mal and Steph: everything was a race, a chance to win, to lead, to shine. Neil was always telling Isaac he shouldn't give up so easily – 'Where's your spirit, boy?' But Isaac was like me. Winning didn't matter as much as making sure everyone else was happy.

All the way home, I held Isaac's hand, stopping to pick up mussel shells, point out orchids and, out of desperation to slow Steph's speed walk towards home, even rabbit droppings.

Steph laughed – 'When did you become such a David Bellamy?'– but my tactic managed to turn a half an hour march into a much longer dawdle.

As we approached the farmhouse, I braced myself for Ben shooting back up the garden, all 'Dad was in bed with Wendy.' But there was just the enticing smell of cooking wafting out.

Steph clapped her hands and turned to Neil. 'See, being a bossy old boot sometimes gets results.'

Neil nudged her. 'I don't know how Mal puts up with it. I'd be booking Evie a one-way ticket to Timbuktu.'

Steph waved him away. 'If I was Evie, I'd snatch it out of your hand and bring the departure date forward.'

I stepped in before Neil turned nasty – he expected everyone to have a thick skin when it came to his witticisms while maintaining the finest of epidermises himself. 'Right, Neil, would you mind asking the boys to wash their hands while Steph and I lay the table?'

I said, steeling myself for ignoring the complicit looks between Mal and Wendy as we headed inside.

Isaac was in the middle of showing Wendy his bandage. 'How did you do that?' she asked.

As he explained, I studied her and Mal for the telltale flash of horror that came with the realisation that we could all have arrived home much earlier. But Mal gestured towards Steph. 'Don't tell me my super-organised wife had a first-aid kit with her?' He went over to where she was folding the paper napkins in half and squeezed her.

I wondered what Wendy thought about that. Clearly Mal hadn't peddled the old crap about 'my wife won't let me near her, there's no love lost, no affection'. I was the last person in the world to feel sorry for her, but it was taking it to new levels of weirdness to have sex with one person in the room and be cuddling up to a different one within an hour. I began to doubt what I'd heard.

Steph turned and kissed him on the cheek, which had me wanting to shrink down under the table and only come out again once everyone had gone home. 'Sadly I'd only taken the antihistamines and the lip salve. But Evie here saved the day and put all that early-morning running to good use. She sprinted back for the first-aid kit.'

Mal stiffened. Wendy carried on stirring the eggs. I clattered about finding the cutlery, hating myself for not making a comment that they would understand but that would wash over everyone else.

Mal recovered himself quickly. 'So when did this happen? You're blessed with fairy footsteps, Evie… you didn't wake me up.' I was sure there was a little note of panic in his voice.

Neil said, 'She obviously makes more effort for you. She and Isaac are like a herd of elephants clumping round the house when I'm trying to get a bit of shut-eye at weekends.'

I wasn't going to put Mal out of his misery. Let him bloody sweat a bit. 'Oh, about an hour or so ago. I wasn't here very long. I heard you moving about, but I wanted to get back to Isaac.'

I watched him intently, examining his reaction but there was nothing concrete to confirm my suspicions.

'You should have told me. I could have brought the car,' he said.

Had I put two and two together and made five? 'It wasn't that dramatic and I don't think you'd have got close enough to where we were to save any time. Steph did a brilliant job patching him up in our field hospital. Flapjack and a first-aid kit were all we needed.'

My heart was thumping with the frisson of confrontation. There didn't seem to be any complicity between the two, though Mal was full of bonhomie, which could be the result of a long lie-in disturbed only briefly by Wendy's need for – early-morning company? A plaster herself? Someone to show her how the shower worked? I knew I was clutching at straws. The most likely answer was post-coital happy hormones.

I sat through breakfast forcing down each baked bean, unable to join in the collective excitement about the birdwatching and the near-severing of the hand experience as embellished and recounted by Isaac.

Steph offered me the tray of sausages. I shook my head. 'God, I wish I had your delicate appetite, Evie. No wonder you're so lovely and slim.'

Neil said, 'That's all the sex keeping her trim. Forget Ryvita and celery sticks.'

Even though the others veered between a polite chuckle and ignoring him completely, I felt myself blush.

Steph tried to come to my rescue. 'Oh, Neil, you're every woman's dream, discussing your sex life over a fried egg. You sound like some backstreet pimp gearing up for a bit of bondage.'

Paul, who hardly ever intervened, said, 'Would it be possible for me to eat my bacon without getting into the details of who does what when?'

Annoyance flashed over Neil's face. He'd be keeping me up half the night tonight 'to give that lot in there something to talk about'.

But I could no longer try and convince myself that I'd misinterpreted what I'd heard earlier. At the mention of sex, Wendy had looked at Mal under her lashes and suppressed a smirk. It had been almost imperceptible, but he'd raised his eyebrows and winked.

I spent the rest of the day and most of the next in a state of constant monitoring. Neil said, 'Thought a weekend away was supposed to be an opportunity to catch up with each other. You're like a Girl Guide volunteering to go with Mal to fetch wood for the fire and peeling veg with Wendy. Next time, I think we'll head off just the two of us.'

I wished Neil was more like Paul, that I could tell him anything and be confident that my friendships wouldn't suffer later because of what he now knew. If I mentioned my suspicions, after a couple of glasses of wine, he'd make some snide remark and no amount of kicking under the table would make him back down if someone challenged him. The strong bond between the women meant we were very forgiving of each other's men. Steph was very pragmatic: 'Paul's a peacemaker anyway, so, Evie, you've just got to keep Neil on board and I'll keep Mal in order.' However, there were limits: we'd all struggle with Neil announcing Mal's infidelity. That would put an entirely different spin on the usual entertainment of Mal and Neil rutting against each other with their knowledge of computers or the best way to barbecue chicken. Or this morning's one-upmanship with Neil boasting about how quickly he could run ten kilometres versus Mal's building up better endurance by cycling forty kilometres. I never dared contradict Neil, who made out he was out jogging every morning before work rather than a dramatic fortnightly run when he'd push himself so hard I worried he'd keel over in the hallway.

Steph suffered from no such loyalty constraints. 'Mal, stop trying to make out you're one step away from the Tour de France. How many times do you actually do a forty-kilometre bike ride? Half the time, the closest you get to cycling is pumping up the tyres on Ben's bike.'

Neil shook his head. 'I'd hate to work with you, Steph. You'd be that colleague interrupting every presentation saying, "That's not strictly true."'

Steph brushed him off with a mixture of impish charm and blatant disregard. 'But if you don't lie, you'd never have to worry about that, so I'm sure you'd love working with me – efficient, organised and I do what I say I'll do. What's not to like?'

I sat there with a big knot in my stomach. Steph would expect me to tell her the truth. But how could I? What if it all snowballed and they got divorced because of what I told her? What if she didn't want to know and blamed me for stirring everything up?

By Sunday afternoon I couldn't stand it any longer. I engineered it so that I had a quick walk with Teresa and the boys to collect wood for the firepit, Steph got on with the cooking and the men chilled out with the papers.

While our sons ran along the top of the dunes, I turned to Teresa. 'I don't know how to say this.'

'What?'

'I'm really sure I haven't got it wrong, but it seems so unlikely.'

'It can't be that bad,' Teresa said, as though she was expecting me to say our sons had found a packet of cigarettes and decided to experiment.

I craned round to double-check the boys were out of earshot. Ben had found a maggot-ridden gull and was busy poking it with a stick, while the other two were covering their noses and shouting about the stink. I rushed out what I thought I'd heard.

Teresa put her hand to her mouth. 'Oh my God. Are you absolutely certain?'

Her shock was so genuine that it made me hesitate. 'I can't really think why else Wendy was in Mal's room and I definitely heard

Mal say something about it being her last chance and Wendy was laughing. And then it went all quiet and neither of them came out.'

Teresa ran her fingers through her hair. 'Wendy's always been a bit of a flirt, but I don't think she'd sleep with other women's husbands. Especially not my friend's husband.' She scuffed the toe of her flip-flop in the sand. 'Or at least not just out of the blue without *some* sort of relationship first. She's only met Mal about three or four times in her life.'

Sometimes Teresa reminded me of a Victorian governess with her limited view of the world. Unlike Steph, who was refreshingly open about the fact that she 'hadn't stinted herself on the men front' before she got married, I suspected Teresa had had a 'no funny business until I know you much better' policy firmly in place.

Teresa put her hand on my arm. 'Don't mention this to Steph. We don't know for sure and she'd go absolutely potty. She'd never speak to me again.'

'I'm not going to say anything to ruin this weekend, definitely not. But if Mal is being unfaithful, don't you think Steph deserves to know? And I hate to state the obvious, but if Wendy is already playing away, it's probably a good idea if she doesn't get married in a fortnight.'

'I just don't think Wendy would do that,' Teresa insisted. 'Even if they did sleep together, we have no proof that Mal has done anything like this before or that he will again. And what if you got the wrong end of the stick, that actually they were just joking and talking and it destroys their whole marriage? For nothing?'

However I looked at it, though, it wasn't normal for a single woman to be giggling away in a man's bedroom when everyone else was out. And that weird silence. 'Just humour me for a minute. If it were true, and you were in Steph's place, would you want to know? If it was just a one-off?'

Teresa shook her head. 'What the eye doesn't see the heart doesn't grieve over. Or let's put it another way. If we told Steph and she left Mal, would she be happier as a single parent trying to juggle all her trips abroad with looking after Ben?'

As I watched Ben hurling clods of sand at the backs of Ross and Isaac, a whirlwind of energy and mischief, I couldn't say with my hand on my heart that one indiscretion merited blowing apart a whole family. Or, at least, I wasn't brave enough to make that call, especially when Teresa was so doubtful that Wendy would have done it in the first place.

Teresa turned to walk back, calling to the boys. She grabbed my hand. 'Promise me you won't say a word to Steph?'

I had no idea whether I was making a promise I really shouldn't keep, but I nodded. 'I'll forget I ever knew about it.'

EVIE

Norfolk, 7 May 1995

I could see that Teresa wasn't herself for the rest of the day and it was a miracle that neither Mal nor Wendy sensed us watching their every move.

Steph, however, picked up on Teresa's mood. 'Hey, are you okay? You're very quiet.'

Teresa yawned. 'I think the sea air has made me tired. Plus drinking two nights in a row.'

'My liver would celebrate if I only drank two nights in a row.' She ushered Teresa onto the sofa. 'Here, you put your feet up with a glass of wine and read a magazine. You are officially off duty while I get dinner ready.'

Paul bent over and kissed Teresa's head. 'Hear, hear. I'll get the firepit going.'

The prospect of a bit of pyromania was enough to entice Ross and Isaac away from Ben's Game Boy and my heart softened as I watched them really listen to Paul's instructions about twisting up the newspaper and making a pyramid out of sticks.

An hour later, the boys had drifted back inside and the adults were all sitting around a roaring fire, laughing about how, when we first met, the pinnacle of our desires was to get all gussied up and go to some posh hotel in London for cocktails. Now here we were a decade later, loving life around a bonfire by the beach in a motley collection of shorts, sandals and sweatshirts.

I was heading contentedly into the phase of recognising that I'd feel a bit ropey tomorrow but accepting that a hangover was part of our weekends away. I had faith that before we left for home the next day, Steph would fix it with one of her legendary brunches.

Ben came out and asked Steph if the boys could have a beer. Before I could stop myself, I said, 'I think you're a bit young to be drinking alcohol.'

Ben muttered under his breath, while Steph said, 'Is it the end of the world if they have a little bottle each?'

There was a silence while we all waited for Teresa and Paul to give their verdict. Teresa said, 'I don't really think we should be encouraging them to drink underage.'

Steph shrugged. 'I don't mind them sharing a beer. The more you make alcohol seem like a big taboo, the more they're likely to experiment as soon as our backs are turned. Italian and French teenagers grow up drinking wine with their dinner and they don't get anywhere near as plastered as the British kids do.'

I looked to Neil for his lead. He said, 'I don't want Isaac drinking at thirteen. He's got plenty of time for that when he goes to university.'

I felt a lurch of fright as Steph frowned and looked as though she was going to argue. Instead she turned to Ben and said, 'Sorry, love, I think that's a no. There's some Diet Coke in the cupboard.'

Ben glanced around the table, gesturing to the bottles of wine and champagne. 'For God's sake. You can all sit there getting off your faces but have a fit about us having a few sips of Budweiser.' Wendy, in particular, was becoming quite loud and lairy so I could see his point, though I was relieved it wasn't my son causing a scene.

Mal tried to be the voice of reason. 'The thing is, Ben, we all need to agree on it and everyone's got different opinions, so it's just not the right occasion to try it.'

Ben was shaking his head as though we were all so lame. 'Dad, you said yourself that you used to go down the pub with your brother at my age.'

I had some sympathy with Mal that a casual family chat had come back to bite him on the bottom. Mal started to argue that it was a different generation but before the discussion got any further, Neil stood up and pushed his face into Ben's. 'You, mate, have been looking to cause trouble ever since we got here. Just remember that it's Evie and Steph's birthday weekend and it's not about what you want.'

I felt a surge of adrenaline as I waited to see how Ben would react.

Unlike Isaac, who'd had many years of practice of sidestepping Neil's temper, Ben clearly hadn't mastered the formula for defuse, appease or disperse and stared straight at him and said, 'Well, at least I won't get so drunk I can't stand up or bore the shit out of everyone talking about my crappy job in advertising.'

'Ben! Don't talk to Neil like that! Say sorry,' Steph said.

Ben pulled a face and said, 'So-rry.'

For one horrible moment, I thought Neil was going to punch him. Instead, he turned on Steph. 'See. This is what happens when you put your career before staying at home and teaching your son respect and manners. Maybe if you spent a bit less time hopping on a flight to discover the best hotel in Portugal and a bit more time keeping an eye on Ben, he wouldn't be quite so rude.'

I knew Steph wouldn't take that lying down. 'Love how you're directing all that at me, Neil. All the boys here have got two parents. So I think that's shared blame between Mal and me at least. Though, to be honest, how we choose to work and bring up our son has absolutely sweet FA to do with you.'

Mal stood up, flapping his hands at both of them. 'Hey, hey, calm down, you two. Come on. Let's just have a nice evening. Ben, go and find something on telly.' For a moment, I thought he was going to argue back again but in the end, he strolled off with a sarcastic 'Have a lovely evening with your, er, friends, Mum.'

Paul and Teresa were huddled on one end of the bench like a couple of penguins sheltering from a storm, looking terrified to breathe in case they ignited Neil or Steph's fury. I willed Neil to sit down and not launch into a long self-justifying dialogue about how it takes a village to raise a child.

Mal, thankfully, took Steph's hand and tried to make a joke of it. 'Teenage boys, eh?'

But Neil wasn't going to let it go. 'It's not all teenage boys though. Isaac and Ross aren't coming out here and making a big fuss about nothing.'

'I can't speak for Ross, but Isaac has his moments, Neil,' I said, in a voice that sounded as though it was creeping about trying not to wake anyone.

Neil darted an irritated look in my direction and said, 'Isaac would never speak to one of our friends like that.' Which, to be fair, was probably true.

Steph took a large slurp of her wine. 'Okay, Neil. So if I accept I've done a crap job with my son because I've been out at work, it must figure that the brilliant job you've done with Isaac is all down to Evie?'

Neil jutted out his chin. 'Evie has done a great job. She's had the time to dedicate to him without pushing him from pillar to post.'

Mal made a warning sound. 'Neil, just drop this. Ben hasn't been pushed from pillar to post. He's spent all of his young years either with me, when Steph's been away, or with his grandma. I think you're overstepping the line a bit.' He held out his hand to Steph. 'Come on, let's just have a walk on the beach for a minute, let everyone cool down.'

'Yep, that's probably a good idea,' Steph said, getting to her feet.

I felt the tight band of fear loosen as she got up. But that old hothead friend of mine wasn't going down without a fight.

'You might think I'm a rubbish parent, Neil, but at least I'm not a horrible bully who goes into a sulk if he doesn't get his own way. Your wife won't even ask if she can come on holiday for a few days to Corfu in case you get your knickers in a twist about it and don't talk to her for a week. I've heard you telling her she's getting a bit chubby in the face, that she needs to get herself to the gym. So, yeah, you can think I'm a poor parent, but you're not the perfect example of a human being either.'

Neil laughed, a harsh, sarcastic sound that made me want to run away from what was coming next. 'Maybe you should have followed my advice as well and signed up for a few keep-fit classes.'

Mal was bristling with fury as he stepped forward, but Steph put up her hand to stop him. She jabbed her finger at Neil. 'You miserable misogynist bastard. Sorry if my not being a size ten offends your panorama. The thing is, Neil, I decided years ago that I would concentrate all my energy on being smart enough to not give a shit what men like you think about my weight or anything else for that matter.'

And with that, for someone who was probably a bottle and a half of wine in, she stormed down the outside stairs at great speed and stomped off to the bottom of the garden.

I longed to go with her, to tell her I was sorry about what Neil said to her, though part of me was furious that she hadn't backed down, if only not to make life difficult for me. But before I could follow her, Neil grabbed hold of my wrist.

'I'm not listening to any more of this tittle-tattle dressed up as facts. Come on, we're going home.'

Paul leapt up and made a plea for us to stay, to sort it out, to not drink and drive. But Neil brushed everyone off. Under the starlit seaside sky of my birthday celebration, he wheeled our cases out to the car while Isaac stood awkwardly in the hallway, as though he was weighing up how to avoid Neil's wrath turning on him. Ben watched with his hands in his pockets, and despite everything, I felt sorry for him. I doubted whether his teenage brain could have possibly foreseen what might happen when two people who had 'always being right' in their DNA were added to a cocktail of wine and parenting opinions.

I tugged at Neil's sleeve. 'I really don't think you should drive. Let's at least wait until the morning when you'd pass a breath test.'

He shook me off. 'I stopped drinking hours ago. I'm not spending another night in the same house as that woman. And if you want to have a marriage left after this, you won't be seeing her again either.'

I knew in that moment that Steph, my funny, loyal but fiery friend, was lost to me. Neil would make me choose. I'd done well to hold on to her for so long. I should never have mixed those two parts of my life, should have tucked Steph away, under Neil's radar for anyone who might encourage me to stand up for myself.

With a weary resignation, I walked out to the car and sat in silence, clutching the seat and watching the speedometer, managing not to ask Neil if he'd seen the car on the outside lane every time he pulled out to overtake. In between times, I was asking myself how life could turn on a pinhead. I stared at the motorway lights zipping past in the dark, tears rolling down my cheeks. I couldn't imagine life without Steph, the week-in, week-out presence of her, the conversations when I felt as though being myself was not just acceptable but welcome. My world would be so much poorer without her relentless optimism and drive.

But at least I wouldn't have to tell her what I had overheard at the farmhouse.

STEPH

Mid-May 2018

In the days leading up to meeting Evie, I became unusually self-conscious about how much I'd aged since last time I'd seen her when I'd proudly told that horrible husband of hers that I couldn't care less what he thought about my looks. And although I'd been serious back then, I did have a little dread that Evie would still have that gorgeous golden skin with barely a wrinkle and long chestnut hair that had somehow escaped the frizz that the menopause had delivered to mine. I inspected my chin for spiky little whiskers that loved nothing more than to glisten in the sunshine.

I tried to pump Teresa for information when we were out walking Gladys. 'Is she still really glamorous? Please tell me she's got wrinkles you could lose your foot down and a great blubbery spare tyre hanging over her trousers.'

But, of course, Teresa frowned and said, 'I don't really notice things like that. She just looks the same to me. Shorter hair. Surely that's not your main worry anyway. Aren't you nervous about seeing her after all this time?'

'A bit, but I don't suppose she would have asked to meet me just to tell me home truths about my shortcomings at this point, would she? What did she say to you?'

Teresa shrugged. 'We haven't really spoken about it.' Then she looked at her watch and said, 'We need to get a trot on. I've got to pick Amelia up from school.'

It would never stop seeming odd to me that eighteen years after our sons left home, Teresa had a child in the sixth form. I'd probably have been a better parent second time around, but I was still glad that I didn't have to deal with a seventeen-year-old in my sixties. Or, even worse, have to teach anyone to drive. I was still scarred from the shouting matches I used to have with Ben: 'Put both hands on the damn wheel!'

'Is she doing exams at the moment?' I asked.

'Yes, just the usual summer-term ones, but she's really stressed about them because they'll be used to predict her grades for uni next year. Newcastle's the current favourite and she's going to need three As for that.'

'Crikey, I'm sure she's capable of the grades, but Newcastle's a fair old trek,' I said.

Teresa smiled. 'She's the total opposite to Ross. Wants to go as far away as possible, see the world. I'm trying not to take it personally that she's mainly chosen universities that are a six-hour drive away.'

I held back a branch for her. 'She'll only be half an hour away from Wendy though. Maybe you could catch up with her a bit more often.'

Teresa sniffed. 'Once a year works for us.'

Given that when we were younger, Teresa was always inviting Wendy to join us, I didn't understand why they saw so little of each other now. She'd never mentioned falling out with her but knowing Teresa, she'd probably keep it to herself anyway. She had an odd sort of family loyalty that made her shut down instantly if she let slip a bad word about Paul, Ross or even that cackling hyena of her sister. Personally, I thought the whole point of friends was to let off steam about everything that got on my nerves about my family, like covering yourself with leeches in medieval times to draw out bad blood. It beat whirling through the house on a rampage because Mal had stolen the de-icer out of my car again.

I let Teresa hold her secrets. 'Lucky Amelia. I wish I'd had the chance to go to university.'

'You've done really well though. Getting to director level isn't to be sniffed at.'

'Thank you,' I said, trying not to sound as though I was puffing as Teresa darted up the hill back to our cars like a light-footed goat. 'But I'm pretty sure I wouldn't have got married at twenty-three if I'd had the luxury of three or four years to experiment with different personalities until I found the one that suited me. That freedom to be yourself and work out who you want to be stops you toeing the line so early.'

Teresa snorted. 'I must ask Mal if he feels you've "toed the line" all these years.'

I gave up pretending to be fit and stopped to get my breath. 'You know what I mean though. We start off full of ideas of how we're going to live our lives, what sort of parents we're going to be, how getting married isn't going to change us, and before you know it, we feel guilty if we go out with our friends midweek and leave our husbands fending for themselves with a fridge full of food.' I tied my cardigan around my waist and started plodding upwards again. Gladys pushed past us.

'You've never been like that, not even when Ben was young. Half the time you were off scouring Europe for new hotels. I was so jealous of you, hopping on a plane like it was a bus to the shops.'

'Yes, but I'd still have filled the freezer with all the meals for the week, arranged for someone to take Ben to Scouts so Mal didn't have to rush back from work, made sure all the sports kit was clean. When Mal went away for his conferences, he just walked out of the door. Still does. And has no problem in staying an extra day at short notice or tagging on a game of golf with someone who might put a bit of work his way.'

Gladys gave me a pause to catch my breath by almost getting her head stuck in some old railings lining our path. 'Go back, you silly dog!' Then she chased off through the woods, offering me a welcome excuse to whistle and call but not climb.

While we waited for her to reappear, Teresa said, 'You'd never have left Mal to get on with it even if he'd wanted to. It's the control freak in you.'

I knew she was right, but it made me want to argue with her anyway. She rarely agreed with me when I moaned about Mal. 'Maybe, but it wouldn't even have been an option. If Paul goes out, you don't shout "What shall I have for dinner?" down the drive after him, do you? But I bet you tell him what he can put in the microwave.'

Teresa smiled but didn't answer. 'I'm going to have to crack on, otherwise I'm going to be late for Amelia.' She leant forward to give me a big hug. 'Hope it goes well with Evie.' There was an edge to her words that I couldn't decipher.

'What's the worst that can happen? She'll be reminded that she didn't like me much anyway and Neil was right about me all along.'

As I watched her making light work of the last bit of the hill, I knew I sounded braver than I felt. My fall-out with Evie and her absolute refusal to stand up to Neil, or even to meet me secretly, was one of the sores I'd carried through life, irrationally furious that Evie had chosen her marriage over me. I'd sent several letters and rung a few times, though on the last occasion Neil had answered when I thought he'd be at work. He swore down the phone at me, leaving me shaky and, to my frustration, tearful.

However, despite Teresa tapping into my misgivings, when Thursday rolled around, I still jumped in the car and drove an hour to Whitstable from my home in Surrey. I breathed in the sea air, with no little envy that coastal walks were right on Evie's doorstep. I pushed open the door to the café she'd suggested, an arty little place scented with cinnamon and designed for the Instagram generation. Teresa's words about it being too late to resurrect the friendship were echoing in my head. All the way here, I'd wondered if the phrase, 'There's no fool like an old fool' was going to be proved true. Evie had sounded pleased – surprised? – to hear from me when I'd phoned her, but she hadn't wanted to chat for long, just to fix a date and meet the following week.

It was so long since I'd felt this nervous about anything, truth be known, so long since I'd cared much about anything at all. It was as though I existed in a perpetual state of low-level irritation at the world, punctuated by bursts of high irritation when some bit of technology that Ben stabbed at and said, 'It's easy!' turned what used to be a two-minute phone call into an endless loop of forgotten passwords, lower case, upper case nightmare. But I'd walked from the car park with a spring in my step, determined to quash the dread that Teresa's doom-mongering could prove correct. Mainly, though, with the tiny squeeze of optimism left in the tube of life, I was suppressing a great gurgle of laughter at all the stories I could entertain Evie with, the sense that I'd burst in and we'd just launch into a condensed showreel of the highs and lows of the last twenty years, with enough distance for even the lows to have been reframed and moulded into something we could find funny.

I didn't recognise her at first, until she stood up and grinned. That easy smile, the one that had tricked me into thinking she was happy with Neil, despite his 'funny ways', as she used to call them. Life had taught me that people like Evie often smile and shrug to stop those around them delving deeper, to prevent them having the courage to ask questions to which the answers would either be a lie or a truth that they'd then have to act on.

Of all the things I could have said, my big fat mouth came out with, 'My God! You've gone grey.' What I meant to say, of course, was 'You are the most stylish grey-haired woman I've ever seen.' And she was. That elfin face of hers carried the pixie cut to perfection.

She laughed and hugged me, still slim but rounder and softer, no longer those coat-hanger shoulders with the deep wells in her collarbones. I caught a trace of her perfume, not L'Air du Temps but something altogether warmer and spicier. A different smell but still a trigger to transport me back to those days in that rancid church hall where the highlight of the whole mum and toddler session was getting to the Fox's biscuits before the Jammie Dodgers ran out. Evie had always managed to look radiant, a waft of scent whenever she bent down to pick up a Tonka toy. Over thirty-four years ago.

'Come on, let's get coffee and you can talk about my wrinkles.'

Her tone was light and teasing but I still felt the need to explain before we got off on the wrong foot. 'Sorry. That came out clumsily. I didn't mean it like that. It's just that I thought you'd be dyeing your hair until you were ninety-five.'

'I don't even wear make-up except when I go out now.'

And over coffee and a huge slab of lime and ginger sponge – more cake than I'd ever witnessed Evie eat in her life – we danced from subject to subject, the boys, their wives, my grandchildren – as though we'd seen each other the weekend before.

I licked the back of the spoon. 'So, the elephant in the room. Neil. You divorced him?'

Evie held my gaze. 'The day Isaac married Rosa, the zip on my dress got caught. It was one of those tricky hidden zips, and I had to call Neil to help me release it. He was always going on about my weight, but that day – I think he was stressed about the whole wedding – he said I'd better take myself in hand because he couldn't see himself staying with a fat bird for the rest of his life. I didn't say anything at the time, just sort of swallowed it down like I had for, well, forever. But when Isaac stood up and said how beautiful Rosa was and always would be to him and just talked about her with so much, I don't know, respect, it shifted something in me. There were a few other things that day that made me see things differently. Six months later, I left him.'

She made it sound so easy. As though she'd just come to a logical conclusion and made it happen. I was properly wide-eyed with wonder. Evie. The woman who would put a biscuit back in the packet if Neil walked in, who'd leap up to make him a cup of tea as though sitting talking to a friend was something to be hidden, to be ashamed of. As though too much leisure and pleasure were somehow offensive, a reminder that Evie had a cushy life 'just' bringing up Isaac, while Neil, poor man, had to work.

Every time I saw her scurrying about, pandering to his needs, it made me so grateful that I hadn't given up my job and that Mal couldn't pull the 'You don't work, so you'd better use your intellectual energy on delivering tea of the perfect strength' card on me. Thank goodness I hadn't blundered into signing up for a lifetime of clearing up someone else's crumbs. Though I noticed that over the years, Mal had gone from washing up after dinner to pushing things in the general direction of the dishwasher without troubling his upper finger joints with the motion needed to open it.

Evie explained how she'd found a good solicitor, dithered for ages but finally taken the plunge and found a flat a stone's throw from the sea in Whitstable and had spent the last four years running an art gallery with a sideline in photography. 'I don't earn a fortune, but it's just me and I've started giving lessons in taking photos.' She looked down. 'You know, nothing to set the world alight, but lots of women our age have a bit more time and want to explore their creative side. And I've always loved how you can see a different aspect of someone in a photo, so…' She trailed off as though she needed to apologise for having the courage to make a living out of something she was passionate about.

I grabbed her hand. 'I admire you. It's brilliant what you've done. How did Isaac take it? The divorce, I mean?'

Evie pursed her lips together as though she was tucking away a specific and potent hurt. 'He was in his thirties, so he wasn't a child. I'm not sure why I held on so long. I had this idea that I didn't want to let him down, that I wanted him to have that one home with both of us, even though he hadn't really lived there since he went to university. Half the time, I think I used Isaac as an excuse because I was scared I wouldn't cope on my own.'

I nodded at her, encouraging her. I yearned for the comfort of knowing that Evie leaving Neil hadn't had a knock-on effect on Isaac, hadn't destabilised his relationship with his own wife. I patted her arm. 'You might be thrilled to know that I am nowhere near as judgemental now as I was back then.' One of the things I'd understood in the intervening years was that women make hundreds of compromises all the time for their children, even when those children are adults, in the hope of protecting them, of letting them live the happy-ever-after fairy tale for as long as possible.

Evie swallowed. 'I was ashamed to admit that I'd chosen badly, that the man who I'd picked to be his dad wasn't very nice, I suppose. I didn't want him to have divided loyalties, to make him feel he had to side with me. I also thought he might be angry with me for not leaving earlier, when he was still at home.' Her voice cracked a little. 'Isaac saw lots of things I wish he hadn't.'

'But he also had a lot of love from you that meant he was resilient.'

Evie's face relaxed slightly and, once again, I marvelled at how much guilt motherhood entailed, however it panned out.

She took a long sip of coffee. 'A bit of me was also afraid that Isaac would be swept along by what Neil told him about me. That I'd refused to work and left all the financial responsibility to him, that keeping me in the lifestyle I "demanded" meant he was very stressed and sometimes that spilt over into family life. Basically, I didn't want to be the bad guy.'

'None of us ever wants to be the bad guy. I do get that. But Isaac would never have thought that. He was always so close to you.'

'As he got older, though, he also started standing up for me, which, as you can imagine, didn't go down well with Neil. I shouldn't have put Isaac in that position. You'd never have been so weak, never needed to rely on Ben to protect you.'

I wished I could tell her. Blurt out all the jealousy I had inside that she'd broken free, sought out new adventures, been brave, moved to the coast. I was supposed to be that woman, the one who strode through life refusing to live in a substandard way. And especially the person who woke up to the sound of waves. I'd talked about it forever.

Instead, I said, 'You beat me to the cottage by the sea.'

She laughed. 'I stole the idea from you. I even chose Whitstable because you introduced me to it. Do you remember staying in those funny little fishermen's cottages, when the kids were small? When we all tried oysters and Ben told Isaac he'd eaten a lump of dolphin snot?'

'Now you mention it, I do. I would never have recalled Ben saying that though.' A collective pool of memories was yet another reason to have lifelong friends.

Evie looked me in the eye. 'Steph, I borrowed the courage to start a new life from you. I kept telling myself that Steph would never stand for this. That you'd hung on to that sense of self, you never gave yourself over to marriage and motherhood so completely you forgot who you were.'

Her blind faith made me feel like a charity worker who'd stolen the collection box but had won an award for her dedication to fundraising. 'God, I thought this first meeting would be a cheery catch-up on the big events. Didn't realise we'd get deep so quickly. Have you met anyone else?'

Evie picked up the crumbs of her cake with her finger. I couldn't get used to this woman who had always impressed me with her ability to eat precisely one chocolate after any dinner we had together. The sort of person who studied the chocolate menu rather than accidentally eating an orange cream, pulling a face and scoffing up a hazelnut whirl to take the taste away. 'No. I haven't looked. I've got an Irish wolfhound called Noel. He's man enough for me.'

'You don't like dogs.'

'Neil didn't like dogs. Turns out I love them.'

I imagined Evie up early, snapping away with her camera, capturing the sunrises, the seagulls, the changing mood of the sea, with her wolfhound darting in and out of the waves, no one to tie her to a timetable. I couldn't go into town to buy a birthday card without Mal ringing me to see where I was. I was delighted that Evie had found the courage to leave Neil. But I was also slightly incredulous that she'd found the gumption to walk out when I had flirted with the idea then shoved it back in the cupboard as soon as it looked a bit messy. It reminded me of occasions at work when someone I thought was a bit rubbish at their job suddenly pulled a brilliant presentation out the bag and I really needed to up my game when I'd been cruising along, safe in the knowledge that I'd be the one to chase.

From the first time I'd turned up to that toddler group, vociferous about how women had a right to hold on to their ambitions, their identity, despite being mothers and wives, I realised that I'd considered myself slightly superior. I'd been so confident that I had the strength to achieve that when so many weaker, less determined women fell by the wayside. Now here I was, sticking with a husband I didn't love in case I rocked the foundations of my whole family. If my disappearing encouraged Gemma to leave Ben, I dreaded to think what his life would be like. He'd probably become a workaholic like Mal and, without Gemma to run the social diary, find himself increasingly isolated. I was doing exactly what I used to despise in other women: putting my own happiness after everyone else's like some martyr prepared to burn on the stake of selflessness.

'I think you've been incredibly brave. Well done,' I said.

There must have been something in my tone that alerted Evie. I'd forgotten how frustrated I became at her skill of asking searching questions but somehow wriggling out of answering them herself. She sat back in her chair. 'So, are you happy?'

I laughed. 'How long have you got?'

She raised her eyebrows. 'Did life turn out the way you expected?'

I swirled the sugar with my fingertip. 'No. It did not.'

She frowned. 'In what way?'

My chest constricted. 'I'm not happy with Mal. I haven't been for years.'

And as easily as that, I spilt out all the thoughts and feelings that I couldn't tell Teresa because she'd counter every 'I'd like to leave Mal' with either a cheery dismissal of my feelings as a big birthday crisis or give me a long list of Mal's good points, which I'd been repeating to myself mantra-like for the last five years. It wasn't enough though. His ability to sniff out the cheapest room rate for an airport hotel no longer outweighed my desire to kill him when he ate an apple within earshot.

All the while the words were tumbling out, I was marvelling that I hadn't seen this woman for twenty-three years, yet I was being more honest with her than I had been with anyone for as long as I could remember. With that came a rush of sadness that I'd distracted myself for decades with friends who didn't answer that need in me, people who I'd tried to mould into soulmates but lacked that specific combination of qualities that were so hard to define and harder to find. The traits that promoted a person who was fun to hang out with to a friend who'd hold your heart in their hands and understand what kept it alive without the need to explain.

Evie sat very still. 'Is there a particular incident that kicked this off?'

I'd always wondered if Teresa had told her, even though I asked her to keep it to herself.

I nodded. 'Understanding that instead of being someone who embraces adventure, I fear change. Realising that we all trolley along thinking we've got decades of life left, that we'll save being happy for when it's convenient and that, right now, we'll just get through because we're too damn busy and too scared to think about how we actually want to spend our time in case the answer means we'll have to make some difficult decisions.'

'That sums *me* up perfectly, but I wouldn't have thought of you like that.' Her head was tilted to one side as though she was trying to match what she was hearing with the person she thought I was.

'Did Teresa tell you what happened?'

Something flashed across her face. 'About when we were in…?' She stopped. 'She never mentions you to me.'

'That I had cancer?'

Her shock was profound and real. She flushed. 'What? When? Teresa didn't say a word. Are you better?'

'I got the five-year all-clear a month ago.' Unexpectedly, I welled up. 'So, yeah, realising that I might not live to be ninety was a bit of a wake-up call. And now I've woken up, I'm caught between being too bloody terrified to get out of bed and feeling guilty for not making the most of every moment of my second chance.'

As I drove home, I caught glimpses of my reflection in the rear-view mirror, my mouth twitching at the things Evie and I had discussed, the laughs, the many truths tucked into our sentences like treats in an advent calendar. I'd sat with so many friends, put on my best face, never once cried in front of them, never offered up anything less than 'fine'. Evie, though, this woman who barely knew anything about my life now, had immediately understood and allowed me to be sorry for myself without requiring me to tie up my pain with a pretty bow so she could bear to listen. She'd offered comfort, words that beat a path straight to my heart in a way that made me feel heard, even after all these years.

But as I turned the corner into my road, the thought that had been circling, weaving its way in and out of the remembered fragments of our afternoon, landed. When I asked if Teresa had told her, she'd hesitated, started to speak, then caught herself. As though she knew something and was waiting to see if I was party to it too.

STEPH

November 2012

I sat in the car watching the November rain splash down onto the windscreen, knowing the worst bit was still to come.

Worse than the consultant asking me if I'd come alone. I'd felt embarrassed then, the middle-aged woman who, after fifty-four years, couldn't rustle up a single person who cared enough to accompany her. I couldn't bring myself to put into words the fact that Mal would have taken charge of the diagnosis. Made it his, demanded a timeframe, a 'schedule', asked questions that I didn't want to know the answers to, reduced the enormity of this news into something tidy rather than a messy bag of emotions that might fall into the category of 'not easily sorted'. Nope. I'd been much happier coming to the hospital on my own, sitting in the waiting room watching the minutes tick past my appointment time without the added stress of Mal saying loudly, 'Do you think they've forgotten you?' and scowling at overworked staff scurrying about doing their best.

Worse than my mind darting down disappointingly banal avenues: the necessity of clearing out my fridge, so if I died, no one would judge me on my out-of-date yoghurts and the bits of chicken I'd put aside for Gladys, forgotten about and which were now growing a mould so colourful I almost felt guilty about throwing them out.

Worse than my body letting me down, the rude realisation that it was refusing to carry on with its job of being a sturdy and capable vehicle that meant I never had to say, 'I'll ask my husband to carry that for me.' Mine was a body built for clearing drains, hauling mattresses upstairs, lugging terracotta urns into the right position. It wasn't a body whose primary purpose was to decorate, to turn heads, to enchant with its lithe limbs or pert anything, gliding about with delicate knitwear on pointy shoulders like an elegant swan. And, in a way that seemed irrational now, I assumed that my carthorse body would be superior to one that required an extra jumper at the slightest hint of breeze, that shivered away from an exhilarating sea swim on a sunny September Sunday.

No, the worst part would be Mal. My drama would become his tragedy. It was so tempting not to tell him, not to tell anyone. To get through it – or die – without the unbearable burden of other people's opinions on how I should be feeling, reacting or 'thinking positive'.

I got out of the car, refusing to duck my head against the rain, resisting the view of myself as someone who was ill. Someone who might die. I'd only just about got the hang of living. That whole whirl of finding any job, then one I was good at. Then sifting through the frogs until I'd met a man who matched me in drive and ambition, a man I could marry, earlier than I expected. After that came the chaos of becoming a parent, evolving from one who felt plunged into deep icy water to one who, on a good day, could make a reasonable stab at a sensible response to lost training shoes, not being invited to a party, first heartbreak. And finally releasing a decent young adult into the world – as vulnerable yet wilful as a puppy, but with enough core sense to marry a wonderful woman. A wonderful woman who also leant towards the drain-unblocking end of the spectrum rather than the flower-expecting type who geared up for wedding anniversary celebrations weeks in advance.

If this was all the living I was going to do, I'd have done it differently. I had a sudden image rush into my head of people singing 'Seasons in the Sun' at my funeral. I told myself off for being melodramatic and made my way to our front door, disappointed to see that I didn't have a heightened sense of colour, that the world around me wasn't enticingly vibrant. The only thing that felt enhanced was the smell of fox poo on the path.

I turned my key in the lock. I wasn't going to cry. I was going to be what Mal would expect. Matter-of-fact. Organised. Hoping for the best but preparing for the worst.

He appeared in the hallway. 'What did the consultant say?'

'That the scan showed a medium mass in my left breast, which doesn't yet appear to have spread into my lymph nodes.'

'Is that what you expected? Are you having chemotherapy? When does it start?'

And on and on, how many weeks, how long, best case, worst case, until I pushed past him and said, 'Could you make me a cup of tea?' I understood in that moment what I'd never understood before: women who didn't carry their own suitcases, who had no idea how to check their engine oil, who didn't do mice or spiders or bins or lawnmowers had an advantage in these situations. No one expected them to get on with it. Their husbands would encourage them to sit on the sofa and 'have a good cry' and, in return, would offer up the thing I really needed, which wasn't advice, or motivational words, or anything involving second opinions or the way treatments were evolving all the time. They would offer a hug, that precursor to the practicalities, the thing that said more loudly, more effectively than anything else, 'We're in this together.' I wanted to put my head on Mal's shoulder and for him to be there for me in a quiet and non-problem-solving way.

I sat at the kitchen table and he put down a mug of tea in front of me.

'Did you find out whether you'd be well enough to work and go out once the chemo starts?'

I shook my head. 'I don't know. I'm not sure it's so drastic that I'll be confined to bed. It depends how I react to it, I suppose.'

'Didn't you ask?'

I sipped my tea. 'No. Funnily enough, I was having to take quite a lot in and didn't pull out a checklist of everything you'd like to know.'

'The only thing is, I'm supposed to be going to that conference in LA just before Christmas. At a push, I suppose Janine could step in, but it's a bit tricky now the team's much bigger. Did he say whether you needed to have someone with you when you have chemo? Can you drive afterwards in case I'm not around to pick you up?'

I leapt to my feet. 'Mal, do you know what? For once, in your whole life, this isn't about you. Don't bother disrupting your working routine for me. I'll manage and I promise you I won't ask you to put yourself out one jot. Perhaps you can schedule in my funeral for a Saturday so you don't have to lose a day's holiday.'

Mal sat open-mouthed as though I'd turned into a madwoman.

I slammed down my mug. 'And another thing, I'm going to tell Teresa, and Ben and Gemma of course, but that's it. No one else unless we really have to.'

Mal frowned. 'But people need to know. They'll be offended if they find out later that you were really ill and we didn't tell them.'

'They'll soon work it out when I start running around in a big ginger wig. My hideous news, my decision how and when and who gets to know about it. So, if you don't mind, I'll keep Teresa in the loop and skip the great big fanfare from everyone else.'

Now my mind was focused on who I wanted to spend time with, in case time was something of a luxury I could no longer afford to waste, I wasn't going to let my days get sucked away in phone calls from people whom, I realised, I didn't even like. And even with the people I did, I wasn't prepared to spend life going over the same old twaddle: 'Yep, cancer, yes, thinking positive, no, I didn't see that article about going on an alkaline diet.' And I definitely didn't want hundreds of bunches of chrysanthemums turning up. They could save them for my funeral.

I stormed up the stairs, reeling from the fact that even in a literal life-and-death situation, Mal's first thoughts were about how my being ill might inconvenience him. I'd expected it but not quite so soon. I did wonder whether that trait, his ability to make everything about him, had always been present but I'd previously mistaken it for ambition and clarity of thought.

I rang Teresa.

'God, you poor thing. Is there anything I can do that would help?'

'Find me a new husband?' I told her about Mal and how he'd immediately started obsessing about how my illness might impact on his life.

'But that's just the way he is. You know he loves you really, he's just not the sort to be making chicken soup and wrapping you up in a fleecy blanket. And you'd hate it if he was hovering over you all the time.'

She was absolutely right that a tilted head and face full of pity every time I walked into a room would soon begin to pall. But in this alien situation when my own mortality was rushing at me with barely an 'excuse me', I could have coped with a smattering of hovering and a bit of 'How do you feel about this?' rather than a brisk rundown of the terrifying statistics that Google had offered up, followed by a dismissive 'You'll beat it. If anyone can, you can.'

I didn't want to have to be exceptional and brave and rely on myself to make me better. That responsibility I wanted to hand over to the oncologists and let them make the decisions. I was astonished that my natural instinct was to say, 'Whatever you think is best'. In normal circumstances I could form a definitive opinion about my favourite brand of tinned tomatoes.

Mal appeared to sense this indecision and against my better judgement, I allowed him to insist on coming to the first chemo with me – 'What will everyone think if I just let you go on your own?' I regretted letting him accompany me when he alternated between moaning about the terrible hospital Wi-Fi and looking like he might throw up himself when the woman in the chair next to me was sick.

When I recounted Mal scuttling down the corridor to escape, Teresa said, 'Give me the dates of your treatments. Tell Mal I'm taking over hospital duty from now on. After Ross when he was little – do you remember? Car sick like nobody's business – I am *immune* to vomit.'

Mal could barely disguise his relief at not having to do the hardcore 'in sickness' part of our marriage vows – muttering a half-hearted, 'Are you sure? I'm happy to come with you.'

Frankly, without Mal in tow, the trauma was halved. Teresa was the perfect chemo partner. She didn't treat me like I was an invalid, didn't fuss – 'Do you need water? Coffee? Shall I get you a sandwich?' – and was quite happy with her Kindle. But most importantly she never sat there trotting out platitudes, doing the whole 'You need to keep fighting', as though a failure to survive would be entirely down to my lack of will.

But the true gold-star excellence as a friend was getting Paul to take Mal out on a regular basis. To the pub for a game of snooker, for fish and chips. Teresa would come to me, Mal would go with Paul. I would sigh with relief when the door banged and I could eat toast and Marmite without Mal telling me that he'd read that tomatoes were good for breast cancer, that I should drink pomegranate juice and that his colleague had an aunt who put her recovery down to cutting out dairy and alcohol. I couldn't bloody wait for him to go out so I could scarf back half a bottle of Chianti in peace and eat Boursin out of the foil with a spoon. If cancer was going to carry me off, it wasn't going to do it before I'd emptied every bottle of wine in the house. There was something a bit decadent about opening a forty-quid bottle of burgundy on a Thursday, especially when my knackered old taste buds could barely raise a hurrah, but the days of saving anything for best were over.

Teresa never passed a single comment about what I ate or drank. 'I guess you've got to have whatever you fancy.' Like a true friend, she organised my freezer and cleared the fridge of the half-eaten hummus and the mouldy blueberries that I'd kept looking at and thought, *Yeah, cancer-beating properties, I'll get to those later, just a little bit of ginger chocolate to keep me going for now*. Most of all, she didn't try to tell me that plenty of people were worse off, that they caught mine early, or produce some horror story of a twenty-year-old niece of a friend of a colleague who'd died of undiagnosed ovarian cancer.

One day, she'd picked me up to take me to the hospital and I'd cried all the way there. 'I'm just so fucked off with this. I don't want to sit there telling the nurses that I've got tricky veins and smiling encouragingly at the women opposite when we all know that the odds are that one of us will probably be dead by Easter.'

She'd parked the car, come round to my side and hugged me, properly opened her arms and let me cry without trying to fix anything. She just stroked my back and said, 'I'm so sorry for you. I wish I could do something to make it better.' I'd teased her that I knew I was in trouble because she was giving me proper hugs, not the ones she normally did, where she stretched her head away, like Gladys when I offered her a piece of cucumber.

She never gave me a rundown of the difficulties she'd faced juggling her physio clients, she never looked at her watch or moaned about the arrangements she had to make for eleven-year-old Amelia to be picked up from school. In fact, she never gave me the impression that she was anything other than happy to be able to do something to help.

She also didn't do Mal's stoking up of my fury. 'God knows why this had to happen to you. It's not like you eat loads of red meat. All those people who don't take any exercise and smoke till they're ninety. It's not fair.' Which probably did reflect what I thought but might have felt more comforting if his outbursts weren't then followed by questions about whether I'd be well enough to be on my own for a few days while he went to Cape Town for what sounded distinctly like a company jolly.

With Paul's blessing, Teresa stayed with me when Mal was away. I was humbled by her offer to sleep on a camp bed in my bedroom. She'd looked horrified when I'd laughed and said I was used to sleeping alone as Mal had disappeared into the spare room within days of my diagnosis: 'You won't want me disturbing you. You'll sleep better on your own.'

What I really wanted was someone who'd be awake with me, who'd reach out a hand and tell me that whatever lay ahead, he'd be right by my side. Someone who would talk about our memories, those little moments – the walks with Gladys, the lazy Sunday brunches, the weekends away with Teresa and Paul – that now I looked back were the big moments. Someone who'd make me feel that even if life stopped now, it had been the best possible version, a free-range, wildflower meadow of a life, rather than a cage-reared alternative, sitting in its own excrement and waiting for judgement day.

When I tried to explain the sheer loneliness to Mal of waking up in the middle of the night with thoughts racing round my head, he said, 'We can't both be exhausted. Someone has got to keep the money coming in. Maybe you should have a mug of milk before bed?'

Towards the end of treatment, I was finding it harder to shrug off the effects of the chemo, which left me wiped out for several days. On one occasion, Gemma had heard Mal going on about how he would have to cancel an important work trip because there was no way he could leave me on my own and she lost it with him. 'You need to listen to yourself, Mal. If I had breast cancer and all Ben was doing was moaning about how inconvenient it was for him, I'd soon be packing his suitcases and showing him the door. Steph's got enough to deal with without you banging on.'

Mal was so surprised that he didn't answer back, just snatched up his glasses and, the next thing, we saw him furiously jet-washing the patio.

Gemma looked at me. 'Sorry. I shouldn't have spoken to him like that.'

I knew there was a reason I loved her. She was still her own woman. She didn't go looking for trouble, but she hadn't yet got to that stage of marriage where keeping the peace outweighed the great liberation of saying what you thought. I hoped she never would. As far as I was concerned, she could carry on giving the men in this family a run for their money for as long as she liked.

'Gemma, if I could cartwheel round the room without throwing up, I would. If I hear "mind over matter" one more time, I'm going to jump in a coffin and bang the lid down myself.'

And with that, she burst into tears. 'Don't say that. You're like a mum to me.'

I put my arms out. 'Come here.'

She hugged me gently. 'I don't want to hurt you.'

'I'm more robust than I look. Don't forget that at this stage, it's the treatment that's making me look like I'm on my last legs, not the cancer. But I do have to say this to you, as Ben and Mal keep sticking their fingers in their ears whenever I broach the subject.'

'What?'

'If I die, and I'm going to try very hard not to, but don't let them bury me. I want to be cremated.'

Gemma started crying again. 'Ben won't like that.'

'Why not?'

'He has some idea about wanting a grave to visit.'

I was astonished that Ben had even acknowledged to Gemma that I might die. If I ever said anything as innocuous as 'Not looking forward to my scan on Thursday,' he'd wave his hand and say, 'You'll be fine, Mum.' Which did nothing to reassure me. Instead it made me feel that the panic that coursed through me whenever I thought about it was ridiculous and I should pull myself together.

Ben had inherited Mal's inability to deal with illness, discomfort or emotions that needed to be examined and talked about maybe more than once before they could be considered 'dealt with'. Last time Ben had come round, I'd left off my headscarf because my scalp was itchy and it was as though I'd greeted him with full-frontal nudity. He didn't know where to look and kept making excuses to get up from the table and stare out of the window. Eventually, he'd started fiddling about with a piece of trim that had come loose under the dishwasher as though it was imperative that it got fixed right now. That was three weeks ago.

I tried to understand that not everyone, including my son, did illness well, but on days when I was strong enough to think about it, I felt like phoning him up and saying, 'I'm sorry my bald head offends you. I'm sorry that you've had to deal with a mother who is ill, instead of one who can pop round and help you put together a new bed at a moment's notice, but, believe me, however hard this is for you, I'm also not having the time of my life.'

But I didn't say any of that. Not to Ben, and not to Gemma, who automatically took on the responsibility of checking in with me rather than forcing Ben to step up. Just as I had with Mal's mother, Janet. I'd been the one to buy and write the cards: Mother's Day, birthday, Christmas. In the end, it was easier than hearing the hurt in her voice when Mal forgot or smothering my resentment at the unspoken accusation that I was a hopeless wife for not getting it sorted. As though sifting through a stand of crappy cards for a message that wasn't an out-and-out lie required special female insight rather than just taking responsibility for your own relatives from any gender.

Which is why I wasn't going to go along with Gemma's charade of 'emergency of guinea pig claw removal/Chihuahua earache/rabbit dysentery equalling Ben being too rushed off his feet to phone his mother'. I wanted Gemma to know I didn't blame her for his behaviour. 'Ben doesn't really do illness very well. I'm afraid he's like his father in that way.' Followed by an immediate regret about being disloyal. 'But he's a lovely man in other ways,' I said.

Gemma sighed. 'To be honest, I think most men don't know what to do when they can't fix something.'

'Which is why I need you to take on board what I'm saying about the whole cremation if it comes to that. If I ever try to tell Mal or Ben, they just say, "Don't talk like that." I mean, I understand it's not the sort of conversation that's going to make your day, but it's got to be had. My life, my death. I don't think I'm going to compromise on that one.'

She squeezed my hands. 'Okay. I'll make sure they know. When's your final scan?'

'Six weeks.'

And by the time I finished treatment, I'd learnt something about my husband and my son that I wished I'd never had to know. My husband apparently found the prospect of me popping my clogs slightly less distressing than the handouts for his next conference being bound in the wrong order. In times of extreme emotion, my son delegated tricky relationship management to his wife. If I ever got well again, I would no doubt spend lots of dawn hours questioning the part I had played in making him like that, while Mal slumbered peacefully in the room next door.

STEPH

24 June 2018

In the weeks following Gemma's work trip to Cheltenham, I monitored every interaction between her and Ben, every comment about her work like a detective building up a case, and I still couldn't decide whether there was an explanation for the rogue text. Today I'd invited them all over for Sunday lunch and felt nervous, as though I was selling our family set-up to her, showing her what she'd be missing. I hadn't said a word to Mal about my suspicions – he never really warmed to anyone who had the temerity to challenge his behaviour – and he was quick enough to slate Gemma as it was. I'd done a huge piece of beef, with Yorkshire puddings, one of the ways I could connect to Ben and guarantee a smile.

Thankfully it was a lovely sunny June day so the girls could run off their energy in the garden, which alleviated a layer of stress as Mal wasn't leaping up every time they went near the TV or any of my houseplants. We had had the cheese plant catastrophe all over the cream carpet last year, so Nell wasn't without form, but the loss of the odd bit of greenery and the occasional carpet clean was a small price to pay for the absolute joy my granddaughters brought me. On the other hand, Mal's 'careful, careful, don't touch that' and the sucking of his teeth every time one of the girls took an overenthusiastic sip of squash as though a splodge of blackcurrant on the table was the end of the world made me want to shut him in the garden shed – without food or water. He justified his grumbling with 'They've got to learn to behave.'

By behaving, I think he meant sitting still for four hours at a time, which always made me rush to their defence. 'They are behaving. Look at them with their please and thank yous and washing their hands. Sometimes, just like you, they make mistakes.'

Nevertheless, every visit was like a set of old-fashioned scales, with the bountiful joy of Dottie and Nell on one side, countered by Mal's miserly dampening down of vitality on the other. I lived in fear that the lovely Gemma would look at us and think – as I often did – are these the people I want to spend the rest of my life with? Who knew what other family might be waiting in the wings with kindness and generosity and appreciation? Rather than Mal moaning about the racket that the girls made on the trampoline (which also created a yellow patch on his precious grass). Or Ben whingeing that the car policy at work meant he was stuck with a four-year-old Berlingo rather than the much-coveted Subaru something or other that would have illuminated his life like a megawatt chandelier and made everything right.

So when Gemma came through the door, I was what Ben would describe as 'overwhelming'.

'Hellooo! Lovely to see you.' I flung my arms around her. 'You smell gorgeous. What's that perfume?'

Gemma said, 'Thank you. It's Red, by Hugo Boss.'

I'd love to have been that person who could turn round and say, 'Aha. I know you're having an affair now because you always wear Chanel/Jo Malone/Miss Dior and that must be a gift from your lover', but, frustratingly, that little bit of knowledge proved nothing one way or the other.

I hugged Ben – 'Hello, darling, you look well.'

'Bit knackered actually.'

I was a bad mother, but Mal had already moaned about me not putting the jump leads back in the correctly coiled position and how he hoped he wasn't getting an ear infection that morning, so my tolerance for anyone else's drizzle on my Sunday sunshine was atrophied. I managed a perfunctory 'Oh dear', or at least I hoped I had. The words that were actually in my head were 'Please don't bore me with any minor troubles that could be resolved with an afternoon nap.' People complaining about their lack of sleep fell into the same category of interest as anyone who wittered on about how long their journey had taken because of the traffic on the motorway, the hideousness of their root canal surgery or ailments of any kind. If it wasn't going to kill them, I wasn't interested. As I got older, I was finding it more challenging to keep the mute button to a permanent on.

I turned to Gemma. 'What can I get you to drink? Is Ben driving? I've got some of that raspberry gin you like, or I could make a mojito with mint out of the garden.'

She laughed and shook her head. 'Early start tomorrow. We've got a team meeting in Bristol.'

My stomach tightened. 'There and back in a day?'

'It should be, but us senior managers have agreed to go prepared to stay over.'

I studied her closely. Not a flicker, not looking away, nothing squirmy. Maybe she was just determined, practised. Or maybe she was telling the truth. 'What about the girls?'

'Ben will have them if necessary.'

Ben said, 'I'll just have to go into work a bit late on Tuesday.' There was an air of 'very busy man making large sacrifice for wife who earns rather less than me'.

'You'll manage as a one-off, won't you?' I tried not to sound snappy, but so many women had to walk that tightrope between family and work, all the time, for doctor's appointments, tantrums outside school, running back for the packed lunch left sitting on the hallway windowsill. Of course, if Ben was currently shifting his appointments to nine-thirty to facilitate Gemma getting down and dirty with another man, then that was a different matter. My problem was that I wasn't sure where I should direct my anger.

I didn't want to allow Gemma even a sliver of an excuse, but I couldn't be a hypocrite. I could never tell her – tell anyone – exactly how well I understood that need to prove that a woman's worth amounted to far more than how efficiently she could facilitate the lives of everyone else around her. I chased the memory back into the corner of my mind, though every time it snowed, I couldn't help smiling to myself.

I wanted to shake my son, to tell him to open his eyes, to be present, to value her before it was too late, before some other man with short-comings she wouldn't discover until our lives had been turned upside down tempted her away with promises of making her feel special, noticed, *heard*. Even if Gemma wasn't involved with someone else, she might turn out to be like Evie and not even need another man to lure her away. The more often I saw Evie and heard about how happy she was without Neil, the more I realised that women could – and did – leave unsatisfactory men without having a replacement lined up.

Thankfully, before I could get sucked any further down that route, Dottie and Nell discovered a worm in amongst my butternut squashes and drew me in with their squeals of horror and delight. Gemma rushed out to join in the excitement, but Ben sat at the table reading the papers with Mal. With a stab of guilt, I remembered being that parent, that huge craving for time in my own head, the space to allow thoughts to waft around without being interrupted. I loved it when my mother sat building Lego with Ben or took him to the farm or zoo on a Saturday so I could get my hair cut or have coffee with a friend, without a time limit or constraint. It was ironic now how I wished Ben would grasp that these worm moments were the important things, that later on there'd be time, lots and lots of time, to do whatever he wanted.

Gemma was already kneeling with them, watching the worm, asking questions about how they thought it moved.

'It's hopping,' Nell said.

Dottie laughed. 'I can hop higher than that!' She launched into a demonstration.

I couldn't help it. I wanted Ben to join in, to not miss this little fragment of innocence. I called to him through the patio doors, 'Come and look.'

He had that reluctance that Mal had, that I'd had. That sense of duty in his walk, that preparation for false enthusiasm. 'What have we got here then?'

I took a picture of them all on my phone, Dottie dangling a worm with them all laughing, almost as though I wanted a catalogue of photos to show Gemma if she decided to leave, a last-ditch armoury of reasons to stay.

After Ben had done his obligatory ten minutes, he started to drift back to the house. I caught him up. 'It's none of my business but…' Wariness immediately spread over Ben's features. I pushed on. 'I do think you could give Gemma a break sometimes. She works really hard and she'd probably like to sit down with the papers too.'

'She loves being with the girls.'

The temptation to grab him by his arms and shout, 'Your wife might be having an affair! Wake up!' was almost overwhelming. Instead, I forced my voice under control. 'Of course she loves being with them, but it's nice to have a bit of time out occasionally. I know your work is full on, but she still comes home to all the cooking and washing and everything else. I imagine she doesn't get to put her feet up much in the evenings.'

Ben scowled, the same expression he'd had since he was a child when anyone told him something he didn't want to hear. 'She was the one that wanted kids.'

Sometimes I couldn't believe how immature Ben was at thirty-six. I sighed. 'Darling, I'm not asking you to become a stay-at-home dad, but no matter how much she loves the girls, it's really important not to feel totally taken for granted. I'm just saying that young marriages come under so much pressure these days and you need to take care of each other. Make an effort to be a couple too.'

'Right,' Ben said, sliding back the French windows.

Sometimes my failure as a mother in training my son to be a decent husband seemed to shine out of Ben in lights so bright that they wouldn't be out of place in a fairground. Only a desire to avoid spoiling the whole lunch stopped me shouting, 'Right? Right? What is that supposed to mean? Yes, I'm right? Yes, you've heard me and agree? Or "right" as in "Right, you have no idea what you're on about" and would like me to shut up?'

Over lunch, I tried another tactic, laying my traps like a poacher at dusk.

I asked them how work was going and, satisfyingly, they both said how busy they were. 'Have you thought about getting some help at home? A cleaner?' I paused. 'Or a gardener?' I asked, putting a funny little emphasis on the word.

I watched Gemma closely. She looked over at Ben, her face blank but her expression was tense. Though whether that was because of 'gardener' or because Ben said, 'I think we'd rather spend the money on other things. Our garden isn't very big and we kind of manage the housework between us,' I wasn't sure. I was pretty certain Ben's contribution to 'between us' was picking up the newspaper off the mat every morning.

'I'm always happy to help out mowing the lawn,' I offered, feeling an irresistible urge to bang my spoon on the table and demand to know who 'Gardener' was in Gemma's phone. Instead I took myself off to the kitchen to fetch some more roast potatoes. When I came back, I said, 'Mal and I wondered whether you'd like us to have the girls for a weekend, Gemma, so you and Ben can go away for your birthday?' I kept my eyes on her.

She smiled. 'That sounds lovely. Are you sure?' I was sieving for any reluctance in her voice. A bit guarded? Or worried about inconveniencing us?

'Of course! It would be my pleasure – *our* pleasure. We'd also like to pay for you to stay in a hotel somewhere. Where would you like to go? The seaside in Kent? Brighton? London?' I could feel

Mal's puzzlement that he hadn't been party to any conversation of the sort, but I'd pay for the weekend myself and he'd soon get back in his box. I turned to Ben. 'About time you had a little break together. It's so important to make space for yourselves. Best gift you can give your kids, staying solid.'

Ben raised his eyebrows as though he was keen for me to relinquish my newly found role of marriage guidance counsellor but, nonetheless, he said, 'I quite fancy Brighton. Good restaurants and pubs. Gemma? It's your birthday, any preferences?' He reached his hand out and squeezed hers. I tried to see whether she squeezed back or tugged her hand away.

At that moment, Mal thrust the gravy boat into my line of vision. 'I think we need some more' – as though the distance between the table and the hob was too much for his knackered knees.

The fury that little gesture engendered in me, that complacency of sitting there, waving his needs in my direction, was quite shocking in its intensity. Since I'd flirted with the idea of leaving, it was as though I needed intravenous antihistamine when he was around. Everything he said, did, the way he laughed – which hadn't changed since I met him, when I found it cute and infectious – plugged into a circuit of annoyance that was getting hotter and hotter, as though it might explode at an entirely inconvenient moment.

I took a deep breath and said, 'Sure, there's plenty in the pan. I'll just go and fetch it.'

And as I picked up my ladle, I heard Dottie say, 'Why does Grandma frown all the time?'

I dreaded the thought that my legacy would, in years to come, be 'You know, Dad's mum, the grandma who scowled all the time.' But there was no way I could plunge the whole family into chaos by leaving Mal if Ben and Gemma were heading for disaster. Frowning, grumpy grandma it would have to be.

TERESA

April 2000

Evie suggested a few days away over Easter to give the boys a break before they took their A levels. I was worried about Ross taking time off from his studies. However, Paul said, 'Probably just what he needs,' so I tried not to be the killjoy as Ross leapt at the opportunity. Neither Evie nor I was good at making decisions, so by the time Evie went to book a cottage in Suffolk, there was only a large house overlooking the beach left.

I was too embarrassed to tell Evie that we couldn't really afford that much so I ended up persuading myself and Paul that it was worth it. 'It's probably the last time Ross will come away with us. He'll be off with his friends after his exams.' I still felt apprehensive rather than excited, in case there wasn't enough to do or, despite the premium price, it was very basic.

In the five years since Evie and Steph had fallen out, I'd really missed Steph taking charge of our weekends away. She always soaked up the responsibility of making sure everyone was happy and we just had to follow along. Steph had a knack of making everything seem like an adventure, even when it poured with rain. The few times we'd been away with Evie's family on our own had seemed a bit flat in comparison.

A week before we were due to go, Wendy phoned and said that she was at a loose end over Easter. 'Can Zoe and I come down and stay with you?'

'We're actually going away with Neil and Evie.'

'Oh no. We haven't seen you for ages. Zoe really misses her Auntie Teresa. Where are you staying?'

I knew where this was heading. 'We're in a little cottage in Suffolk.' I tried to make it sound as though it was a tiny place we were all shoehorning into.

'I've never been to Suffolk. Is there any chance you could squeeze me and Zoe in as well? She'd love to spend some time with you. She hardly ever sees you.'

I didn't know how to say no. Since Mum had died the year before, I felt horribly guilty about Wendy being up in Durham with a four-year-old and no support. One of the last times I saw Mum before she died, she said, 'You make sure you look out for our Wendy. She pretends to be tough but she hasn't got the family you have. That useless husband of hers, leaving her with that wee one.'

I came up with lots of objections – that it wasn't fair on Evie and Neil to invite her at the last minute, that a four-year-old girl would want to do vastly different things from two eighteen-year-old boys, that it was probably our last holiday with our sons – but Wendy woodpeckered away until I gave in, like I always did.

Paul frowned, then put his arms around me. 'You're my favourite soft touch.'

I dreaded telling Evie, especially after the Norfolk debacle, but she laughed and said, 'At least Mal won't be there.'

'Don't. I've never had the courage to confront Wendy about that.'

Evie shrugged. 'At this point, it's probably better to leave well alone. Mind you, that's easy for me to say as I'm probably not likely to cross paths with Steph again.'

I nodded and changed the subject, surrendering to the stab of regret that our happy band of three no longer existed and of guilt that I'd done nothing to facilitate bridge-building. I half-wished we'd brought it all to a head at the time, that we'd let Steph, Mal and Wendy sort it out between them, instead of having to carry this sickening anxiety that the truth would come out one day and I'd look like the worst friend in the world.

Thankfully, the house was big and beautiful, right on the beach in Shingle Street. The irritation that Wendy had muscled into our weekend subsided as Ross engaged with his cousin. Both boys took it in turns to give Zoe piggybacks to a backdrop of great squeals of laughter. The weather was blustery and our days passed in kite-flying, walking and hot chocolate drinking. Apart from a few spats over who'd used all the hot water, I was unwinding nicely and enjoying the satisfaction of eating hearty dinners after long days in the fresh air.

On Sunday evening once Zoe was in bed, we started making chicken curry. As Wendy chopped the onions and Evie measured out the spices, our conversation meandered backwards and forwards, with Evie making a huge effort to include Wendy. 'Do you find it hard taking all the decisions on your own for Zoe?' she asked. Evie had been quite taken with the little girl, which made me think she would have loved a daughter.

'A bit. But I've been by myself since she was about a year old so I'm used to it. It's lonely though. It wasn't so bad when Mum and Dad were alive, but I can't afford babysitters, so it's much harder for me to go out in the evenings now. I don't know how I'll ever meet anyone else,' Wendy said.

Neil caught the tail end of our conversation. 'Why don't you look in the lonely hearts column? Isn't there a "searching for love" section in the local paper? Or what about internet dating? That's supposed to be all the rage now.'

'Meeting random strangers off the internet? Wouldn't that be a bit dangerous?'

During dinner, the conversation turned to Wendy's potential partners. Fuelled by wine, we all piled in, with much hilarity about whether Wendy was more likely to meet a Tom Hanks type or end up with a bloke who still lived with his mum at forty-two and wore Superman pyjamas. Paul was very much against the idea – 'You'll end up locked in someone's basement' – whereas Neil was all for Wendy disappearing to the library to sign up to a dating site on one of their computers. 'Spread your wings. Why not? You're far more likely to meet someone decent that way, it's like a checklist for a boyfriend. Much better than hoping to bump into your soulmate in a pub.'

Ross looked positively disgusted at the idea of his aunt talking about men at all, especially when she winked at Neil and said, 'You never know, I might find one as sexy as you.'

Neil raised his eyebrows and said, 'I'm one of a kind.'

I glanced at Evie to see if she minded, but she pulled a face as if to say, 'Too right there' and started clearing the plates.

As Ross disappeared off with Isaac to play *Tomb Raider*, I was disappointed that the highlight of their weekend was the discovery of the PlayStation, rather than any coastal walk or beautiful sunset over the sea. On the upside, not having to worry about Ross being bored allowed me to keep an eagle eye on my sister. She was clearly enjoying being the centre of attention, but a knot of tension was tightening in my stomach as she filled her glass again. Nine o'clock. There'd be no chance of shuffling her off to bed before eleven.

I stood up. 'Right, shall we watch a film? There are quite a lot of DVDs through there.'

I signalled to Paul to support the idea, but he was blokily oblivious to my semaphoring. 'Aren't we okay just chatting?'

Through gritted teeth, I said, 'I fancy having an open fire in the sitting room at least once before we go.'

Thankfully at the word 'fire', Neil became all hunter-gatherer and beckoned Paul through to discuss kindling and log arrangement techniques.

Wendy wandered off to join them without bothering to help finish clearing up. I took the opportunity to whisper my apologies to Evie, who said, 'Don't be silly. She's fine. I've enjoyed having a little one around again, though I'd forgotten what hard work it is. Just having to keep your eye on them all the time. You forget that you're constantly watching that they don't fall in the water or touch something hot.'

I nodded. 'She's as good as gold, but I do feel sorry for Wendy on her own.'

'Doesn't Zoe's dad help out?' Evie asked.

'He does a bit but, of course, he didn't live with her that long. As far as I understand, he visits and has days out with her, but she never stays with him. Maybe that will change when she's a bit older.'

'She seems really well-adjusted to me. Wendy must be doing something right.'

I was just thinking that the weekend had exceeded my expectations and I'd assuaged a bit of my auntie and sister guilt, when Paul came through, looking flustered. 'I think one of you needs to rescue Neil. Wendy's had a bit too much to drink.'

My heart sank. We both followed him through to find Wendy attempting to lure Neil away from his fire-making duties to dance with her. She was wiggling her hips in his face to 'Dancing in the Moonlight', trying to get him to stand up.

He was saying, 'I'm not dancing, Wendy. You need to go into the kitchen with the girls.'

Wendy wasn't having any of it, tugging at the back of his jumper. 'You're teasing me.'

Neil stood up. 'I'm really not. I'm deadly serious. I'm not dancing and I'm not teasing you.' He had an edge to his voice that I'd heard him use with Evie when she did something he didn't like and it made my stomach flip with apprehension. The concern on Evie's face that Neil would suddenly lose his temper galvanised me.

I marched over. 'Wendy, come on. Let's go and get some coffee.'

'I don't want coffee. I want to dance with Neil.'

Paul came to my rescue and we manhandled her into the kitchen. I shut the door. 'You can't behave like this. It's embarrassing. They're my friends and you just can't start flirting with other people's husbands and expect them not to mind.' My tone was gentle, but inside I felt as though flames were licking dangerously close to igniting a firework of home truths.

'Oh lighten up, Teresa, I was just having a laugh. You've always cared about your friends more than me. You weren't sticking up for me when they were all taking the mickey out of me about how I'll only meet weirdos and axe murderers.'

I tried. I really tried to see her point of view. All I'd seen over dinner was her loving the attention and laughing at everyone's suggestions for her profile.

Paul stepped in. 'It was just a bit of fun, Wendy. You were joining in. We didn't mean to upset you.'

'How would either of you know how I feel about anything? You never show any interest in me or Zoe. Since Mum died, you've been to Durham twice – and one of those trips was for the funeral.'

'I don't think any good is going to come from this conversation tonight. Why don't we talk about it in the morning?' I suggested.

'You just want to get back to your stupid friends.'

I snapped. 'No, actually, Wendy, I want to make sure my best friend is still talking to me after you hit on her husband. What do you think Evie thinks when she sees you hanging off Neil like that?'

'He's not really my type anyway.' I should have known that an apology would be beyond her, that she'd default instead to petulance.

Paul grabbed her by the arm. 'That's enough. Upstairs to bed with you.' She resisted and started flopping about, refusing to budge.

'You never did put me first. Always trailing round after that Steph like some simpering lapdog. You can tell her from me that her husband knows what he's up to in bed.'

Wendy was wearing that expression I remembered from childhood. More defiant and determined than abashed. The temptation to shake her until her brain shuddered in her head was almost overwhelming.

Paul looked completely stunned, but I could only focus on Wendy and the realisation that for the last five years, I'd been hanging on to a vain hope, convincing myself that she wouldn't, couldn't have done something so despicable.

'You little cow. Evie kept saying she thought she'd heard you two together, but I wouldn't believe her because you were getting married in a fortnight. Why? I mean, literally, why would you do that?' I had the irrational thought that this woman couldn't possibly be my sister, that my mother must have picked up the wrong baby in the hospital.

She still looked rebellious. 'I don't know. Just wanted to check I wasn't making a mistake before it was too late.'

Paul was frowning, gesturing to me as though he wanted confirmation that he had heard correctly.

Wendy starting shouting. 'You've no idea how I felt growing up with a sister who does everything right. Everyone always rolling their eyes as though "Wendy has gone and done it again". Can you imagine what it was like when I split up with Glenn after less than two years? "If only you were more like your sister" was written all over my mother's face. And would have been over Dad's as well if he hadn't been dead!'

I was trembling. 'You're so selfish, Wendy. You always have been. What part of you thought it was okay to come away with me and jump into bed with my friend's husband? If Steph ever, ever finds out, I'll lose her. Steph is not the sort of woman to take this lying down. She'll make us all take sides.'

Wendy leant forward. 'I don't suppose Mal's ever going to tell her, so unless you and Paul do...'

'Evie knows you slept with him.'

'Yeah, but that's old news really, isn't it? It's, what, five years ago? She's not likely to bother bringing it up now.'

My mouth dropped open at Wendy's definition of 'old news'. 'You haven't exactly got her onside this weekend by trying it on with her husband.' I knew I should stop, resume the discussion in the morning when she'd have half a chance of remembering some of it. But I couldn't overlook her casual attitude to the fact that we all had to cart her betrayal around with us. 'You've put us in such a difficult position. What are we supposed to do? Every time I see Steph, I'll know that I'm keeping a great big secret from her that could wreck her marriage.'

Wendy shrugged. 'You've got two choices. You can either tell her, and, I guess, knowing what a tyrant Steph is, she'll dump Mal and never speak to you again, or you can keep quiet and accept that it's none of your bloody business!'

Paul looked so disgusted with Wendy that, for a second, I had a brief flicker of fear that he'd divorce me just for being related to her. He was going to be furious that I'd never told him my suspicions earlier.

I turned to him. 'You go and apologise to Evie and Neil, I'll get Wendy to bed.'

Thankfully, Paul was a man who knew how to pick his moments, so he sighed and headed back into the sitting room.

Contrarily, as though she was content with the havoc she'd wreaked, Wendy went singing up the stairs without a word of complaint. I, on the other hand, plodded up behind her, weighed down with the burden of being stuck between two unpalatable choices.

TERESA

August 2000

In the four months since Wendy's revelation, every time I saw Steph, I was plagued by the sense that I might burst out with what I knew, then watch her face pass from shock, through to disbelief, to settle in fury.

In the end, I told Evie, who was surprisingly sanguine. 'We sort of knew already. In some ways, I'm glad to have it confirmed, to have the proof that I wasn't making it up.'

'I didn't think you were. I just didn't want to believe it.'

We talked at length about what I should do with the knowledge. 'It's up to you. Obviously my friendship with Steph has already hit the buffers.'

'I need to think about it,' I said, knowing that I would probably take the easy way out and do nothing, while convincing myself that keeping Wendy's secret was the honourable thing to do.

When Steph held me to an idea we'd vaguely discussed – walking the Camino de Santiago in Spain as soon as our sons disappeared off to university in the autumn – I justified my decision. This was a fresh chapter of our lives and dragging up the past didn't seem relevant to the future. The present was tricky enough – Paul's work as a lecturer had taken a hit just as we'd taken the plunge and put down a deposit on a clinic so I could set up my own physio practice. I kept putting off telling him that I wanted to spend money on going away with Steph. In the end, I tried to ease my conscience by suggesting to Steph that we invited our husbands.

She was having none of it. 'Can't we do a bit of a Thelma and Louise? We'll have done eighteen years of child-rearing. This should be the start of a new era. I'm going to become a *lot* more selfish.'

I'd laughed but kept my counsel, as, in my opinion, she'd always been quite rigid about pleasing herself regardless of Ben and Mal.

Urged on by Steph – 'It's our reward for all those bloody hours spent making pigs out of plasticine' – I'd finally got round to mentioning to Paul what we wanted to do. He'd surprised me, which only added to my guilt. 'I think it's a great thing to do to mark that transition. Especially as you're going to be working flat out all next year and beyond to get the clinic up and running.'

Steph appeared to have no such qualms. 'If Mal, at forty-two, can't feed and clothe himself for a fortnight, that's not my problem.'

I envied Steph and her dogged determination to be her own woman. I'd done so much more because she'd been my friend. She always had to tease me out of my instinctive reluctance to leave Paul and Ross to their own devices: 'Come on! It will be fun. It's not the end of the world if they eat pizza and don't change their underpants.'

Once we'd committed to our Camino de Santiago adventure, I then turned my attention to fretting about what I'd let myself in for. Steph morphed into trip organiser extraordinaire, telling me where she'd managed to blag free accommodation through work, a little complimentary wine-tasting in Bierzo – 'You'll have to pretend to be my assistant' – and how one of the final stages, Arzúa to Lavacolla, would be on horseback, the prospect of which was both thrilling and terrifying.

I found myself wishing that Evie could come with us, a companion in the cautious corner. A wish quickly swept away by the shameful rush of relief that Evie didn't have any contact with Steph any more. The last thing I needed was Evie letting slip what had happened between Mal and Wendy on a wine-fuelled evening under a Spanish sky.

I pushed those thoughts away as I met Steph for a drink at the pub to finalise who was bringing what for our trip. It was only 7 p.m. but I was already yawning, weary with all the extra shifts I'd done during the summer in an effort to plug the hole in the family finances. When I'd told Paul I was worried about keeping up with Steph, who never seemed to need to rest, he said, 'I think you need to get your hormones checked. You might be starting the menopause. That can make you tired.' I'd felt ridiculously offended, as though he didn't appreciate how hard I was working and just dismissed it as me getting old.

'Forty-five is a bit young for that,' I'd said, marvelling at my ability to be embarrassed about discussing 'women's things' with my husband of nineteen years.

I wasn't going to tell Steph any of this. I didn't want her to feel as though she was going to be carrying dead wood through Spain. In truth, though, I knew that I'd agree with whatever she decided. She'd always swept me along with her, stopped me turning into a mother who measured her self-worth in how many A*s Ross pulled out of the bag at GCSE and whether he continued with the violin in the sixth form. 'He's had so much attention and love. He'll find his way, he's got such a good base to start from. You can't take responsibility for every last detail.'

There was no doubt that in Steph's slipstream, I became more. More adventurous. More open-minded. More carefree. My natural bent was towards planning, booking and checking rather than towards Steph's angst-inducing assertions that 'something will turn up, let's see how it goes'. Steph had brought lightness and joy and colour to my life. I couldn't lose her.

Within minutes of settling down with our drinks, we fell into our usual pattern of me greeting any of Steph's plans with caution before surrendering to whatever she suggested.

I baulked at her foodie tour of Galician delicacies: 'Goose barnacles? Fried milk? Really?'

I also had reservations about the tour of the vineyards by bike given that the last one I'd been on was probably a Chopper, but she waved me away – 'I'll haul you out if we end up in a ditch.'

We were like an old married couple – 'I'm not sure about that.' 'You'll enjoy yourself when you get there.' And she was spot on. I usually did.

She pulled out her list of essentials. 'We don't want to be carrying more than we need to.'

I took out my pen and wrote down *picnic blanket, water bottles, blister plasters,* keeping a running total in my head of how much I'd need to spend on supplies, while Paul was at home combing the *Times Educational Supplement* looking for extra teaching work.

We ordered some food. 'Ha… can't wait to be eating tapas in the sunshine,' Steph said.

'Well, I hope I can keep up with you. I'm falling asleep on the sofa at ten o'clock.'

'You'll get energy from doing something different. Before you know it, you'll be flamenco dancing on the tables.'

I didn't dare contradict her in case she made it her mission to make it happen.

Just as my scampi arrived, I felt an odd sensation, as though I was either going to wet myself or be sick. I jumped to my feet. 'Just popping to the loo.'

As I got up, Steph gasped. 'Teresa, you've got blood all over the back of your trousers.'

'Oh God. Sorry.' I dashed to the loo, like a schoolgirl bleeding all over her uniform and having to wear her PE skirt for the rest of the afternoon. I'd begun to think that Paul was right and that I was having an early menopause because it was a few months since I'd had a period.

The blood had soaked through my pale trousers. I hoped it hadn't leaked all over the pub chair. I tried to limit the damage with a handful of paper towels, cursing the indignities of being a woman.

I sidled out of the loos with my back to the wall, when the room started to spin and I stumbled into a chair, knocking it over. The next thing I knew, Steph was kneeling beside me, along with a young woman who was feeling my pulse.

'You passed out. Lie still for a minute.'

I struggled up onto my elbow, aware of half of the pub craning round at the middle-aged woman collapsed on the floor.

Steph had draped her jacket over me. She felt my forehead. 'You don't have a temperature. Do you think you need a doctor?' Steph's voice had an undertow of panic. She indicated the woman crouched next to me, who was lifting my legs onto a pile of cushions. 'This is Lyndsey, she's a trainee nurse at the Royal Guildford.'

'Sorry about this.'

Steph squeezed my hand. 'Only you could apologise for being ill.'

The nurse was asking me questions. 'Do you feel sick?'

'I did but I don't now.'

'Do you normally faint when you have a period?'

'I've only ever fainted once before. When I was pregnant with Isaac. That was eighteen years ago.'

She frowned. 'And you're not pregnant currently?'

'I've just bled everywhere. My periods are so irregular now. I think I'm going through the menopause.'

But her words played on my mind long after I'd managed to drive myself home. When I told Paul about the fainting, he was really concerned. 'You've been working too hard. Do you think you need to take some supplements? Perhaps you're anaemic.' I was too embarrassed to tell him about the whole bleeding through my clothes thing, so I muttered something about it being my time of the month.

I tried to put the nurse's comment out of my head, but the following day when, at Paul's insistence, I made an appointment for a blood test to see what was happening with my hormones, I kept thinking that my coffee was tasting a bit odd. In the end, like a fifteen-year-old sneaking into Boots in her lunch break, I bought a pregnancy test, annoyed with myself for wasting money but wanting to dismiss the possibility before my clients noticed that I wasn't as engaged with them as usual.

When I got back to work, I peed on the stick, glancing casually at it after a few seconds to see a very, very definite blue line. I stared. I picked up the box and re-read the instructions, to check that in the years since I had Ross the 'double line means pregnant' hadn't changed. Nope. I was definitely pregnant. Or had been at least.

I told the secretary to cancel all my afternoon appointments and went home. As I walked through the door, Paul smiled. 'Have you taken the afternoon off?'

I burst into tears. 'I'm pregnant. Or was pregnant.'

Paul's face froze. 'I thought you'd stopped having periods.'

Even in these extreme circumstances, I saw the effort he had to make to say the word 'period'.

'I have. Because I'm expecting a baby. Not going through the menopause.'

He blinked long and hard.

'I don't want this child, Paul. I really don't. I can't cope at this stage of life. I'll be sixty-four before it leaves home.'

Paul's face went from stunned to horrified. 'Let's sit down.'

He fussed about making tea while my mind veered down all sorts of dark alleyways, from fearing that the bleeding meant I'd lost the baby anyway to hoping I had, to feeling like a terrible person for not rushing straight to hospital the minute I saw the test result.

I filled him in on the bleeding in the pub the day before.

'And you didn't think you needed to mention that to me?'

'I thought it was my period. I never usually announce it to you.'

'Come on, I'm taking you to A&E right now.'

I nodded and followed him out to the car.

Paul drove carefully, pulling away slowly from junctions as though I was in labour.

'If I haven't already lost the baby, I don't want to discuss it with anyone, until we've thought through all the options.'

'What options?'

For the first time ever in our married life, I felt as though we were standing on the opposite sides of a raging river. 'I'm not sure I can have this baby. We're too old. You'd need a badge saying, "Father, not grandfather". And we're already struggling for money. Our best chance of being financially stable in our old age is for me to make a bloody great success of the new clinic.'

'You're not suggesting getting rid of it?'

'I'm not suggesting anything yet. But I'm not ruling anything out either. We could consider adoption.' I was pleading, panic flooding through me. I couldn't get my head round another eighteen years of child-rearing.

'I'm not letting you kill or give away our baby, Teresa.' There was a strength and steel in his words that I didn't think I'd ever heard before.

And when we walked out of the hospital three hours later, a healthy heartbeat confirmed, Paul turned to me and said, very gently but with great conviction, 'I won't be able to stay married to you if you don't keep our baby. It would eat away at me until it tore us apart.' His voice broke. 'We can get through this. We'll love him or her. It's just the shock. Of course, it's not what we expected at our age, but you've been a brilliant mum to Ross and you will be again.'

In the face of such opposition, such intensity of feeling from Paul, I desperately struggled to cling on to hope that he'd miraculously see my side of things, agree to explore other possibilities with me. But however hard I argued, often into the early hours of the morning, hissing at each other in bed in a way we rarely had before, he never showed the tiniest chink of surrender.

So I packed all that ambition, all that want, all that selfishness away, allowed Paul to tell everyone how happy we were with our 'late gift' and smiled coyly when people congratulated us. It was only in the early hours of the morning that I allowed myself to worry that I'd never love my baby and that it would sit in the middle of my marriage like an infected sore that refused to heal.

Steph was very subdued when I told her, failing to disguise her disappointment. 'Of course the baby is more important. We can't go off hiking for hours at a time if there's a chance that you're going to start bleeding. That would just be irresponsible.'

But her words were lacking enthusiasm. I could tell she was frustrated. She'd spent years fantasising about what we'd do once we had an empty nest, where we'd go, how we'd trek in Thailand, India, maybe even Nepal, and meet our husbands in posh hotels at the other end. I'd managed to encourage her to consider the tamer option of Spain to begin with and now we couldn't even do that.

Steph stopped short of announcing, 'Rather you than me', but I felt as though she was already running through her mental contact list of who could take my place as her preferred playmate. Even when our sons were young, she'd often shut down conversations and taken them in a different direction with 'That's enough talk about Ben' when really she meant, 'Let's *all* stop talking about the kids.' Sometimes when she'd had a lot to drink, she'd say, 'But honestly, child-rearing is a bit tedious, isn't it? I kind of thought I'd decide what was important, put it into practice and Ben would just be that person.' Which, for an intelligent woman, made her sound rather naïve.

Steph leant towards me. 'How did Paul react?'

I had the distinct impression she wanted to ask, 'Are you definitely going to keep it?' but even Steph lacked the bluntness to pose that question. 'He's worried, of course, because, let's face it, forty-five isn't an ideal age to have a baby from a risks point of view. But I think he's quite pleased now the shock has worn off. He said he'd always regretted being too sensible and deciding that we couldn't afford to have another baby after Ross.'

'What about you? How do you feel about it? Out-and-out excited?' She didn't quite manage to neutralise the false note of interest in her voice.

I wanted to tell her the truth. Explain to a sympathetic ear that I'd given my all to bringing up Ross, got up at the crack of dawn to trolley him all over the country to play football, taken it as a personal point of pride that he'd learnt to read early, that he'd made it to grammar school. That I hadn't minded fetching him from parties at two in the morning so he wouldn't be in a cab on his own. And while I was doing that, Paul had – until recently – progressed at work, and I'd witnessed his satisfaction at a successful piece of research, lit up by a promotion, a wage rise. He'd worked hard, and we'd moved into a bigger house, in the catchment area for the grammar. He'd been so proud when we'd got our house with an en suite. 'Get us! No more shouting at Ross to get out of the bathroom!'

I'd loved the bigger house, but I was also ashamed that I'd envied him. That freedom to stay at work for as long as he wanted, until it was done. I, on the other hand, was juggling my patients, stressed about not being able to schedule any appointments beyond three-thirty, rushing home to host play dates with rude and rough boys, monitoring vegetable intake, making sure Ross had a decent breakfast on the mornings of his GCSEs. I'd felt the privilege of it, but also the weight. Whenever I thought about Ross leaving for university, I could cry – the empty bedroom, the lack of trainers in the hall, all the things that irritated me suddenly precious markers of his presence. But undeniably my own kernel of ambition was ready to emerge like an earthworm squirming in the daylight.

I swallowed and said, 'I'm really disappointed about the trip, and I'll have to pull out of setting up my own physio clinic for a few years, but we always wanted another baby.'

Steph looked more like she was preparing herself for a funeral than the celebration of a new life. I was right not to tell her the truth. She'd give my doubts oxygen, shake them free into the air, where they would swirl around Paul and me like angry wasps. 'Could you get a nanny and start the clinic up anyway?'

It was like walking through the woods trying to avoid falling into a trap covered with branches. If I was too keen, she'd badger me with suggestions: 'A woman I work with is looking for a nanny share.' If I said I was going to stay at home with my baby, she'd do that quiet face of disappointment that I was failing to be my own woman. I didn't know why I was finding it so hard to lie to Steph because I was already lying to myself.

STEPH

August 2018

When my mobile rang and Ben's name flashed up, I had the immediate thought that he was phoning to tell me Gemma had left him. The realisation quickly followed that even if that was the case, he'd probably leave it to her to break the news. I wasn't sure when I'd become that woman who always jumped to the worst-case scenario. Even though I'd paid forensic attention to the tiniest detail whenever I'd seen them over the last few weeks, there was nothing specific to trigger any further cause for concern. But I couldn't shake off my unease. I reassured myself that they'd both come back quite enthusiastic about Gemma's birthday weekend in Brighton a couple of weeks earlier.

Despite trying to outwit my worries with logic, I still answered my phone with a panicky, 'Are you all right?'

Ben's response was a bemused, 'Yes, why wouldn't I be?'

It took all my restraint not to say, 'Because I'm pretty sure your marriage is going down the pan, your wife is in love with someone else and unless you pull your finger out, you're going to be that bloke standing in the hallway surrounded by her cases, shaking your head and saying, "I didn't see that coming."'

Instead I managed, 'You don't often phone me on my mobile.'

'Sorry but I needed a quick answer. Gemma has got to go up to London for a meeting unexpectedly and I'm on evening shifts this week. I wondered if you could have the girls tonight? Sorry. I know it's short notice.'

'What meeting has Gemma got?'

Ben sounded annoyed that I wasn't just offering up a straight yes or no. 'I don't know, something to do with budgets for next year.'

'Don't her bosses realise she's got a young family? There must be loads of women who don't have childcare at a moment's notice.'

Ben remained silent. I wanted him to be asking himself these questions, to open his eyes to what was going on around him.

I couldn't help it. 'Is everything all right between you?'

'Fine.' Was he matter-of-fact? Defensive? I still wasn't a hundred per cent certain I hadn't got the wrong end of the stick. 'Why?'

My turn for silence. I should have thought this through. I abandoned several openings before finally settling on, 'You're both working so hard, you never have time for yourselves, you just seem like ships that pass in the night.'

'That's life with young kids when you're building careers, Mum. I did all that training, and I need to make some money now so I can set up on my own or I'll spend the rest of my life working for someone else. I want to provide for my family, you know.'

His voice was snappy and irritable, but if I was going to stop waking up at 4 a.m. to toss and turn about whether Gemma would disappear off with Dottie and Nell, I needed to seize the moment. I was going to have to be blunt. 'You need to stop taking her for granted. She's a lovely woman and you won't be the only man in the world who thinks that.'

'What do you mean by that?'

'I just don't want you to get so blinded by work that you forget what's really important.'

'I'm at home more than Dad ever was. Or is.'

I wanted to scream, 'And look how well that's panned out' down the phone.

'Different generation, Ben. Women expected to carry the burden of the household even if they worked. I'm trying to help you here. I just want you to be happy.'

He made a sound of disbelief. 'I've got to go, a dog's come in with a cancerous toe. Need to decide whether to amputate or not.'

Mal came in and started semaphoring at me. I turned my back on him.

'Shall I pick the girls up from their holiday club, then?'

The relief rushed out of him that the immediate problem was solved. 'Thanks so much. Gemma will drop their stuff round after lunch.'

With that, he rushed off.

Despite everything, I allowed myself a smile at the sudden image I had of Ben as a little boy leaning over a hedgehog with an infected wound on its stomach. He'd bathed it in saltwater to try and heal it. The hedgehog died anyway, but I'd been astonished by his patience and kindness, which weren't his most obvious qualities. He always appeared more at ease with animals than his peers. They appreciated his absolute certainty that he was right, that he knew what he was doing, unlike humans, who seemed to find him a strange combination of arrogant and awkward.

Mal said, 'We're not having the girls again, are we? We've done more childcare for Dottie and Nell than we did for Ben.'

One of the knock-on effects of deciding to leave Mal then feeling I couldn't was that even when I agreed with him, I still contradicted him. 'It doesn't really affect you though, does it? And I like having them here.'

'It really annoys me that they assume we've got nothing better to do.'

'What have you got on that's so pressing?'

And we carried on goading each other until I resorted to lobbing in the grenade that always livened up any marital disagreement. 'Anyway, given that we're having the kids so often, I'd really like to think about buying somewhere near the seaside before they get much older.'

Predictably, Mal said, 'We're not having this conversation again, are we? People who retire then leave behind everything they know are asking for trouble. It's so important to have a social network.' He then mentioned the names of various acquaintances who'd dropped dead within months of relocating to Cornwall or Devon. 'There's all the stress of moving, then not having any friends. Not surprising they keeled over.'

'I'm not asking you to retire. Nor am I suggesting we move. I'm just saying that with my mum's inheritance, I'd like to buy somewhere on the coast where I can take the girls. Close by, Kent or Sussex.'

'Just go to a hotel for a weekend.'

'I think my mum would love the idea that I'd bought a little place by the sea. She loved going to the beach.'

And like all long marriages, we assumed the dance positions that either shimmied away from confrontation or waltzed towards it. My frustration with Ben at not seeing what was happening with Gemma and my fury with her for thinking about herself instead of her girls, let alone my son, made it easy for me to take it out on Mal. I quickstepped into territory that would only have one outcome.

'I love how you were quite happy to buy yourself a new motorbike. Another one, in addition to the two you already have sitting in the garage like a shrine to a midlife crisis. How much was that? Fifteen grand? Depreciating as soon as you drove it out of the dealer's and likely to kill you? Whereas I could buy a little bolthole, great investment, and we'd just watch it appreciate, year on year.'

Mal shook his head. 'You don't know that. What if there's a property crash? We've already got enough maintenance here. Our roof needs looking at.'

'If we use that logic, you should have bought yourself a pushbike rather than a new Ducati. How come it's okay for you to spend your money however you want but you feel entitled to a say in how I spend the money my mother left me?'

And so it rumbled on until Mal marched out the room, saying, 'I'm not listening to this.'

I slumped down in the chair, knowing that I was taking my anger out on the wrong person. I did wonder, though, how, in a marriage where both people have worked all their lives, the final say about how the money was spent rested with the man. I'd worked all through Ben's childhood because my mother had drilled into me the need to have some money of my own. It was her mantra after a lifetime of my father dictating how many bars she could have on the electric fire 'as he paid the bills'. I'd watched him snap the heating off as soon as she stopped turning blue, inspect her shopping list for frivolous items – 'Brie? What's wrong with good old English Cheddar?' – and seen her putting money by all year to make sure she could buy Ben a decent Christmas present. Yet, when he died, all that resurrecting of yellow broccoli and black bananas turned out to be the work of a man who had a portfolio of shares that enabled my mother to live a merry widowhood and still leave enough for me to buy the cottage of my dreams where I could hear the waves at night.

She'd have been disappointed to know that in the end, for all my bravado, I didn't have the guts to stand up to my husband and say, 'Tough. You do what you want with your money and I'll do what I want with mine.'

I was just examining what was actually holding me back when Gemma rang the doorbell. She pushed a big bunch of freesias into my hands and popped the girls' bags down.

'Have you got time for a coffee?' I asked.

'I need to get going really. I'm not sure the trains are running smoothly today.'

There was an energy, a restlessness, an eagerness to leave, to be on her way to whatever – whoever – made her feel alive. The person that allowed her to hold on to who she was, bringing her back from that brink of fading into the woman who defaulted to 'I don't mind' just to keep the peace, the woman whose usefulness was often distilled down into an ability to get paint off a school uniform and to interpret the purple and orange splodges on a piece of paper as Grandma's dog.

She was sparkly, reminding me of when I first met her, when she walked that fine line between familiarity and respect, so confident about her place in the world. And that spilt over into how she handled Ben, not afraid to stand up to him but with this lovely sense that anything she challenged came from a genuine interest in his welfare, in supporting his dreams.

I'd had years through school, persuading him to join the karate/football/cricket club, encouraging him to see if sons of friends wanted to go out for a drink. I'd pushed away my feelings of jealousy when Ross went camping with a group of lads, off to a festival in Cornwall. Or driving Teresa mad with all his twenty-something friends traipsing through the house, emptying the fridge. Then like a magical answer to where Ben would find his niche in life, Gemma appeared. The sister of someone he was in veterinary college with. Smart, kind, capable and in love with my son. The full responsibility for helping him find his way in the world no longer rested on my shoulders.

Without warning, I blurted out, 'You don't have to do this.'

Gemma frowned. 'I really do have to work, Steph. I love the girls. You know that. But I was always clear from the beginning, with Ben, with everyone, that I would carry on with my career. I love what I do. It's part of who I am. You of all people should understand that.'

'Of course I understand, but that's not what I meant—'

She pulled her phone out to check the time. 'I've got to run. Thank you for having the children.'

'Gemma, think very carefully about the choices you're making.'

For the first time ever, Gemma snapped at me. 'I don't make any choices. Ever. I work, I run around after the girls and, if I'm lucky, Ben takes them out on their bikes for an hour at the weekend so I can order my Tesco shop in peace.'

Her eyes filled and I backed down. 'Just remember Ben loves you. I love you. We all do.'

Gemma brushed impatiently at her tears and turned to go.

I didn't know what else to say. I watched her climb into her car and reverse out, shouting after her to drive carefully.

I went back into the house. If I was wrong, Gemma would probably tell Ben I was going a bit doolally. If I was right, she'd know I was watching. I hoped that might be enough to provoke her into calling a halt to whatever was going on.

On impulse, I dialled Evie's number. It was only a week since I'd last seen her but this conversation required someone I could trust and who, unlike Teresa in her blissfully happy marriage, understood that it was possible to behave terribly and still love your spouse.

'Can I come over? I need your advice. I can't talk about it in front of Mal.'

An hour and a bit later, I was sitting in her little flat on the edge of Whitstable. I still couldn't get used to how much Evie had embraced colour. She had that leaning towards the greys and whites and neutrals that characterised her last house but now there were splashes of brightness that I never associated with her. When I complimented her on it again, she smiled and said, 'I don't think you're here for the décor.' And after all these years it was like slipping into a warm bath, to tell her my worries and feel there was somebody there who understood. Evie didn't make me feel I'd failed. Over home-made carrot cake – when did Evie learn to bake? – I told her my suspicions about Gemma.

'Oh my life, what a horrible worry. I'd be devastated if I thought Rosa was going behind Isaac's back. I thought there was something you weren't telling me.'

'I didn't want to be disloyal to Ben. He'd hate it if he knew I was talking about his marriage like this.' If I'd known what a huge relief it would be to speak my fears out loud, I would have done so earlier.

Evie tipped her head on one side. 'I'm going to play devil's advocate,' she said. 'Assuming that she's not going to leave Ben for this other chap, if there is another chap, is any useful purpose served by telling Ben? Or shall I put it another way: would you want to know if Mal was being unfaithful to you?'

I managed a half-smile. 'Good question. Now, maybe. It would give me carte blanche to end my marriage without the guilt. But would I have wanted to know when I was thirty-five and had a young son? If it was just a fling, probably not.'

An expression I couldn't quite read flashed across Evie's face, almost one of relief, as though she'd heard something she hadn't expected.

We talked around the subject, examining everything from sitting them down together to taking Gemma quietly to one side. The conversation wasn't just about what we were discussing. Underneath it was the sense that we were continuing our discovery about each other, feeling our way as we learnt how the other one thought at the age of sixty, as opposed to thirty-seven.

Evie fiddled with her silver bangle. 'What did Teresa say?'

'She doesn't know yet.' I felt the shift as Evie recognised that I'd chosen her to confide in. With a rush of disloyalty and a pressure to explain, I said, 'I'm never sure Teresa understands the grey areas of marriage.'

Evie nodded.

I carried on. 'She's lucky to have found her soulmate. The downside of that is that she probably doesn't realise that your average marriage isn't a straightforward series of cosy evenings in and exciting weekends away.'

Evie immediately made me feel small by saying, 'She was very supportive when I was leaving Neil, even if she assumed, the way happily married people tend to, that leaving a crap marriage is easy – your husband isn't very nice so clearly you'll be better off on your own. But no one realises how lonely it is out there. When you're married, you never have to think about what you are going to do on a Sunday or how you're going to fill the hours between six o'clock and bedtime.'

'You mean, once you don't have someone ridiculing your choice of programme, frowning at what you've cooked and making you feel that anything you say is about as interesting as the word of the day on last year's calendar?'

Evie laughed. 'I didn't say there wasn't an upside. But back to the matter in hand. What would happen if you confronted Gemma?'

'I just tried to broach it, but I'm not sure I was blunt enough. I hid behind the "be very careful about the choices you're making" and she sort of stormed out, which isn't like her at all. More like Ben, to be honest. And he isn't listening. I've tried to warn him about taking her for granted. But what if I'm wrong? Is it really any of my business anyway? Can I make my daughter-in-law stay married to my son if she doesn't want to be?'

'Marriage is hard, especially when you're young and you still feel like there are lots of choices out there or other paths you could take. From what you've told me, Gemma's got a lot going for her and, let's face it, it's tempting to spend time with someone who's not balancing their charm and passion with needing a round of applause because they've cut the lawn.'

Despite asking Evie for advice, I felt my maternal defences rear up in case she found fault with Ben. But she didn't.

'You've got very good instincts, Steph.' Evie pulled a face. 'For a start, you never liked Neil. But that aside, you're not prone to worrying unnecessarily and looking for problems where there aren't any. So there probably is something not right if your alarm bells are going off.'

'I love that you think I'm not prone to worrying unnecessarily. Christ, since I had cancer, I go from nought to sixty over nothing. I bet if they tapped my veins they'd find I was running on pure adrenaline and cortisol.'

'All the more reason to live the life you want, Steph. We all bumble along labouring under the illusion that we'll put off being happy until everything else is sorted. That's why I ended up leaving Neil. After I'd watched Isaac on his wedding day being so kind to Rosa – she accidentally knocked a glass of water into his pudding and he didn't flicker, didn't hiss, then glance round to see if anyone was watching before adjusting his face for the audience. And I thought to myself, I'm fifty-four. I'm assuming that I'll live for another thirty years. But what if I only live for two, three? And this is it? A life with a man who doesn't really like anything about me. I told him when we got home that night.'

'Was he angry?'

Evie considered my question for a moment. 'Disbelieving. Sad. Then angry. Angry when he realised he'd lost his power over me.'

I couldn't help noticing that I'd come here to talk about Gemma and Ben but the conversation was heading towards my own dilemma about splitting up from Mal. I felt as though I was balancing on a precarious edge between finding as many reasons to leave as to stay and not knowing which way to jump. Oddly, Evie's encouragement to live the life I wanted made me keen to defend the one I already had.

'Mal's not as bad as Neil. He's had a lot of respect for me over the years. Maybe I forgot to have a midlife crisis and now I'm having a senior citizen one.'

'Mal doesn't belittle you in public, no.'

Again, I had this odd sense that she was holding something back, something more she'd like to say. I didn't know how to challenge her without damaging the fragile bonds we'd started to weave between our hearts again. What I did know was that Evie, the woman I'd always pitied for putting up with such an arrogant, rude man, had found her courage in the end. I, on the other hand, had made preserving my son's marriage a convenient excuse not to rock the status quo.

All the way home, Evie's words about assuming we'd live for another thirty years and waiting to be happy buzzed around my brain.

Of all people, I couldn't take that for granted.

STEPH

May 2008

A week after my fiftieth birthday, I found myself on a familiarisation trip to Finland. All the other travel product specialists were in their twenties and although I was used to being the oldest on most of the trips I went on, I just couldn't engage with the stories of falling asleep on the train back from London and ending up in Brighton after a night on the cocktails. Or that women their age were doing online dating. I thought that was the preserve of divorcees in their forties. Why weren't they meeting men in pubs and clubs? When I asked that question, they caught each other's eyes as though I still believed in being a virgin on your wedding night and collecting embroidered tablecloths for your bottom drawer.

One of them laughed and said, 'We do meet men in pubs and clubs but, you know, just checking out the ones we might otherwise never meet.'

I felt frumpy and ancient next to these women who seemed a world away from how responsible I'd been at their age. Though, of course, I'd been married for six years with a school-aged child by then.

I found them a bit vacuous, discussing who was going to buy an iPhone 3G when it was released and casting pitying looks at me whenever I fished out my BlackBerry. They never remembered their gloves and held us up every morning with a giggly 'I need them on a bit of elastic like a schoolgirl!' as though being disorganised was somehow endearing. Nevertheless, I was envious of their vitality, the way they laughed so easily, lost themselves in the joy of the moment rather than spoilt it by wondering how long an injury would take to heal if they stumbled while snowshoeing and twisted their knee.

The one saving grace was that our host, Ari, was about forty and also appeared to suffer from youth overload, shuffling in next to me at dinner and at the bar afterwards. And this evening, our last before the flight home the following afternoon, he'd been particularly attentive, all floppy dark hair and scruffy Nordic charm. He'd been catching my eye all through dinner. It felt good, astounding even, that he'd noticed me against the backdrop of these smooth-faced women with hair that didn't have a wiry mind of its own. I experienced a pathetic twinge of gratitude for him being able to see beyond the magnolia of my middle age, for not being dazzled by these carefree beings who leapt on their snowmobiles with the recklessness reserved for those on whom no one depends.

I wasn't sure when I'd changed from the woman who was always up for anything – paragliding, abseiling – to someone who started saying, 'I'll sit this one out.' It wasn't lack of courage exactly. More a concern about who would run my life if I couldn't. Unlike me, Mal wasn't going to trek down to be insulted by his mum in her nursing home on a regular basis. Plus I held a strong suspicion it was better for my marriage to avoid the absolute proof of how little Mal did around the house despite his loud lip service to equality.

While the group of girls engaged in a 'worst date' competition, I went outside to cool down, to get some fresh air away from the blazing fire in the lodge. That was the lie I told myself. The truth was that I'd set a little test, to see if I could still tempt a man outside with me, if I still had that power, with no intention of taking it anywhere.

Five minutes and there was Ari leaning against the pillar, his eyes locking on mine as the snow fluttered down. He wasn't lying to himself. Not at all. 'Hey.'

I immediately pretended his arrival was a surprise to me. 'It's really hot in there.' I just reined in a joke about my own menopausal furnace providing me with all the heat I needed. Oh sexy lady.

He raised an eyebrow, which didn't feel as though he was going along with my performance. 'So, Stephie.'

The expectation of a wise or entertaining observation hung in the air. I was at least ten years his senior and decided that I'd leave the rules of flirting to the people who still did it. 'So, Ari.'

He lit a cigarette and offered me one.

'You'll die young,' I said, shaking my head.

'And you, Stephie, how will you die?'

It was so long since I'd needed witty repartee that I nearly blurted out the truth: 'Slowly withering to the floor and not bothering to take the next breath because Mal has taken apart his motorbike on the patio and left it there for three weeks.' Instead, the thoughts that I had been stroking, like a cat purring away contentedly on my knee, burst out into the chill air. 'Having exciting sex in a field of wildflowers.'

Ari guffawed, a deep and genuine laugh, the sort that erupted when you get an entirely unexpected answer.

I laughed and laughed, mainly to cover my acute embarrassment that he now knew for sure that I hadn't been holding on to him just to stay alive on the back of the snowmobile, but also from the relief that the me from long ago, the feisty, flirty, anarchic twenty-five-old, was still hanging on in there somewhere.

'You are a wild one, Stephie. Who knew there was all this fire behind such a proper exterior?'

Wild. Clearly Ari hadn't been party to the Sunday evenings where I sat matching up socks in front of *Gardener's World*. Very anarchic as I simultaneously admired the plants Monty Don managed to grow in the shade and muttered about the mystery of all these single socks. Wild. I was going to hold that adjective in my heart and warm myself with it every time I looked at the shower screen and thought, *I must get some limescale remover on that.*

He stepped towards me. 'Do you want a kind of trial run tonight, where you don't actually die but just test out the method?' He blew out a puff of smoke. 'See if the strategy is a good one?'

I nearly said, 'Yes, what the hell, why not?' fast-forwarding in my mind to the next morning when the other women would be holding their hangovers and coffees and I'd be replenishing my energy with a plateful of ham and cheese and having little flashbacks with a secret smile all day long.

But for all my bravado, I had a fundamental belief in fidelity, in doing the right thing. In marriage, actually.

I laughed as though he'd made a joke rather than a proposal. 'I didn't see that on my itinerary.'

He stepped forward, snowflakes glinting in his hair like fairy lights. 'You obviously didn't get the updated version.'

He flicked his cigarette out into the snow, then pulled a hip flask out of his pocket and handed it to me.

I took a large swig, not sure whether I was hoping to get drunk enough to do what I shouldn't or whether I didn't want to look like his Great-Aunt Brenda who could only drink out of a bone china teacup.

My eyes watered. 'Christ, what is that?'

'Vodka. Special Finnish vodka. My uncle makes it.' He swigged and then beckoned to me to follow him. 'Come on.'

That was definitely my moment to say, 'I need to go back to the others.' I shook my head, feeling my younger self slumping in despair at passing up the possibility. 'I'm going to go back to my cabin now. It's an early start for husky sledding tomorrow.'

He smiled and pulled at my sleeve. 'I just want to show you one thing. Then I will walk you home and, I promise, that is it.'

And that lingering, treacherous ten per cent of me that loved a risk and subscribed to the 'I'll sleep when I'm dead' philosophy, whispered its challenge into my ear.

'Is it far?' I asked.

'Ten minutes. Bed by midnight, no later.'

We crunched through the forest, Ari lifting branches heavy with snow out of my way until we came to the edge of a lake.

'Shall we go for a swim?' he asked.

'Yeah, right.'

'I mean it. We Finns like ice-swimming.'

'We English do not.' Freezing my backside off in icy water didn't really fit with the moonlit stroll peppered with flirtatious banter that I'd envisaged.

'Try it.'

'I'm not wearing a swimming costume.'

'You British. Go in your bra and knickers. There's only me and the reindeers to see.'

I loved the way Ari didn't make that sound like a problem.

'How long do we stay in for?'

He chuckled. 'You'll know when enough is enough. Probably about three seconds. Come on! It's so good for you, you'll live to be a hundred and five and you'll feel seventeen. I'll go first. Then we go there.' He indicated a shed. 'It's a sauna. That is the reward.'

This was all moving too fast for me. I'd half-agreed to something that might shorten my life rather than prolong it. And I'd also realised that I was about to be cooped up in a sauna without the benefit of a beautician's tidy-up beforehand. But there was no time to worry about an unruly bikini line as Ari clapped his hands. 'I'm going in. As soon as I'm in the water, you throw your clothes off and follow. Keep your hat, gloves and socks on.'

I peered into the dark hole in the lake. What if I got sucked under the ice, what if my heart stopped, what if there was a fat ice eel in there… or what if, just this once, I did the wild thing?

Ari was suddenly skidding across the snow in his boxers and lowering himself down the ladder. 'Come. Now!'

There was nothing for it. I threw everything off and ran. I dithered on the edge before deciding that it was worse to be standing with my stomach hanging over a not-quite-matching pair of pants than to freeze to death.

'Slowly down the ladder. Feet, knees, bottom…'

I was shrieking and laughing. 'I can't, I can't.'

'Let go, let go.'

I released my grip more out of a desire to get it over with than a desire to go in. Instantly, I lost all the air in my body, gasping and flailing.

Ari grabbed my hand. 'I didn't think you'd do it! Take deep, calm breaths.'

I was battling with myself, trying to stop hyperventilating and thrashing about, though the tiny bit of my brain that hadn't seized up was euphoric at my daring.

Ari guided me back to the steps. 'That's enough for the first time. Sauna.'

He pulled a towel out of his rucksack and passed me some flip-flops.

'You came prepared,' I said.

'I always carry these things with me. I go ice-swimming several times a week.'

As we walked the short path to the sauna, my body was on fire, every nerve ending alive, as though the cells circulating lazily around, required to do little more than digest a bit of breakfast, had suddenly snapped to attention, bringing the world into sharp focus. I was so invigorated, by both the water and the glorious proof that I was still me, that I could still surprise everyone, including myself, with a bit of bravado.

Ari opened the door to the sauna shed and handed me a thick towelling robe. 'Here. Put that on while I sort out the coals.'

I peeled off my gloves and socks and studied the mottled pink of my skin, trying to blame the icy water for the tingling of desire. Until today, I would have said that the part of my brain responsible for still fancying men resembled the desiccated crescent of a marigold seed.

Before I could dissect that thought, there was a fierce hiss of steam and Ari – thankfully but disappointingly not naked – was waving me onto a towel on the bench. 'You're going to feel amazing after this.'

I shrugged off the robe, the heat of the sauna hitting my freezing skin like a thousand tiny wasp stings. I tried to sit in the most elegant way, hugging my knees to hide the stark evidence of my 'I don't want to be thin at the expense of enjoying myself' philosophy. Ari wasn't perfect either, but his height and confidence tricked my mind into assuming I was in the presence of a Nordic god.

He was so easy to chat to that I was almost able to pretend that I was simply enjoying a traditional Finnish experience, which would then translate into an extra marketing tool for customers. Which in a way it was, as I learnt about how he played the drums in a band – 'You know, it's something to do in the evenings. Finland is famous for its heavy metal bands – we have a festival in Helsinki every year.'

I nodded enthusiastically, omitting to mention that I only ever listened to Smooth Radio now on the grounds that I'd turned into my mother, greeting every other radio station with 'What's this racket?'

In return, I told him about where I'd visited for work, my favourite places – 'In Europe, I'd have to say Sardinia, very specifically, the Spiaggia Rosa, the Pink Beach. The water is so clear, and the sand is made up of coral, granite and shells so it has this lovely rosy hue. You can only get to it by boat, but I don't think you're allowed to disembark there now. They're trying to preserve it. I went years ago.'

Ari fidgeted about on the wood and, for one second, I was terrified that he was going to move closer, but he just wiped his face with a towel. He had the most striking eyes.

I babbled on. 'Outside of Europe, I love Sydney. All that outdoor living and sunshine. No offence, but I could never manage your long winters.'

Ari leant forwards. 'None taken. We find ways to cope.' He raised his eyebrows and that was the point where I should have said, 'Well, I think I've had enough heat, better get back to my cabin and do the sudoku.'

But clearly the thrill of the freezing water had gone to my head and when he shuffled up to me and wound a strand of my hair around his finger, then leant forward to kiss me, I shut my eyes and allowed myself to be that woman, the one I hadn't connected with in quite some time, whose primary purpose was not to pay the paper bill and never run out of liners for the recycling bin but to feel desired. Maybe not desired. Noticed.

And in that blissful moment, with my skin not knowing whether it was hot or cold, my heart was beating faster than was required for pumping blood into my extremities. My mind was not analysing or protecting but just melting into the sensation and I was reminded of what it was like to feel special. I wondered where that went in marriage because courtship didn't usually start with a pledge to change the towels twice a week and a commitment to decanting the All-Bran into a Tupperware container so it didn't go stale. But after a few seconds I pulled away.

He sat back, his eyes questioning.

'I have a husband.' I scrabbled together every last shred of conscience.

'I know.'

'I think I should leave now.'

'That is disappointing news.'

With the contrariness that had dogged me all my life, I felt mildly insulted that he made no effort to change my mind. He took me by the hand and said, 'You have a choice now. The ice hole again or a cold shower.'

'I think I've lost my nerve. I'll take the shower.'

He nodded. 'I think you have lost your nerve too.' His voice was teasing, but kind.

Ari had found my Achilles heel. No one had ever accused me of not being brave enough. Stupid, yes. Reckless, yes. But not cowardly.

He switched the shower on. 'After you,' he said as freezing water poured out of a huge rain head.

I didn't hesitate. I marched in, clamped my lips together and internalised the shriek as the water flooded over my body.

When I opened my eyes, Ari was grinning. 'A woman of courage.'

He stepped towards me and my resolve weakened. I moved over to make room. And somehow we managed to kiss, the icy water raining down on us, without drowning, in a scenario that if Mal had suggested it to me would have had me craning round to see if he'd cracked his head on the garage door. The temperature served to heighten every sensation until Ari pushed his long hair out of his eyes and said, 'I mustn't send you home with a cold' and directed me to a changing room to get dressed.

I was grateful for my big coat disguising the fact that I was braless. It wasn't really a look I'd pulled off with any aplomb in my twenties, let alone at fifty. He pulled my furry hood up over my head and jammed a woolly hat over his wet hair and we walked towards my cabin, with the snow landing lightly.

I fished my key out of my pocket, not daring myself to speak in case I forgot – even more – what marriage meant.

'I can offer you the warmth of my cabin and some hot chocolate,' Ari said.

I wiped a snowflake from his cheek. 'I can offer you my thanks, my regret at being unable to take up your suggestion and my gratitude for sharing an insight into a Finnish tradition I might otherwise have missed.'

'Are you sure?'

'Don't ask me twice.'

He bent his head and kissed me gently. 'A loyal woman of courage.'

And I lay smiling to myself into the early hours, darts of guilt casting a fog over the slideshow of images whirling through my head. Darts that were easily silenced by how liberating it had felt to be myself without Mal reminding me to talk more quietly, laugh less loudly, to 'leave the daredevil stuff to the youngsters' when I suggested we should learn to snowboard. For one glorious evening, it was as though the cataracts growing over my life had been removed. Ari had exposed the glittering possibility that just because Mal found my stories tiresome, especially when I talked about places I'd travelled without him so he couldn't parp up with his expertise, *someone else* might find me interesting.

The following year when Ari was hosting a trip to the Northern Lights, I sat on the invitation, clicked on it every day for two weeks, gazed at the photograph of him next to a reindeer and battled with my desire to hear again the words, 'a woman of courage'.

On the day before the deadline to RSVP, I forwarded it to our newest employee, a lad straight out of university, who'd won me over at interview by telling me his favourite sensation in the whole world was the adrenaline rush of landing somewhere he'd never been before and feeling that it was all to discover. 'Please go on this familiarisation trip on my behalf.'

And then I took myself, courageous woman that I was, to Waitrose to buy an amaryllis for Mal's mum and drove to her nursing home. I sat with her and painted her nails, listening to her version of the world. 'My son's been to see me every day this week. That horrid wife of his – Sonia, Serena – I can't remember her name. Awful woman, she never comes. Too busy to bother, he told me. He should have married someone else.'

'You're right, Janet, he should have done.'

If I tried to pass the buck back to Mal and suggested he did actually go and visit, not every day, but at least once a month, he said, 'You're better with her than I am.'

In my next life, I was going to be so awful with everyone, even my husband would have to step up to the plate.

STEPH

Mid-September 2018

I wasn't naïve enough to expect that now Evie was back on the scene, the three of us would slip back into a regular pattern of weekends away. However, I had hoped that we could all have at least a few evenings reminiscing about when the kids were young without letting the mere fact that Evie and I hadn't spoken since they were thirteen get in the way. I always said that the first ten years of child-rearing were so intense as to count for double time. That without friends to keep you sane with wine and stories of when they, too, had failed to stick to the 'Let's all sit down calmly and explain how we feel' in favour of 'Because I bloody said so!', no mother – or marriage – could survive.

When I mentioned an evening out with Teresa to Evie, she seemed quite enthusiastic. 'I'm always up for that. Now I've ditched the husband, there is so much more that I can do in my evenings. It's been quite a revelation to be able to go home when I want to. I can't believe I was ever that pathetic. Honestly, I love walking into an empty house knowing that I won't have to use energy to understand the subtle shift in atmosphere.'

I struggled not to feel that I had swapped roles with Evie.

However, when I suggested going out as a threesome to Teresa, she'd say, 'Oh I'm still doing a few physio clients in the evenings. I'll have to have a look and see when I'm free.' Or she'd make some excuse about needing to be there for Amelia. My memory of Ben being seventeen was faded, but I knew enough to be sure that Amelia wouldn't give a hoot if Teresa wasn't at home for a few hours. It was one of the ironies of life that just as offspring became very interesting to parents, parents had a stink-bomb effect on children.

So on Monday morning when Teresa came to walk Gladys with me – 'It's the only exercise I do – my clients would be horrified if they knew how little I move, despite all my professional advice' – I'd decided to pin her down to a date or have her explain to me what the problem was.

Normally we bounced from subject to unconnected subject as old friends do – her sister's daughter who'd snagged some mega job straight from university, my peony that had refused to flower this year, random people who annoyed us half to death – but today Teresa was really hard going. I felt I'd been quite entertaining about Dottie and Nell, but maybe I was falling into that trap of thinking that my own grandchildren were super cute and everybody else was dragging their backsides along the floor with boredom the second I mentioned them. In the end, I said, 'Is everything okay? You seem a bit preoccupied.'

With that, she burst into tears. 'I'm not supposed to say anything. Just in case she changes her mind.'

'Who changes her mind?'

'Amelia. She's pregnant.'

I came out with the first unhelpful thing that sprang to mind. 'I didn't know she had a boyfriend.'

Teresa stared at me. 'She doesn't. Or not one who's interested in facing the music anyway.'

'Oh you poor things. Have you looked into, er, options?'

Teresa started crying even more. 'She's determined to keep the baby. And she's already fourteen weeks. I keep hoping she'll see sense. She won't even be able to take her A levels, let alone go to university.'

I grappled around for a 'let's look on the bright side' comforting comment but was still fumbling for some upside when Teresa burst out with how she had really wanted to have an abortion when she was pregnant with Amelia. How she'd felt guilty about it all the time Amelia was growing up, how she'd wondered whether she loved Amelia as much as she loved Ross. 'I really don't want her to have to wrestle with all that, to feel guilty and resentful. Or to miss out on exploring all the paths that she could take in life, rather than this baby dictating everything she does in the future.'

I had that sense of everything I'd taken for granted being shaken about and presented to me in an entirely different way. 'But I remember you being thrilled when you fell pregnant with Amelia, you called her your "late gift". I admired you for not being upset about missing out on our hike along the Camino de Santiago. You seemed so flexible in your thinking, so ready to surrender the freedom that we'd been looking forward to.'

Teresa looked down. 'Paul was furious with me for even considering a termination or giving her up for adoption. He said he'd have to leave me if I did. It took him months, maybe years, to forgive me. He just couldn't believe that a woman in a happy marriage, who is financially stable, could even contemplate getting rid of a baby. He couldn't understand – at all – that I'd put so much into motherhood first time around, I felt if I did it again, I would lose myself completely.'

'But you don't regret it now, do you?' I was raking through my memories. How had I not noticed, not given Teresa a chance to talk about how she felt?

'Of course not. I love Amelia, but I definitely didn't put as much effort in with her when she was little. I was older for a start and I couldn't be bothered to go to the playgroups and coffee mornings like we did. But Amelia is younger than I was when I had Ross. Don't forget I was twenty-six.' She sobbed with despair. 'Seventeen, Steph. Seventeen. With the whole world at her feet, university, the lot.' She stopped to sniff some buddleia. 'Can I say something really selfish?' Her voice was small. 'I know that if she has a child, whatever anyone else says, I'll end up making all the sacrifices so she can live the life she wants. I know you wouldn't do that, that you'd be much stronger and firmer and be clear upfront about the consequences of keeping the baby – then stick to them. But I don't know whether I'm that person. I'm not sure I'll be able to stand by and watch her waste her potential.'

I was so relieved that Teresa had small, selfish thoughts too. I'd always felt that in comparison I was the meanest-spirited mother that ever stormed around the earth.

'Firstly, I'm sure she could still do her A levels and go to university somehow. She might have to think a bit creatively about how full-time she could be or whether she does a mixture of attending and online, if that's possible. It's not like when women of our generation went to university, when everything was handwritten and computers didn't exist. She can probably do it from home. Christ, these young people spend enough time gawking at their phones and laptops, there has to be some upside. And I think they have nurseries at some places too. Secondly, as far as my being able to enforce any boundaries, you're talking to the woman who drops everything to look after Dottie and Nell at a moment's notice. I can't deny Ben, or even Gemma anything. I might not have given that impression when Ben was young, but I was still clinging on to the deluded idea that I'd be able to separate my son's happiness from my own.'

Teresa rubbed her eyes. 'I gather from Evie that you're worried about Ben and Gemma.'

Despite her own distress, there was a definite pissed-offness in her voice. I gave her a rundown of what was happening, adding, 'I just happened to have arranged to have coffee with Evie on a day when it was really bothering me.'

'But she also said that you were thinking of leaving Mal?' She did a funny little laugh, as though Mal and I had become fused together like two candles left on a sunny windowsill. I should have been a bit more explicit with the 'Don't mention this to Teresa' instructions to Evie. I was much more comfortable talking about other people's chaos than examining my own.

We finished our climb to the top of the hill and flopped down onto the bench. I stared out over the South Downs. 'I can't go back to the person I was before I had cancer. I can't accept things the same way. Can't just think this is my lot – a husband who barely looks up when I come in. He sparkles like a sequin when we go to the golf club for lunch, quite the charmer with Eddie's wife, who's as soggy as a rotting cucumber, but grumps about if I ask him to help me shift the sofa, as though I'm just another thing to schedule into his day.'

Teresa smiled. 'But he's always been a bit selfish with his time. I suppose he had to be. That's how he was single-minded enough to get to the top of his profession.'

'I get that he's always been like it. But I'm sixty, Teresa. With a second chance at life and a husband who drove me to one chemo session. One! You did the rest. I've tried being grateful for the mere fact of being alive but, sadly, that doesn't seem enough for me. I want another shot at life. A challenge. Or at least a life where the man I live with doesn't start singing "Always Look on the Bright Side of Life" when I get a bit stressed about my next scan.'

'Maybe that's just his way of dealing with his own anxiety.'

'Maybe it is, but what about my bloody anxiety? A man I've been married to for thirty-seven years ought to be able to say, "Poor you, love. It must be really frightening." A bit of compassion instead of making me feel that I'm just a spineless wuss.'

Teresa snorted. 'No one could accuse you of that!'

I had the weird sensation that I would regret putting all these grievances out into the atmosphere, but it was as though the thoughts I'd been dismissing as 'just married life' had queued up to be released and were now going to tumble out whether I wanted them to or not. 'I mean, whenever I end up staying for dinner with you and Paul, he listens to you, asks you questions, teases you, but not in an unkind way. Mal is always making jokes about how my brain has atrophied now I've retired, and how I'd better start doing the crossword if I don't want to be gazing vacantly into space. He knows full well that me "retiring" was a bit of a "let's make way for some youngsters who aren't likely to keel over from cancer". I mean, it kind of suited me, but it wasn't exactly the career high I'd hoped to go out on.'

'Paul can be a bit careless sometimes too.'

I loved Teresa for trying to make me feel better, but I was pretty sure Paul's carelessness amounted to forgetting to cut her toast into triangles. I wasn't sure I'd ever seen a husband whose happiness was linked so closely with his wife's. In all the years I'd socialised with Teresa and Paul, I couldn't remember a single occasion when Teresa had wanted to go home early and Paul had said, 'You don't mind if I stay?'

Teresa lifted her face to the autumn sun. 'Got to get my vitamin D.' She carried on, 'Would you really want to live by yourself? How would you meet someone new?'

I shifted on the bench. 'Evie's happy on her own. I've got the grandchildren and Ben and Gemma. I've discovered after all these years of flitting around being busy and feeling like a loser if we were in on a Saturday night that I don't really like many people. So I've had the cancer cull – all those people who were quite happy to come and drink my wine in the good times but didn't have the dextrous ability required to drop me a text to see whether I'd gone bald yet or not. I could have the divorce cull now.' I laughed. 'I'd probably only have you left.'

'And Evie,' Teresa said, looking for all the world like a cockatoo on a crowded perch, ruffling its feathers to get the interlopers to back off.

I turned to her. 'Look, I'm not going to pretend that it's not nice to have her back in my life, but she'll never be as close to me as you are. You've been here through thick and thin.'

'I'm glad you're back in touch.'

I stopped myself saying, 'Sounds like it,' and returned to our original subject. 'Don't you think Wendy might see Amelia getting pregnant as a good opportunity to relocate down here now your parents have passed away? You always gave me the impression she didn't really want to move back to Durham but just did it so your parents could help with Zoe. She always loved little children, didn't she? I remember how good she was with Ross when he was tiny. Perhaps she could help out with Amelia's baby while she finishes her education.'

Teresa shook her head. 'No way. I can't see her settling in the south-east.'

'I thought you said she wanted to be nearer to you?'

'She didn't mean that she'd live in Surrey. At most she might come two or three hours further south. The Midlands or somewhere like that.'

'Has she got friends there?'

'No. But she was always good at making a life for herself.'

I knew I shouldn't propose this without checking with Mal but I owed Teresa. Without her, I wasn't sure how I'd have kept going through my chemo. 'The tenants on our little flat in Redhill have given us six months' notice. Why don't you suggest it to her? I can do mates' rates.'

Teresa's reaction surprised me. 'No. No. Wendy is not coming here.'

'Well, keep it in mind.'

She grunted and got up. 'I need to get going.'

And then I had that feeling of being really annoyed that I'd made a generous gesture and Teresa hadn't appreciated it. My mum's words popped into my head: 'You've got to give because you want to, without having an expectation of how other people are going to receive.' Mum was always so much nicer than me though. I liked a bit of gratitude.

We trundled along in a grumpy silence.

Then, as if she'd realised that she'd been rude, Teresa said, 'Thank you for the offer, but I don't think Wendy coming to live here will work.'

And although both Evie and Teresa teased me about how no one ever dared challenge me for fear of me turning the gun turrets on them, Teresa's ability to finish a sentence leaving a punchy 'and that is the end of that conversation' hanging in the air was starting to make me feel that I'd lost my touch.

EVIE

22 December 2018

Now I was single, I was always suggesting things that Steph and I could do at the weekend. I invited Teresa with us, but she never accepted, and, surprisingly, even Steph, who'd always been up for anything, was weirdly concerned about leaving Mal at home on his own all day on a Saturday or Sunday. Jokingly, I said to her, 'Does he make sure you've got someone to play with when he's away?'

I knew I'd hit a nerve when she said, 'If I'm going to stay, I have to make some sort of an effort. I can't just pretend he doesn't exist. He gets so grumpy if I'm out for too long.'

I didn't remind her how scathing she used to be about Teresa, who stuck to two weekends away a year with us when we had young kids, on the grounds that she didn't want to take advantage of Paul. 'Take advantage? Is that how you see it? I just regard it as a father taking as much responsibility as a mother.' Teresa, in her quiet but firm way, would not budge.

I finally managed to entice Steph up to London on the last Saturday before Christmas when Mal was away for work.

'What businesses are still even open on 22 December?'

Steph fluttered her fingers. 'Oh goodness knows. Some place over Bristol way, I think. They're installing a new computer system and need it up and running by the New Year.'

'Do you mind him being away so much still?'

She pulled a face and said, 'That'll be a no. It's like being set free.'

We headed over to the Victoria and Albert Museum. I was in my element, looking at all the costumes. Steph had always been interested in anything and everything, her taste as eclectic as a jumble sale. From there, we walked through Knightsbridge to look at the Christmas displays in Harrods, then through Hyde Park to see the lights on Regent Street.

After fighting our way round Hamleys so that Steph could get a jewellery-making kit for Nell, we admitted defeat and retreated into a little French wine bar. Over platters of ripe Brie and cured ham, we put the glitzy glamour of the day to one side and sank into a philosophical conversation about life, love and the universe that I remembered of old.

'Are you happy with what you've achieved in your life?' I asked.

'Broadly. I wouldn't say no to one last adventure. Just to prove that I haven't become totally timid.'

I laughed. 'Timid? You? I can think of lots of adjectives to describe you, but timid wouldn't be in the top five hundred.'

Steph surprised me by shaking her head. 'I wish. Sadly, whereas I used to believe I could either buy myself out of trouble, or think myself out of trouble, I've come to understand that some things depend entirely on luck and good oncologists.'

I still hadn't made this adjustment to Steph as someone who could ever feel vulnerable. When the kids were little, Teresa and I confided in each other about how we imagined that every tiny spot heralded the beginning of meningitis and how we stood with our fingers under our sons' noses at night to check they were still breathing. I could have never said that to Steph. She would have ridiculed my 'vivid imagination'.

Now though, there was a softness about her, a tolerance for other people's foibles that I didn't recall. I'd always had the distinct impression that she thought people – including me – who didn't make the most of life needed to pull themselves together. When I told her that, she said, 'It simply hadn't occurred to me that other people already knew there isn't always a safety net. I was viewing the world from a position of privilege – I had a good job, I'd never had any big problems in my family, so I was quite smug, I suppose. Boringly, I've discovered that some people find it much harder to take a risk because they've already used up their resources just surviving to date.'

'But you're still really brave, aren't you?'

She flopped forward, smoothing her eyebrows with her fingers. 'I'd love to say yes to that. But, honestly, when I remember how I used to race up to Gatwick at the last minute to hop on a plane to Mexico to negotiate with hotels for the next season, I barely recognise myself. If I catch the train to London, I have to check my tickets about five times between home and the station in case they've somehow leapt out of my handbag.' Steph always exaggerated.

I leant in. 'So let me ask a different question. What do you think life will be like in ten years' time?'

Suddenly, she lost that air of laughing at herself. She sighed. 'I might not even be alive then.'

I'd already learnt not to dismiss her concerns and tell her not to be silly, but I wanted to pin her down. 'But if you are, do you think you'll still be married to Mal?'

She looked me straight in the eye. 'It turns out I'm not as courageous as you.'

I had such a strong memory of her saying in front of all of us – Mal and the other men included – that she'd never bought into the fairy tale, believing that there was one man, for one woman, forever. Neil had slapped Mal on the back and said, 'Think you're being given fair warning there, mate. Shape up or ship out.'

Mal hadn't missed a beat. 'Works both ways. Not much point in staying together if you can't stand the sight of each other.'

I didn't want to push her too hard as we were still doing the delicate dance of bridge-building, but this new, resigned Steph was alien to me. 'What's actually stopping you leaving? You seem quite clear that you don't really love him any more.'

'You can't just get up and leave for no real reason though, can you? "Do tell me why you split up with your husband, Steph." "Oh, I found the way he shuffles across the kitchen floor in his slippers unbearable." Otherwise half the women our age would be packing their bags and setting up a commune with their girlfriends. I mean, it's not like I'm twenty-eight and want to find a new man to have a family with.'

I laughed. 'I quite fancy living in a commune with my girlfriends, but even if that's not an option, if you'd be happier on your own, I don't see why you – of all people – would drift along in some kind of half-life.'

I now understood why Steph used to get infuriated with me when I was married to Neil and I was always coming up with a million reasons why I couldn't do things, making excuses for why he was the way he was, why changing my circumstances was impossible.

But the thing that made frustration bubble in every vein was Steph repeating over and over again, 'I don't know. I've become the eternal malcontent since I had cancer. He's not perfect, but he's a very good man. And, anyway, as we are all well aware, the grass is never as green as we think it will be.'

'But something must have made you consider leaving. It was one of the first things you said to me when we met up again.'

'Evie, after all these years, you should know that I'm a great one for flip-flopping about. I'm just a drama queen – one day I think I'll get a divorce, the next I can't imagine watching Netflix on my own.'

Her words didn't convince me. I couldn't remember the Steph of old ever voicing anything with as much conviction as she had when she told me she wasn't happy with Mal.

I prompted her. 'I have a really clear recollection of Mal saying that marriage was like a job – that you should only stay in it as long as the rewards are fair for the hours put in.'

Even Neil had clapped him on the back when he announced that and said, 'You old romantic, you.' Steph had made a joke about how he was living on borrowed time.

I trod carefully. 'Do you think you might both feel the same way? That the marriage has run its course? He might even be relieved.'

Steph immediately reverted to the person I recognised. 'I don't know any man who is relieved by losing the person who does all the cooking, cleaning and unclogging of plugholes.'

'Right there, you see, that's a reason to leave him. That's a blue job.'

Steph did her comedy glare. I knew straight away that I'd lost any credibility. She had always been rigid about insisting that all jobs were equally shared according to skill set, rather than gender, and being female didn't preclude using a drill. I didn't dare tell her I'd missed Neil the most when I was trying to put together a flatpack wardrobe in my new flat.

As we ordered more Chablis, I couldn't shake off the sense that this woman, this whirlwind, who scooped up life and sucked the juice out of its bones, was rusting away like a vintage car neglected past the point of no return.

The next day, I popped round to see Teresa on the pretext of dropping off a panettone. After we'd done the obligatory moaning about how much preparation there was at Christmas for what was effectively just one big roast lunch, I broached the subject that concerned me.

'Steph isn't who she was.'

Teresa shrugged. 'None of us is.'

'She's so beaten, so lacking in energy.'

'I don't view her like that. Maybe you notice it because you haven't seen her in so many years.'

'No. Steph always had a core belief in herself. That's why she got so frustrated with me putting up with Neil. She always believed she would survive on her own. It's what I most admired about her. She wasn't afraid to say what she thought because she felt her opinion was as valid as Mal's and if he didn't like it, too bad. She was never supposed to be running around appeasing a man. Now look at her. She's trapped in a weird existence where she can't wait for Mal to disappear off to work. She told me she only feels really happy when he goes out for the day.' I took a slurp of coffee. 'You don't feel like that about Paul, do you?' I felt entirely safe asking that question.

Teresa screwed up her face as though I was just wasting air.

'Right. But Steph is really unhappy with Mal. She seems paralysed though. I don't even think she's telling me the whole story.' I paused. 'We should probably tell her that Mal had that thing with Wendy. I've always felt guilty for not saying anything.'

Teresa jumped up. 'No. Absolutely not. That was decades ago. What would be the point of raking it all up now? It's too late. She'd definitely shoot the messenger.'

Teresa did have a point that Steph welcoming our honesty was not guaranteed. 'I should have told her once we knew for definite, after that weekend in Suffolk, when Wendy was all over Neil. I should have got back in touch with her. I actually thought that a woman was better off putting up with a philandering husband, or a bully like Neil, than being a single parent. I don't know what planet I was on. Mal shagging your sister, Neil telling me how fat I was, belittling Isaac, convincing me that I was so thick that I'd never be able to survive without him.'

Teresa was shaking her head. 'You were right to leave Neil, but what good would it do Steph to know about Wendy now?'

'I'm pretty sure Wendy wasn't the first one or the last. He responded so calmly when I told him that I'd been back at the farmhouse when he was in bed with Wendy. I definitely got the sense that he was used to thinking on his feet.'

'How can you even remember what he said now? If you don't mind me saying, I think you're just seeing everything from your own perspective of being happier without Neil. It's easy to start looking round and assuming everyone else should follow your lead. Steph and Mal have always had a robust relationship. Of course it's not okay if he's sleeping around, but we don't have any proof it was anything other than that once. We should either have spoken up at the time or forever hold our peace.'

I overlooked how much I minded her effectively accusing me of wanting everyone to ditch their husbands just because I'd freed myself from mine. 'It would more than likely give her the courage to leave and I honestly believe that's what she wants to do. She's got so used to putting everyone else first over the years, I think she's forgotten what her own happiness feels like.'

'No. Please don't do it. I know Steph. I know her much better than you do now. She will not thank you for this.' Teresa's colour was rising, along with her voice.

'But if it wasn't your sister, would you tell Steph?'

'I wouldn't deliberately wreck anyone's marriage.' Teresa sounded both panicky and belligerent.

I wanted to let it drop, but I had an overwhelming sense of needing to come clean, even if it led to me and Steph being estranged again. In an odd sort of way, I felt I owed it to her, a payback for trying to help me realise how unhappy Neil was making me all those years ago, when I was too blind, or too scared, to see. 'I don't think she'd be any unhappier than she is now.'

'Promise me, Evie. Promise me that you won't tell her. It's just not fair for you to turn up in her life after all these years and start stirring things up. I really can't cope with the worry of it all. I've got enough on my plate trying to make sure Amelia has a future. We still don't know whether she'll be allowed back to school after the baby's born. And if you won't do it for Steph, do it for me, because if you say anything, she'll never speak to me again.'

I'd never heard Teresa more definite or determined about anything. With a heavy heart, I nodded.

STEPH

3 April 2019

As it happened, when my mobile went at 5 a.m., I was lying awake, thinking about whether my complicity in Gemma's deceit – if that was what it was – would protect Ben or irrevocably damage my relationship with him. I still didn't have any concrete proof that she was having an affair but over the last six months or so, she'd definitely been spending more nights away for work than she used to. Whereas before she would hang around delaying saying goodbye to the girls for as long as possible, she seemed much keener to get on her way. So many times it was on the tip of my tongue to ask her outright. But whatever answer she gave me, I was damned if I did and damned if I didn't. If I was barking up the wrong tree, I'd have destroyed the trust between us. And if she was being unfaithful, I'd be backing her into a corner and forcing her to take action. Action that might not fall in Ben's favour.

In the end, I took a gamble that 'he' – if he existed – was probably also married. Hopefully he would gather his skirts like a nun on the run if Gemma suggested anything more permanent, but it would be unreasonable to expect Ben to forgive me if he found out I had known and kept quiet for so long. Or at all. He was very black and white: even got outraged about me talking about what sort of dog I might get once Gladys died, as though being realistic was tantamount to disloyalty.

My maternal instinct was to tell him, to not let anyone make a fool of my boy, but my 'seen a lot of human behaviour and often doing nothing is the best option' instinct was winning. Currently, anyway. I was glad I'd never had a job where my hand had to hover over the nuclear button, especially in the unpredictable days of the menopause. Who knew what I might have blown up just for the fun of it?

Alongside the fear of losing Gemma from our lives, my mind kept mining back through the years, when Mal was my first port of call for discussing anything that was bothering me. I was always confident that we were a team, that he had my best interests at heart. Where were these turning points in marriage, these forks in the road, where suddenly, instead of walking along holding hands, we found ourselves stumbling off on separate journeys, a sad little rucksack swung over a shoulder, with a small bottle of water and a yoghurt for one?

But before I could indulge in any more of the navel-gazing that Mal detested, this crack of dawn phone call shot me into action. I dashed out onto the landing where my mobile was charging to see Teresa's name flash up on the screen. I had a short burst of relief it wasn't Ben, telling me that Gemma had left. Then I panicked in case something had happened to Amelia and her newborn baby. I couldn't think why else Teresa would call me so early. I immediately heard a sob, followed by, 'It's Paul. He's dead.'

I couldn't get any more out of her. Except that she was at home. 'I'm coming over.'

I woke up Mal. 'Paul's died. I'm going over to Teresa's.'

He was slow to come round. I'd always admired his ability to switch off so completely rather than sleep – as I did – as though it was just a matter of time before a lorry careered into the house or the dishwasher burst into flames overnight. Now though, it was pure good fortune that I didn't have a bucket of freezing-cold water to hand.

He struggled onto his elbow. 'Paul's dead? What? How did he die? Shall I come with you?'

The fact that he wasn't already pulling on his jeans and rushing to be with our friends of thirty-five years incensed me to such a degree that I said, 'No, it's fine, you go back to sleep.'

'What happened?'

'I don't know. Teresa can't speak. I just need to get over there.'

'Are you sure you don't want me to come?'

That moment had expired. In fact, I could immediately see the benefits of dealing with Teresa without Mal having an opinion on what we should be doing or feeling.

He'd wriggled into a sitting position. 'Give me a ring if I can do anything.'

I had a strong suspicion that as soon as I left our bedroom he would snuggle down under the duvet for another couple of hours' kip, reassuring himself that he was fortifying himself with enough sleep to help everybody else later on.

I ran down the stairs and out into the rainy April morning. My sadness for Teresa and Paul was only just taking priority over my deep and frightening dislike for my husband. By the time I reached the end of the road, I'd dismissed Mal and was forcing myself not to dissolve. What lay ahead did not require an extra person to weep and wail.

I drew up outside her house. All the lights were on. I walked up to the front porch, taking deep breaths as an image of Paul coming to the door in his trademark checked shirt to welcome us darted through my mind.

I let myself in and found Teresa in her sitting room. Paul's big leather armchair was already announcing his absence. She pushed herself up and I held my arms out to her. Her grief was so intense, so palpable, it almost had a shape of its own, fleshing out every last nook and cranny in her angular body. As I released her, I held on to her arm and guided her back to a chair in case she crumpled to the floor.

On the other side of the room, Amelia sat on the sofa cradling Violet, her four-week-old baby, rocking her and shushing her with tenderness, while swiping at the huge tears that coursed down her face and onto the soft blanket below.

I had a flashback to Mal teasing Paul for drinking so moderately when we were in a hotel with copious bottles of wine on New Year's Eve. Six? Seven years ago? Before I had cancer anyway. Paul never seemed to take offence at anything, just replying, 'I've got a daughter who's still at school. Got to live a long time. I want to walk her down the aisle.'

We all thought he was being a bit dramatic and over-serious, but now my heart wept with the knowledge that he would miss out on so much. Back then, Mal had poured another glass of Rioja and said, 'I'd rather live well than long.'

Paul had smiled and said, 'But your son is already an adult. He can manage without you.'

Although I'd been nowhere near as dismissive as Mal, remembering it now, how we'd shrugged and thought, *All the more wine for us*, made me yearn for the naivety of the person I was then. The me that hadn't yet had proof of the precariousness of life. My mum was still alive, breast cancer was something that happened to one in seven women, but, of course, I'd expected to be in the lucky six. Ben had just married Gemma, who I knew at once would be the perfect fit – both for him, and selfishly, for me. I'd dreaded Ben hooking up with some prissy, houseproud woman who'd be inspecting the sofa for Gladys's hair before she sat down.

But now, now I understood the fragility of life. How money gave you a few more choices in tough times, but when push came to shove and cancer came calling, it didn't matter whether you turned up at the hospital on the number 260 bus or in a vintage Daimler, you were still in the hands of the gods and oncologists.

And Paul's daughter hadn't had my luxury of getting to fifty-four before discovering that life can turn on a sixpence. She'd only just turned eighteen and she'd already seen her life swerve from its expected track. One day, she'd been planning to go to university, the next she'd found herself responsible for keeping a tiny human alive. And now, she'd had the added proof that you can say a casual goodnight to your dad, a bit grumpily, a bit irritated by his question 'What time do you need to get up tomorrow?' – as though there was ever a chance of a lie-in once you had a baby – and that was the last time you'd say anything to him, slipped past, unnoticed and without fanfare. Eighteen was so young to lose a parent, to learn the grown-up lesson that learning to live with loss was the unmistakable drawback of love.

I went over and put my hand on Amelia's shoulder. 'I'm so sorry, love.'

'Thank you.' Her voice was strong though. 'At least he got to meet Violet.'

I ran my finger down the baby's cheek. Already there was something steely about Amelia, something I'd never associated with her before, a departure from that self-effacing demeanour that I'd privately found a bit disappointing in a woman of her generation. There were several times when I'd been chatting to her and she'd put herself down, practically apologising for her own ambition. Now I could see that youth's impetus to survive had worked its magic. She wouldn't shrug off the loss of Paul, but her focus was on Violet, what came next, not what had come before. She had a grief barrier, a self-preservation that would enable her to keep going for her daughter. The circle of life right there. Unpredictable, unwieldy, unrelenting.

I made tea and fetched a blanket for Teresa from the cupboard in the hall. She sat on the sofa, unable to tell me anything beyond, 'He had a heart attack, which led to a full cardiac arrest. I couldn't save him. He was dead by the time the ambulance got here. They tried to resuscitate him but it was too late.'

I sat holding her hand while she cried. Her hand never relaxed in mine. I realised, with a burst of bemusement, that Teresa had never been someone I'd linked arms with as we walked or given anything more tactile than a perfunctory kiss on the cheek. She'd always had that self-contained aura: Teresa's love language was definitely not my hugging and enthusing and laughing way beyond the moment that everyone else found something funny. She had shown her love by forwarding me the number of a good plumber, being five minutes early whenever we met – and never ever making me feel as though I was clogging up her calendar with my chemo. But actual hugging, that had been Evie's department way back when, and more recently, Gemma, Dottie and Nell's.

'Does Evie know?'

Teresa nodded. 'She's on her way.'

The three of us were finally going to be in the same room. I felt guilty for how often I'd moaned to Evie about Teresa not appearing to be interested in us all getting together. This wasn't the joyful Three Musketeer-style reunion I'd envisaged.

'Can I make you some toast?'

She shook her head. 'I can't eat. Maybe for Amelia?'

I busied about in the kitchen, glad to escape the feeling that I was failing to find the right words, the right actions. I should be much better at this. I had a sudden rush of compassion for the people who practically jumped in hedges when they saw my bald head advancing down the high street. What words would comfort Teresa? Even after thirty-eight years of marriage, she'd still done a little half-smile when Paul's name flashed up on her phone. Whereas I was like an eager spaniel straining at the leash to have a break from family life for a weekend – 'Don't worry if you don't hear from me, not sure what the mobile reception will be like' – Teresa would be texting Paul as we drew into the hotel car park to let him know she was there safely. I'd been both critical, vacillating between thinking that the way they depended on each other was one step up from writing your boyfriend's name inside a love heart on your schoolbooks, and envious because Mal might not notice I'd gone until he needed the password for Netflix.

Thankfully, there was a knock at the door and Evie walked in, her face crumpling as soon as she saw Teresa. She was so much less awkward than me, avoiding the reluctant hug and going straight for the grasp of the upper arms and a heartfelt 'I'm so sorry, T. Tell me what you need me to do.' Even crack of sparrows, straight out of bed, she brought knitwear glamour to an otherwise sorry tableau of fleeces and dressing gowns. And fresh croissants that she'd picked up from her friend who owned the bakery next door to her photographic shop.

I popped them on a baking tray, embarrassingly keen to make a start on them despite feeling that I should join Teresa in losing my appetite. Sadly, in times of crisis, my gene pool seemed to lean towards the carbohydrate storage system to survive, rather than living off current fat stores to become a fleet-of-foot fighting machine.

Once we'd had breakfast, we gathered in the sitting room, alternating between cuddling Violet, shaking our heads in disbelief and reassuring Teresa that she didn't need to sort through Paul's filing system this very minute, that she should take time to absorb the shock, that we'd help her through everything when the moment came. However, after Teresa's reluctance for the three of us to be reunited, it felt surprisingly normal to be together. Evie and I slipped into our old roles in the group, as though the intervening years had never happened. Evie magicked up the delicate words to express her feelings and reflect Teresa's, while I blundered about, nervous of saying anything in case I made her cry again. On the other hand, I hit my stride when it came to making a list of people to contact and what needed to happen next.

Evie was way ahead of me in terms of the nitty-gritty of death though. When Teresa asked Evie to fetch her reading glasses from the bedroom, I was jittery with relief that I didn't have to go as I wasn't sure whether his body was still up there. When she came down, Evie whispered to me that the paramedics had already taken him to the mortuary.

The phone rang and I leapt up to answer it.

A shrill voice rattled down the line. 'Who's that?'

'It's Steph, Teresa's friend.'

'Is Teresa there?'

I had no idea whether this rude woman knew about Paul or not. 'May I ask who's calling?'

'It's Wendy, her sister.' Clearly she hadn't joined the dots when I introduced myself the first time.

It wasn't the moment to have a little trip down memory lane and remind her that we'd met. 'I'll pass you over. Teresa, Wendy for you.'

As soon as she heard Wendy's voice, Teresa dissolved, sobbing out the bare facts. Evie and I allowed ourselves to cry and gasp about the shock of it all, trying to talk loudly enough so that Teresa wouldn't feel that we were earwigging on every word. Even though we knew the extent of Teresa's grief, it still felt somewhat voyeuristic to listen openly to her account of Paul's death. 'He asked for a Rennie, he thought it was indigestion.' 'I know, he'd just bought a new mountain bike.' 'This afternoon, I think, I'm waiting for the funeral director to call me back.' 'Steph and Evie. No, I don't know whether they are staying.'

The thing that made me stop my half-crying, half-mumbling and swivel my head right round so as not to miss a word though was Teresa's change in tone from desolation to a rather aggressive 'You're already at Grantham? No. I don't need you to come down now. There's nothing you can do. *No*, Wendy. Well, I'm sorry you've had a wasted journey.' Teresa walked out to the kitchen, where she hissed, 'It's not about putting friends before family.'

I caught Evie's eye. She leant towards me and whispered, 'The last thing Teresa needs is her turning up. Don't you remember how she wouldn't stay overnight alone in her own home?'

'Don't suppose she'd be Teresa's first choice for sleeping in a house where someone's just died?' I said, perilously close to laughing hysterically.

Evie knew me of old, the inopportune giggler, and stopped speaking to me.

Teresa was practically shouting now. 'No, Wendy. You can come for the funeral of course. You know why!'

I went through and put my hand on Teresa's shoulder. 'Shall I deal with her?' I mouthed.

She waved me away. 'I'll talk to you later,' she said and finished the call. 'God, I don't need her pitching up and making the drama her own.'

I knew Teresa and Wendy didn't get on very well, but when Mum died, I really wished I'd had someone to share the burden with. I had never felt my lack of siblings more than when Mal looked like he might throw up when the undertaker suggested going to see my mum in the chapel of rest. Thank goodness Ben had found a wife who appeared strong of stomach and a sleeve-roller-upper in a crisis.

'You might find Wendy's a real help to you, Teresa,' I said. 'Someone who knew Paul well. She could support Amelia a bit too, another person to look after the baby.'

But Teresa was adamant.

We went back through to Evie, who wanted to know what the deal was with Wendy.

Teresa shared the gist of the conversation, adding, 'I can't cope with her hysterics just now.'

'I think you're right, T. Wendy isn't going to add value, at least not yet.'

I agreed. 'Maybe later on.' When it came to sorting out stuff with a sentimental rather than actual value, I was absolutely in favour of the 'many hands' approach. When Mum died, Teresa had been a godsend in stopping me cluttering up my house with Mum's zoo of pyjama cases – dog, tiger, giraffe – and the teddies that she'd kept on her bed. I turned to Teresa and said gently, 'Would you like us to be here when the funeral director comes?'

She nodded and dissolved into tears. In the days after Mum died, I'd frequently found myself wondering how so much water could make its way to the eyes, puzzling as I cried into Gladys's neck about where the liquid came from, imagining a little reservoir tucked behind my jaw like the one in my Mini for windscreen wiper fluid.

'Is there anything in Paul's papers that might be useful to know before the funeral director gets here?'

Teresa looked bemused.

'Like what sort of service he wanted?' It felt too soon to say the words, 'cremation or burial?' out loud.

Teresa looked dazed, as though the words weren't making any sense to her, but Amelia stood up. 'Shall I get the blue file?' She handed Violet to Evie, who was a natural with her, cooing and rocking. Despite having my own son and my two granddaughters, babies could smell my awkwardness a mile off and used me as proof to their parents that their lungs had developed perfectly the second I clutched them woodenly.

Amelia came back in with a big box file, which was a glory to behold in its organisation, with neatly labelled dividers for everything from house insurance to car tax and, now the most relevant, wills.

Teresa pushed it towards me. 'You have a look. He wrote down all his passwords for everything in a little book. I wonder if he had a premonition. He made sure I knew where everything was a few months ago.'

It was funny how the traits I'd mocked in life – Paul's Captain Sensible approach to everything – suddenly transformed themselves into sanity savers in death. I had absolutely no clue what Mal's passwords were and only a one-in-four hit rate of remembering my own.

I didn't suppose there would be any shocking revelations skulking about in Paul's paperwork given that he'd met Teresa in his early twenties. It was, however, a reminder for me to have one last read of the letters in the old cigar box in my desk and save Ben from any posthumous revelations from my youth. How quickly the years passed. From wearing flip-flops from a beachside market stall all summer long with no thought for arch support to feeling inside a shoe to judge the likelihood of being able to walk round London without limping.

I turned my attention back to Teresa, who'd taken Violet from Evie and was nuzzling into her wispy blonde hair, the little girl she'd feared would ruin her daughter's future. Life was terrifying in its ability to deliver a perspective readjustment without warning. Right now, Violet looked as though she was the lifeboat that would keep Amelia and Teresa sailing forwards.

I slid the folder in the 'Wills' section out, still numb from the slap of realisation that Paul was gone. I kept feeling as though I was watching what was going on from afar, rather than witnessing the pitiful aftermath of the loss of a soulmate.

As I riffled through the papers, Amelia crumpled and sobbed, 'I wish I'd said goodbye properly.'

Evie put her arm round her. 'Shall we go and get some fresh air? Let's take Violet for a walk.'

Amelia nodded and reached out for Violet, whose eyes widened with delight as her mother came into view. Amelia pressed her lips into Violet's cheek, then strapped her into her buggy. Deep in my heart, I felt a tug of regret for not savouring those moments with Ben. I'd listened to Evie talking about how she loved the middle-of-the-night feed, cherished that special time in the early hours, alone with Isaac, when no one else was awake. I, on the other hand, had resented every moment that I was up in the night with Ben, watching Mal packing in a solid eight hours, fresh as a summer meadow for work the next day, while I sometimes had to sneak out of work at lunchtime for a nap in the car. If only I'd known how fleeting that moment of lighting up someone's world just by being there was.

As Amelia wheeled Violet out of the door, Teresa sighed a thank you to Evie, the sound of someone who was on the last teaspoon of resources for coping with anyone else's distress.

I turned back to the pile of papers, but just as I started to flick through the will to see if we could shed any light on Paul's wishes, the doorbell rang.

Teresa looked as though the arrival of the funeral director was another notch in making her nightmare real.

I jumped up. 'I'll go.'

I opened the door. 'Wendy!'

I didn't have time to announce her arrival before she pushed past me and marched into the sitting room, flinging her arms wide, sucking in Teresa and crying at a pitch that matched that silly squeaky laugh of hers I remembered from years ago. She was obviously one of these women who didn't feel they were having an emotion unless everyone else was aware of it.

I made myself scarce in the kitchen, banging about with the kettle but could still hear Teresa saying, 'You shouldn't have come.'

'You're my sister. Paul is…' She let out a screeching sob. '… my brother-in-law. You know, family?' She was really annoying me now. I'd worked with so many people like her who vied for the top slot in other people's tragedies, when, in ordinary life, they'd be reluctant to lend them a stapler. Although Teresa was very loyal, she'd let slip that her mum had paid Wendy's rent while she brought up Zoe. Wendy had also wangled a way to inherit two-thirds of the estate when she died. It was a credit to Teresa's generous heart that she hadn't completely fallen out with her.

I slammed some chocolate digestives onto a plate and carried through the tea tray.

'I might pop home, you know, give you a bit of time. Just text me when the funeral director gets here and I'll come straight over.'

Teresa nodded. 'Okay. Thank you.'

I was glad to escape the Durham dramatics, though once I got home, I was irrationally enraged to discover Mal carrying on as normal. He was sitting at our kitchen table with a smorgasbord of cold meats and smoked salmon for lunch.

'You poor thing. What's happened? Do you want some food?' he asked, fetching me a plate.

I swallowed my irritation and sank gratefully onto a chair, then spoilt the moment by moaning about him opening a new Brie, Cheddar and the Ossau-Iraty, instead of finishing the ones that were already open. I did feel short-changed that the post-cancer 'lucky to be alive' euphoria had not translated into long-term 'Don't sweat the multiple cheese openings'.

Mal waved me away. 'Never mind about that. Just tell me what's happened.'

Another wave of sadness rushed through me. Paul had never made himself the centre of attention but he'd always been there, in the background with calm, kind words, happy to help out whenever he could. 'He woke up in the middle of the night complaining of chest pains. They both thought it was indigestion and by the time Teresa realised it was serious and called the ambulance, he'd gone into full cardiac arrest.'

Mal put his head in his hands. 'That's so unfair. He was always the one drinking sensibly and going out on his bike even when it was chucking it down. I thought he'd live to be a hundred and ten.'

'Me too.' I cut off a large piece of cheese, brooding about the ridiculousness of depriving yourself of wine, chocolate or anything that was bad for you if you were going to drop dead at sixty-four.

'It's good in a way that Teresa's got Amelia and the baby at home. At least it will be company for her initially.' Mal passed me the grapes.

'Wendy turned up too, though I got the impression Teresa wasn't overly thrilled about that,' I said.

'Wendy?'

'Yes, you know, her sister. She came to Norfolk years ago with us. Silly squeaky laugh? A bit of an idiot.'

Mal frowned. 'I vaguely remember her. How long is she staying for?'

'I don't know. Probably until the funeral.'

'But that might not be for a while if they have to have a coroner's report into Paul's death. They do a post-mortem when it's sudden. She's younger than Teresa, isn't she? She must have a job to go to?'

I stared at him bemused by his sudden interest in a woman he'd met about three times in the last thirty years. I shrugged. 'I think she's a dental hygienist. Do family members get special leave in these circumstances? Perhaps she's taken holiday. I don't know,' I said, already bored.

Mal jumped up and started packing away all the lunch things. 'Anyway, I need to get on. I've got a proposal to proofread this afternoon.'

'Are you going to pop round to see Teresa?' I asked.

'That would just be awkward. She won't want me there, not today. There's enough going on without having to entertain me.'

'But you should at least make some kind of contact. You were one of Paul's closest friends.'

Mal seemed more interested in polishing off the last two olives than seeing if he could do anything to help Teresa.

'I got on with him well enough, but we didn't really have that much in common. It was more because you girls were friends. I wouldn't know what to say to her.'

Rage was fermenting in me as Mal defaulted to doing what he always did, distancing himself from anything that might require tolerating someone else's unhappiness without thinking about how awful it was for him.

I called Gladys and escaped into the garden. We walked down to the fishpond, where I immediately felt calmer. People laughed at goldfish for their small brains, but I envied them, how little they needed to be happy. A few ferns, a couple of mates and someone to chuck in some food pellets now and again. That sounded much more appealing than my brain spinning round, chasing one thought after another.

I was just watching the tadpoles darting round the pond when, over the top of the hedge, I caught sight of Mal's car reversing out of the drive. So much for his proofreading. God knows where he'd gone. Probably running off to the osteopath for a massage to help relieve his stress. Thank goodness I'd been spared the 'Feel my shoulders. Do they feel tight?'

Twenty-five minutes later, a text arrived from Teresa. *You don't need to come back today. Evie's here and is happy to help with the funeral director, and of course, Wendy. Thank you for coming over though. xx*

I stared at my phone. It wasn't as though I was desperate to put in my tuppence-worth about the merits of 'The Lord's My Shepherd' over 'Amazing Grace', but my nose felt well and truly out of joint. I'd obviously appointed myself Chief of Grief and was put out to discover that Teresa thought the other two could fulfil that role. Who knew that I could even get competitive over who got to advise on a cremation over a woodland burial? No wonder Ben's PE teacher had described him as 'pathologically ruthless in his determination to be first'. We'd all laughed about it – Mal thought it was the best compliment ever – but now I was beginning to feel sorry for the legacy of his double-whammy cut-throat genes.

I replied, *Are you sure? I'm more than happy to pop round. Just let me know what works for you. Otherwise see you tomorrow?*

Absolutely sure. Thank you. xx

I told myself that there shouldn't be a hierarchy in helping someone who'd just lost their husband, that the best outcome was the best possible help available, whoever it came from. Nonetheless, I was like a thirteen-year-old girl whose friends had all clambered into a Waltzer without realising there'd be no room for her. I'd show her that I was bigger and better than that. Food. That's what people needed in times of stress.

I was frying up some garlic and onions for Teresa's favourite in my repertoire – slow-cooked beef with mustard dumplings – when Mal came back in.

'Where have you been?'

'Just popped in on Teresa, like you said. Helped her choose the hymns for the funeral. Didn't stay long. Quick chat with Wendy and Evie. Nice to see them after all this time.'

I dropped the beef sizzling into the pan. Why didn't Teresa say Mal was there? I forced myself to smile. 'Well done. She will have appreciated that.'

I stirred in the tomato puree with a ferocity that threatened to scratch the enamel off my crock pot.

'Perhaps we should take this over tonight and have dinner with her.'

Mal shook his head. 'No, she'll want to be with her family.'

'I'm the closest thing to family that she's got. Much closer than her sister.'

Mal shouted at me, properly lost his temper. 'For God's sake, listen to yourself. A fucking opinion on everything. Have you stopped for a second to consider what Teresa wants? If she'd wanted you there, she'd have bloody invited you.'

He slammed the kitchen door, making all the utensils in the jar by the cooker rattle. I struggled to remember a time when I'd ever felt lonelier. At some point in our marriage, the magnet that had pulled us together had spun around and repelled us in different directions. With Teresa down the road broken-hearted about Paul, it felt entirely wrong to wish I could just pack my bags and never have to withstand Mal's disappointment in me, never have to feel as though everything about me was so unappealing. Never have to see him again, in fact.

STEPH

17 April 2019

Six days before the funeral, I forced Teresa to let me come round to firm up what sort of food she wanted for the wake. She was procrastinating, saying that she couldn't think about it yet, that maybe she'd just go to the supermarket and buy a load of quiches and sausage rolls. In the end, I'd persuaded her that I really wanted to do it – 'My parting gift to Paul.' But pinning her down to when I could pop by to discuss it was another matter. I knew that Evie had been round a few times to flick the Hoover about and clean the bathroom and kitchen and I was trying really hard not to be offended by Teresa's unwillingness to let me visit. She'd been the first person I'd turned to when I got cancer and I'd assumed – wrongly – that she'd be leaning on me in a similar way. Instead, that role had gone to that puerile sister of hers, who had rarely sullied herself with coming down south to visit in the last twenty years and – according to Evie – was barely bothering to make her a ham sandwich to keep body and soul together.

I was treading a fine line between letting Teresa get there in her own time and panicking about how the hell I'd get everything organised. When Ben was young, I'd learnt very swiftly that tight deadlines at work usually had a direct knock-on effect to how much I shouted about mud trailed across the carpet and milk left out of the fridge. I'd done my best to build in a wobble factor ever since. While catering for a wake wasn't going to be the most ambitious cookery challenge, I wanted to feel I'd given Paul a good send-off, rather than scrabbling about for a few pork pies just within their sell-by date and whispering, 'Family hold back' to Amelia and Ross.

As Teresa let me in, she murmured, 'Save me from my sister. She's driving me mad.'

I tried to deny the childish satisfaction at the fact they hadn't all been a happy little team in my absence, then gave up and embraced the warm glow of romping to the rescue.

I put my best face on, greeted Wendy and then started to discuss possible options for food. 'It depends how long you expect people to stay? If you want to do a quick in and out, a slice of cake and a cup of coffee, I can make some sandwiches, a few quiches and a Victoria sponge? Or if you intend to settle in for the long haul without people falling flat on their faces, then maybe a lamb casserole with rice?'

Before Teresa could answer, Wendy piped up. 'You won't want people hanging round all afternoon. You'll be exhausted. A few sandwiches and cake will be plenty.'

I acted as though she was supermarket music and waited for Teresa to answer.

'I'm not sure. Lots of Paul's relatives are coming down from Scotland. I don't feel I can fob them off with a cheese sandwich and a packet of crisps. And his cousins aren't the sort you can offer a glass of milk. They'll be expecting to send him on his way with at least a couple of tumblers of whisky.'

'Okay, so something fairly substantial.'

Wendy huffed. 'God, if you start giving them loads to drink, they'll never leave. That Eric drank nearly a whole bottle of whisky to himself at Amelia's christening.'

Teresa didn't quite snap but managed a fairly terse, 'They are driving all the way from Aberdeen and staying in a hotel overnight. As far as I'm concerned, they can have whatever they want. Eric and his wife have always been ridiculously generous when we've been up there.'

I really hoped that when I pegged it, whoever was in charge of post-crem jollities would over-order the booze by fifty per cent on the grounds that it wouldn't go to waste rather than see my demise as the signal to start curbing everyone else's enthusiasm for life. A reminder to take the joy when it presented itself, rather than the starter gun for clipping out discount vouchers for vol-au-vents.

Wendy didn't back off. 'I think you should put a time limit on it. Tell everyone they can come between three and five.'

Teresa slumped back into her chair. 'But then I'll be sitting here all evening on my own. I've got the rest of my life to do that.' Her voice caught. 'I don't care if they stay till late.'

Wendy looked offended. 'But we'll need some time together as a family. Amelia won't want a load of people she hardly knows hanging around. Nor will Ross.'

This woman was royally getting on my nerves, dictating to Teresa what she had to do on the day of her husband's funeral.

I got out my notebook. 'So how many people do you think will come back to the house?'

Teresa handed me a list. 'These are the ones I'm inviting, so about forty-five, and then there might be a few more on the day.'

'Forty-five? Where are they all going to sit?' Wendy was like a wasp at a summer barbecue.

I glared at her. 'Most people don't expect to sit. They don't usually stay for very long either. As long as there's room for the oldies to perch somewhere, everyone else will just mingle standing up.'

'Aunt Edie won't be able to stand. Nor will Maud.'

I turned to her. 'We'll reserve them a space on the sofa. I'll put a notice on the cushions.'

Wendy frowned, as though she wasn't sure whether I was joking or not.

I made the most of the temporary closure of her mouth to settle on a menu – a stomach-lining fish pie, plus a lamb stew – and to agree the wine and whisky order.

The reprieve from Wendy's petulant suggestions was short-lived. She was soon puffing about how much it was all going to cost. 'You need to think about the pennies now, Teresa. Just like I've had to all these years without a husband to provide for me.'

Teresa's eyes started to fill. 'I know, but I want to celebrate Paul's life and we were going to have a party for his sixty-fifth next year, so I'm going to spend the money on this instead.'

Gesticulating as though Teresa had only known five-star luxury, Wendy said, 'You've never had to worry about bills because there's always been two of you, but you'll see now what it's like, trying to make ends meet with one income.'

I would have bet my house on the fact that Wendy never rejoiced in other people's good fortune. I couldn't help myself. 'Wasn't it lucky you had your parents to pay your rent?'

She narrowed her eyes and said, 'I saved them a fortune in nursing-home fees.'

Out of deference to Teresa, I smothered the knowledge that Wendy had used that fact to sway the inheritance in her favour, but it nearly choked me.

Wendy got to her feet. 'Right, if that's sorted, Teresa and I are going to make a start on clearing out Paul's stuff.'

'Already? Paul's only been dead a fortnight. Are you up to that, T?'

'I suppose we could leave it until after the funeral. I might feel a bit stronger then.' Teresa looked punch-drunk, as though her brain couldn't make a decision about what would make her feel better. Mainly because right now, nothing could make her feel better.

Wendy was having none of it. She clapped her hands. 'Teresa! There's no time like the present. You can't possibly start moving on while all his clothes are hanging there every time you open the wardrobe door. As for all his toiletries in the bathroom, sorry, but that's just a bit creepy.'

Much to Evie's horror, I'd never being the sort of person to make memento boxes or cling on to sentimental souvenirs. Evie had made a beautiful scrapbook of Isaac's drawings, handprints and Mother's Day cards. My approach to memories was far more eclectic. Occasionally I'd stumble across Ben's first curl of hair at the back of my desk drawer, or a tiny little toy car that I couldn't bear to part with in the sideboard. However, even I felt that it wasn't unreasonable to take a beat to decide on the right moment to adjust to a toothbrush-for-one panorama. Wendy seemed under the impression that coming to terms with losing a husband of thirty-eight years was just a question of pairing up the moccasins, tossing the shaving foam in the bin and donating his ties to Oxfam.

I patted Teresa's arm. 'Do you really want to do this now? I'm happy to help you at a later date.'

Wendy moved towards the door. 'Why don't we at least see what there is to do?'

Agreeing which food to serve at the wake seemed to have sapped Teresa of any energy. 'Do you need a rest?' I asked.

'Getting things sorted is energising in itself,' Wendy said.

Teresa dragged herself to her feet.

'Would you like me to help as well?' I asked, ignoring the fact that Wendy was passing me my coat. 'Many hands make light work.'

Teresa said, 'That would be great, if you're not too busy? I've no idea what to keep.'

She led the way upstairs, each step appearing an effort, as though grief had seeped down into the very heart of her and filled her limbs with lead. I recognised that sluggish daze from when my mum died, when the days that had seemed way too short to allow me to visit as often as I should have suddenly expanded into long and loud hours to observe her absence.

Teresa sank down onto her bed. Even after all these years of friendship, there was something slightly awkward about being in her marital bedroom. I didn't want to intrude by understanding which side of the bed Paul used to sleep on. I shuffled about, trying to decide the least excruciating starting point. Not the bedside table. Definitely not that.

But Wendy was like the leader of a kids' club who wasn't going to rest until everyone had nailed the actions to 'We're Going on a Bear Hunt' to her satisfaction. 'Where shall we start?'

Teresa pointed to a wardrobe.

I hoped we weren't going to stumble over some rusting sex toy leaking battery acid. Or worse, some terrifyingly hi-tech update with a smorgasbord of multi-flavoured potions that would forever change my view of Teresa and Paul. One glimpse of caramel latte lubricant and I was out of there.

Wendy was gathering up armfuls of his suits and shirts and piling them on the bed. Teresa sat with tears trickling down her face. I hugged her. 'You just say when you've had enough and we'll stop.'

She nodded.

Wendy scrabbled about at the bottom of the wardrobe, flinging out all of his shoes. 'Steph, you pair up the shoes and put them in separate bags. There's a recycling bin at Sainsbury's. You could pop them in there on the way home.'

I realised in that moment that being very senior at work meant that no one had given me an order they hadn't bothered to dress up as a polite request in about twenty years.

Wendy wasn't worrying about hierarchy sensitivities. She was formulating her next diktat. 'Teresa, you sort through the shirts and suits and put out a pile for Ross. Though Paul wasn't exactly cutting-edge trendy, was he? Do you think Ross is likely to want anything?'

Teresa reached out a hand, caressing the collar of a dark suit.

Wendy rattled on, like a demented knitting machine. 'Teresa! Come on. That can go in the charity pile. I don't think wide lapels like that are going to be Ross's thing.'

Teresa obediently started checking the pockets of the suits, while I knelt on the floor, resentfully stuffing shoes into bags as per Wendy's instruction. In the meantime, Wendy was pulling out a heap of jumpers, tracksuit bottoms, cycling gear and demanding answers from Teresa. 'Keep for Ross?' 'Charity?'

When Teresa reached out for an Aran cardigan and pressed it to her face, Wendy said, 'That's definitely charity.'

Teresa did up the buttons. 'Mum knitted this for him. I thought he looked like Val Doonican, but he showed me a photo of David Beckham wearing one just like it. So old-fashioned he'd become trendy.' The longing in her voice made my eyes prickle.

Wendy did a little scoff.

I couldn't believe my gentle friend was related to this self-obsessed cow. No wonder Teresa always went up to Durham rather than inviting this tyrant down to visit. 'She's not so bad on her home territory.' Frankly, Teresa deserved a medal for not falling out with her completely and Paul a posthumous tolerance award for spending a week up there every summer. Whenever I'd tried to lure him into being disloyal about Teresa's family, he'd always said, 'But they're important to her. It's only a few days a year.'

I'd tried not to compare his attitude to Mal's whenever I'd said Mum was coming over. He'd made exaggerated sinking-to-the-floor-in-despair gestures. Over time, despite my determination that he should just suck it up, I'd slowly seen less of her and lied to myself that I was too busy at work to have her over for dinner every week.

I did my best to let Wendy's banalities wash over me. And, reluctantly, I could even agree that there was a flickering of determination from Teresa that made my heart both ache and lift. As though she was on the cusp of a delicate shift from submerging herself in grief to raising herself into survival.

I allowed my mind to flit between memories of Paul to block out Wendy drivelling on. I switched from pairing shoes to folding up his ties, against a rolling backdrop of images of Paul fixing my sunglasses, patiently searching out the set of tiny screwdrivers that only he would have and know where to find. Paul explaining how a jumbo jet took off to Ben. Paul taking Amelia for a walk as a toddler so Teresa could finish lunch with us in peace. All those New Years we spent together, with him kissing Teresa so tenderly at midnight, as though each year held the promise of so much to look forward to with her.

I snapped out of my thoughts when Teresa burst into noisy sobs.

Wendy was shaking an old T-shirt at her. 'Don't be silly. The collar on it is all frayed.'

Teresa reached for it, but Wendy was pushing it into the charity bin bag. In between sniffs of despair, she said, 'Paul was wearing that when Amelia was born. You remember she was early? He'd been clearing the gutters and my waters broke suddenly.'

'You hold on to it if you want to. You can get rid of it at a later date, but you don't have to make the decision now,' I said, just moments away from getting into a tug-of-war with Wendy.

Wendy rolled her eyes. 'Christ, if you hang on to every last ancient T-shirt, you're going to end up with a house full of old clutter.'

And that was it for me. This bossy bloody woman telling my friend what she could and couldn't keep. 'Just shut up. Let her do what she likes. Who are you to tell her what she has to throw away? If she wants to sleep with his holey old underpants under her pillow, what does it matter to you if it gives her comfort? She's just lost her soulmate for God's sake. She hasn't even had the funeral yet.'

Teresa curled up on the bed, sobbing into the duvet. The shame at my loss of temper was immediate, a picture flashing into my head of Teresa and Paul sidling out of the room whenever Mal and I started to go at each other in a way we wouldn't even have considered particularly vicious.

I sat down next to her. 'Sorry. Sorry. I know we're all doing our best here. Everyone copes in different ways.' I lifted my face to Wendy. 'My apologies for snapping. Stress doesn't bring out the best in me.'

But I'd obviously tipped Wendy past the point of no return. 'Yeah, Mal said that about you.'

'Mal?' I screwed up my face. He'd obviously slipped in a whine about his wife when he popped in the other day. 'Yes, he probably does say that about me, but I doubt you have any idea what his opinion is.' I was trying to keep my voice neutral, but she was really beginning to be horseradish up my sinuses.

Teresa leapt off the bed. She grabbed Wendy's arm. 'Right, you go downstairs and make some tea. We'll finish up here.'

Wendy swung round. 'You've always been like this. Always prized other people above family. Never inviting me and Zoe down here to visit. You've spent more time with Steph's son than you have with your own niece!'

Teresa didn't respond. Just stood, defeated, with tears pouring down her face, my kind-hearted friend having to listen to Wendy's grudges when it was all she could do to hold her heart together.

I stepped forward. 'Wendy, I don't know what your problem is but can you save it for another time? Perhaps wait until after the funeral of the husband that your sister has *just lost*, before you get into your own family grievances? You might not have found a soulmate, but let's have some respect for the woman who did, yeah?' Something about the stand-off reminded me of the old-fashioned set-tos we used to have over the park with the kids from the estate on the other side of town. I clearly hadn't lost that 'You and whose army?' instinct when the right buttons got pushed, no matter how many organic blueberries I sprinkled on my steel-cut oats.

Wendy obviously hadn't been a pushover on the Witch's Hat either. In that split second, I recognised the crazed recklessness of the kind of lads who'd try and make the swings go over the top bar.

'You think you know it all. You don't know anything. I bet you think Mal is *your* soulmate.'

I was just working out how to avoid giving her the satisfaction of admitting that, actually, my soul shrivelled a little when he walked into the room, when Teresa grabbed Wendy's arm. 'Stop this. Both of you.'

But Wendy did one of those triumphant smiles, the sort that people do when they know you can't outplay them. 'Your husband is the father of my daughter, Zoe. She was twenty-three in January. And until she was eighteen, Mal visited her at my house twice a month. All those weekends he was away "working" – he was down the park with our Zoe. He's paid for her. All. These. Years. Supported her through university. Took her away nearly every year. France. Italy. We had a lovely holiday in Majorca when she was about twelve.'

I stood stunned in front of her, my brain barely bothering to stir itself to work out whether the accusations of the crazy lady could be true. My first inclination was to laugh. But before I could muster up any reaction, Teresa screamed at Wendy to get out, slammed the door behind her and collapsed onto the bed in fresh tears. 'Oh Steph, oh no, I'm sorry.'

'You knew?'

This friend of mine surely couldn't have been lying to me all these years.

Her head slumped forwards. 'No. Not really.'

There was a silence, one of those moments laden with the sense that something unpleasant was about to follow.

'I didn't know Zoe was Mal's. I thought she was Glenn's.'

'But you said "not really"?'

'I only knew that something had happened between Wendy and Mal, that weekend in Norfolk, when you and Evie fell out.'

'That was nearly twenty-four years ago!'

'But I didn't know for definite then.'

The length of betrayal, the scale of it, was like a dual conduit to both intense fury and oddly, very un-me-like, a wish that I'd never found out about something that had its roots in so long ago. I felt cold, shivery, as though I'd got soaked through to my bra on a walk with Gladys.

'You didn't tell me. You didn't *tell* me.' Despite the many things on the tip of my tongue, when it came to it, I couldn't do it. Couldn't say the hurtful and spiteful accusations that were threatening to surge out into the bedroom she'd shared with Paul, that space where she would – without consciously realising it – still be waiting for the clink of the water glass on the bedside table, the creak of his wardrobe door, the sigh as he stretched out in bed. There was plenty of time to scorch the earth of our friendship.

Teresa's shoulders were shaking, her voice was coming in bursts. 'I didn't want this. I only found out for certain when I had that horrible weekend in Suffolk and I fell out with Wendy because she was flirting with Neil. I still didn't know Zoe was Mal's.'

'Did Paul know?'

'Not about Zoe, but what happened in Norfolk, yes.' She knotted her fingers in one of Paul's T-shirts. 'It was a real bone of contention between us. We kept arguing about it right up until he died.'

'I didn't know you had any arguments.' It was one of the things I'd found utterly weird about them. They were never short with each other. Unlike me, who, whenever Mal said, 'I've emptied the dishwasher *for you*', 'I've put the food in the fridge *for you*' – I rarely managed to say, 'Thank you', preferring instead to point out that he also ate the food in the fridge and, last time I looked, was also using crockery and cutlery rather than scooping up his soup with his fingers.

'We didn't row about anything really.' Her eyes filled, but she forced herself on. 'Just this one thing. He was entirely at odds with me over it. You know how black and white he was about everything.'

I nodded. The only time I'd seen him get close to falling out with anyone was when Mal let it slip that I'd taken his speeding fine and put the points on my licence. 'But that's illegal. And dishonest.' Mal had argued that speed cameras were just a money-spinning exercise, dismissing Paul's claim about the reduction in accidents as though he was just a killjoy old uncle, moaning about the younger generation. Unlike Mal though, Paul would back down at a touch of the hand and a gentle frown from Teresa.

She carried on. 'I didn't tell you because I wasn't brave enough to destroy your marriage. But, most of all, I didn't want to lose your friendship. I couldn't imagine how that wouldn't happen then and I can't imagine it now.'

And there, in that shuddery sobbing heap, was the woman who'd bolstered me over the years – when Ben was constantly in trouble at school – 'He'll make a wonderful adult' – who'd held the sick bowl for me when chemo had got the better of me, who'd watched daytime TV to keep me company instead of going to work. And also, now, the woman who knew that my husband, my own husband, had slept with someone else, her sister no less, and *didn't say a word.*

My thoughts felt as though shock had beaten them so flat that nothing other than the basic instinct to survive was squeezing through.

I stood up. 'I'll still do the catering for the funeral. Just make sure Wendy doesn't try to talk to me. Because I could not give a shit what she has to say.'

Teresa was trembling and attempting to speak through her tears, but I needed to leave before my words returned and cornered her with a viciousness that even I wasn't cruel enough to deliver. Not today, anyway.

TERESA

17 April 2019

After Steph marched out, I drifted down onto my bed as though all the necessary forces to keep me anchored in my life had disappeared in the proverbial puff of smoke. I lay, letting my limbs fall heavily onto the mattress and wondered whether I'd ever find the momentum to get up again. I stayed there until it got dark, my mind floating off to obsess over whether there was any salt in the garage to grit the drive when it snowed and, if not, where Paul ordered it from. What the tyre pressure was on my car. Which knob to turn on the boiler when the pressure dropped. These small and resolvable worries seemed the most my mind could handle. Not how I was going to survive the next few decades without Paul. And probably without Steph, the one person who would definitely have been an asset in navigating my new and alien landscape.

When Wendy finally poked her head around the door to see if I was coming down for dinner, my grief reared up and broke free of a lifetime of peacekeeping.

The F-word had long been Steph's favourite expletive. Over the years, I'd learnt not to flinch every time she uttered it, but I still couldn't stop myself from shushing her when she said it in public and turning around waving apologies to anyone over the age of twenty-five in the vicinity.

But today, I appreciated the power of its profanity, galvanising myself to leap off the bed and scream at Wendy, unleashing a torrent of abuse that was strangely satisfying. To her credit, she didn't interrupt but waited until I folded onto the floor, spent with the effort.

She wasn't, however, anywhere near as contrite as I expected. 'I would have told you that Mal was Zoe's father, but Mum was already so mortified that I'd left Glenn after less than two years that I thought she might keel over if I then brought Mal out of the woodwork.'

'Did you know straight away that Zoe was Mal's?'

'I wasn't sure initially. I thought there was a good chance she might be, because she was a bit early to be Glenn's. I hadn't had sex with Glenn in the lead-up to getting married because he'd been away on the stag do, then after that he had a terrible cold and I was sleeping in another room because I didn't want to catch it just before the wedding.'

'Does Glenn know she's not his?'

At last, a flicker of shame passed over Wendy's features. 'He didn't to begin with. I thought I'd be able to pretend that Zoe was his daughter and no one would be any the wiser. But I couldn't. I mean, she looks just like Mal, with those almond-shaped eyes and strong chin.'

I felt sick. I hadn't been a big fan of Glenn's, but I couldn't imagine how painful it must have been to discover the truth. And I'd helped it happen. I'd opened the door and allowed Wendy to march into Steph's life, taking whatever she wanted, and ruin Glenn's into the bargain.

'And Mal's role in all of this? Apart from the obvious? I mean, do you have a relationship with him? Or is he just a part-time father to Zoe?'

Wendy folded her arms. 'I know you don't have a hope in hell of understanding this.' Her voice dropped. 'You had Paul. Not everyone is that lucky.'

I had to work hard not to fling my arms out in despair and howl about the unfairness of the universe, that I had lost him so early. 'Help me understand then.'

'I wasn't prepared to facilitate Mal seeing Zoe, turning up on high days and holidays, without some kind of relationship.' She gave a bitter laugh. 'Let's just say he did his duty. Until Zoe was eighteen, anyway. Sod's law that she can't stand me and adores him.'

Despite the fact that Paul had just died, that Steph's marriage was in smithereens, that Zoe had grown up knowing her father had another, more important family, the person Wendy felt most sorry for was herself. I knew in that moment, that if I had to take sides, Steph would win over my sister.

STEPH

17 April 2019

Mal's car was missing when I got home. Which meant I had a great swirl of adrenaline coursing round my body with no outlet. This was it. I could leave. Guilt-free. No one would blame me. In fact, people would expect it of me. But before I could do that, I'd have to get a handle on what Gemma was planning. Leaving aside the imminent implosion of his parents' relationship, if Ben was to have news of Mal's second family, of his half-sister, thrust upon him, he needed Gemma to help him make sense of it.

I stood in the hallway, looking at the photos of us on the wall. Mal laughing with his arm round us, on a Suffolk beach. Ben would have been about fifteen. Zoe, one? Two? Had Mal simply been doing the honourable thing as far as Zoe was concerned? Or was it conceivable that he was in love with Wendy? The latter possibility was the hardest to entertain. Mal was a bloke's bloke. Came alive with debates about football, the state of the economy, the failings of our local MP. He had utter disdain for women who did a dying duck over a lack of roses on Valentine's Day, or who started dropping hints about Christmas earrings in October. And Wendy was the epitome of needy – 'No one appreciates how difficult life has been for me.'

I tried so hard not to go down the route of 'I could understand it if she'd been gorgeous'. Before finding out that my husband of nearly thirty-eight years had had some sort of other family for over half of our marriage, I'd always erred on the side of 'But life is not really about looks in the end. It's a special chemistry that no one can account for.' Pah. And here I was in full blown 'What an insult! All that codswallop about liking women with a bit of substance and you end up with some skinny little bint with hair so scraggly it looks like it's been sucked up a Hoover.'

My mind rushed about, searching for all the nasty comments I could make about Wendy, of which, disappointingly, a good eighty per cent related to how she looked and laughed. I'd hoped to be more sophisticated in extremis but, sadly, 'must have been like having sex with a washing line' was jostling for dominance over 'I would have thought you'd have gone for someone more intellectually stimulating.'

I walked through the house, thinking of all the times Mal had come back from conferences or meetings. We'd melt into a Friday night over a bottle of Rioja and one of his favourite chicken curries that I'd thought about and prepared, maybe raced to the supermarket after work to make sure he came home to something a bit better than cheese on toast. How often had he sat down at our table – the one that Ben had written his name on in biro, that Nell had scratched a little flower into – having said goodbye to his daughter, his other family, that very morning?

How had he done it? And knowing what I knew now, did it make everything else a lie? Was all the time with us – poking about in the rockpools in Cornwall, pretending to be lost in the Hampton Court maze, looking for conkers in the Winkworth Arboretum – under sufferance, a performance rather than a pleasure?

I couldn't cry. The scale of betrayal was so huge that neither anger nor despair seemed the right response. I wondered whether I was even a normal human being with normal reactions. I couldn't work out if shock had sent my heart into the equivalent of a medically induced coma or I actually couldn't be bothered with the upset, couldn't muster the necessary outrage. About Mal anyway. Maybe it was a bit like finding a coat you once loved in the recesses of the garage, savaged by damp and mould. Alongside regret, there was a slight relief that you could throw it out rather than confront the reality that you'd never wear it again, that the part of your life when you wore leopard-skin coats with huge fur collars was gone.

Life was going to change. Now it was here, now I could no longer stick my head in the sand and find a million reasons to preserve the status quo, I was astonished to feel so little.

I pottered about, nothing like the wild woman I would have expected, throwing in a load of washing and deciding that leaving out Mal's socks and pants would just be childish. I made tea and stood dispassionately in front of the cupboard, thinking about which mugs I'd like to keep. Mal could have the ones with the wishy-washy landscape scenes.

Before I could get as far as divvying up the teaspoons, Gemma appeared at the French windows with a tray of lavender. I unlocked the door. She leant in to give me a hug and instinctively I drew in a big breath, as though I'd be able to smell the aftershave of anyone who wasn't Ben on her.

'Hey, how are you? Brought you these. They were two for one at Morrisons and I knew you wanted to put them along the path.'

'Thank you, darling, that's very kind of you.' I paused. 'Come in, come in.' I held up my entire existence and pulled the pin on it. 'I've just found out Mal has got another family.'

And saying it out loud made it real, made everything I'd considered as my family, my life, the scaffolding of my world feel insubstantial. All the 'I'll fob Mal off with the plain white dinner plates whilst I have the lovely artisan pottery ones' fell away and pain, sharp as a paper cut, engulfed me.

Gemma stood motionless while I battled to hold back my tears, then gave up, bypassing the tissues and going straight for the tea towel.

'Another family? Who with?' Thank goodness she sounded astounded. Amidst the notions crashing around my head, I'd half-formed the idea that maybe Ben knew, that he had been sending birthday cards to Zoe for years, perhaps even asking if he could get a stamp out of my purse, while I stirred onions and garlic into a casserole and thought I was as happy as the next person.

'He's got a daughter. She's twenty-three. Twenty-bloody-three!'

Gemma led me to a chair and sat holding my hand. I poured out my thoughts as they arrived, from what Ben would say and whether he'd want a relationship with his half-sister – 'It would be the icing on the pissing-me-off cake for Wendy to have you all up to Durham for Christmas' – to how Teresa had known that Mal had had a fling with her sister and lied to me all these years. 'My best friend!'

'Did she know Wendy's daughter was Mal's?'

'Apparently not. She thought Wendy's ex-husband was the father. But still. She knew Mal had been unfaithful. I don't know why she didn't tell me.'

'Did you ask her?'

'She said that initially she wasn't even sure whether it was true and she didn't want to be responsible for wrecking my marriage. I was working abroad a lot, Ben needed another parent around, hundreds of plausible excuses, but what it *feels like* is that she has lied to me forever – the one person I really trusted. That's leaving aside the fat lies that my husband has told me every day of his life. But I already knew from when I had cancer that he didn't have my back.'

Now the confetti that we sprinkled over our realities had blown away, the truths beneath were brutal. I'd spent the last five years saying, 'I think Mal struggled a bit when I was ill. It's hard to face up to the fact someone you love might die. And he's always been squeamish.' I wouldn't bother with letting him off the hook any more. Perhaps something more like, 'Yeah, when I was bald and throwing up, he was completely crap and had already lined up my replacement.' Might not be the exact truth, but if I was going to emerge from this as the cuckolded idiot, I wasn't going down without a spectacular fight.

Gemma's grip on my hand loosened, but I felt her body stiffen next to me. She cleared her throat. 'It's a big decision to tell someone something that will put them under pressure to act. You can't let what you know now negate all the rest. Ben had a great childhood – he's always telling me about the activity holidays you went on, all the sailing and canoeing, and how amazing you were – and are – at getting everyone together and making everything fun. You can't regret that, can you?'

'I'm losing everything, Gemma. Not just my husband – the jury is still out on whether that's going to be a big deal long term – but Teresa, she's the closest thing I've got to a sister. It's not like when you're young and there's time for several changes of friends – the ones you make at school, college, when the kids are small and maybe work… if you're lucky, you keep a few along the way and start sieving out the ones that were only in your life for a season.' I wiped my face with the tea towel. 'That kills me. She was brilliant when I was ill. I depended on her. Those sorts of friends don't come along that often. They take years to make. There's a special sort of chemistry to them, a magical mixture of a meeting of minds and shared experience. And I'm running out of time and inclination to go through that whole palaver of presenting myself in my best light and remembering not to swear. I'd earmarked who I was going to trust with the tweezers to pluck my whiskers in the old folks' home. And now, I find that my very best friend has kept a secret from me for decades.' I tried to make a joke. 'And I might need a magnifying mirror for my own whiskers.' I didn't pull it off, just choked and sobbed at the sharpness of her betrayal.

Gemma stood up and wiped her hands down her jeans. She looked at me, straight in the eye. 'But if she thought it was a one-off? If she didn't realise Zoe was Mal's? Don't people sometimes keep secrets precisely because they hope to save the people they love from getting hurt?'

I couldn't ignore it. I didn't know whether she was taunting me or verifying something that I didn't want to acknowledge.

'How do you mean?'

'I think you might be able to guess.' Her voice trailed away. 'I'm sorry.'

Even though I'd expected confirmation of my suspicions one day, the hard evidence still came as a shock.

'Is your affair over?' It was nothing short of a miracle that the question came out so calmly, because behind it, there were plenty of unkind comments queuing up to hurl themselves out.

She nodded. 'I finally came to my senses.' She looked at the floor. 'I'm so ashamed. I'm not sure what came over me.'

'Does Ben know?'

'Not yet.'

'Do you have to tell him? Does the other bloke's wife know?' Despite everything, the tension in my chest was easing as though unpalatable certainty was preferable to speculation laced with unlikely hope.

'No. Obviously she's aware things are not right between them, but she doesn't know specifically about me.'

'In that case, count yourself lucky and sit on your guilt. That's your burden. No one else's. Find somewhere to bury it, somewhere where you can bear it all on your own. I know he's not the easiest person to live with, but he loves you. And those girls. Don't make them pay your price. Look how long my marriage has survived while I've been oblivious to the truth.'

Gemma paced about, tears pouring down her face. 'I'm sorry. I've let you down. Let Ben down. I can't explain it. I just wanted to feel more than someone who remembered to buy new tights for the girls and set up a direct debit for the TV licence. Ben – sorry, I know he's your son, but he makes me feel so invisible, as though he wouldn't notice I wasn't there until he ran out of dishwasher tablets or one of the girls was ill and he had to cancel his surgeries at short notice.'

On one level, it was the whole 'my wife doesn't understand me' in reverse. But the thing was, I got it. I wanted to find Gemma selfish and feckless and disloyal. But she wasn't. She was generous-spirited and funny and kind. And I thought – hoped – she still loved my son. The boy that between Mal and me, we'd made a mixture of direct with his opinions but sparing with expressing emotion. I was sure that, in his own way, he loved deeply, but I doubted he articulated his feelings to Gemma on a regular basis.

I pushed a box of tissues towards her.

'I just wanted to feel like someone was interested in me for who I am, not what I can facilitate.'

There it was. The abyss that so many mothers stare into. The challenge of preserving a sense of self, to separate their own happiness from their children's, to avoid slowly suffocating in all the little details – shepherd's pie without peas, night light on the landing, World Fricking Book Day tomorrow – squeezing out the space where being interesting to a husband or even to oneself used to be. And where, dangerously, treacherously, a man who reminds you of who you were once, who you'd still like to be, could infiltrate with ease. Without much more than a couple of glasses of wine and an appreciative laugh at one of your witty asides. A complicit glance across a meeting, a suppressed smile when the boss neither of you respects talks about the unity within the team. Suddenly, you're not just the person who can find a missing dolly's shoe or come up with a half-baked explanation that might make sense to a five-year-old about why Matilda's daddy is marrying Freya's mummy and Matilda's mummy was saying rude words about them in the playground.

Then he comments on your gorgeous hair and incredible eyes, the things men always commented on but you'd forgotten about in the battle to lose the baby weight, which was nearly achieved when you got pregnant again. And what with work and the kids and never having time to exercise, the only thing you ever notice about your appearance is the way your bra digs into the fat on your back and the resemblance between your stomach and the roman blind in the downstairs loo.

I studied Gemma. Those kind eyes, her face quick to crinkle into a smile, her confidence to connect with people, to ask a question to which the answer might require a nimble response, her ability to draw people out. The way she had with Ben, making him less serious, softer, easier to be around.

'I wanted a family where we worked hard but we were growing together, does that make sense?' Gemma asked.

I understood so completely that my heart ached for this woman, who at just half my age was already twice as wise. It was perverse how perfect she was for my son, for all of us, and how little any of us had appreciated her until someone else had stepped in to do our job.

'Gemma, it's not too late for you. This—' I didn't even want to give it gravitas by naming it out loud. 'Marriage is hard, my love. But the answers aren't always in leaving, nor in telling the whole truth and nothing but the truth. Sit down with Ben, tell him how you feel and work out how you can make a change going forwards. Obviously, don't bother enlightening him about the other thing.'

She smiled at that. 'You must be the only mother-in-law in the whole damn world who sanctions lying to her son.'

'Practical, darling.'

Though it was sheer practicality rather than sentimentality that had landed me where I was now. I hadn't got the balance right, but maybe they could. Mal and I had been heading in the same direction, united by ambition, admiring of and excited by each other's drive. We'd been like a corporate partnership striving for equality between the sexes rather than a cocoon of two people who loved each other. Mal wore his stints with the bleach and his ability to hang out the washing as something that made him different, special, a badge of his uniqueness rather than a deeply held belief that all the boring crap shouldn't fall to women.

And I was rushing past, too busy keeping a tenuous grip on everything that had to happen before I could concentrate on work, to notice that our paths were running parallel rather than intertwining, the kindness and selflessness of our relationship brushed away in who was doing what when and who had a gap to pick up the slack with Ben.

Until that day. That night with Ari. Nearly eleven years ago. I thought about it every time it snowed. Until now, with ninety per cent regret and a ten per cent admiration for my fortitude.

Gemma leant forwards, stopping that memory gaining traction.

I pulled her to me and said into her hair, 'I can't condone what you did, but I understand far more than you think. It's what happens going forwards that matters now.'

'Thank you.' There was a brief silence, then she asked, 'What are you going to do about Mal, though?'

'Honestly? I don't know. I haven't got my head around it yet. I'd already made the decision to leave him a year ago.'

The relief of saying that out loud. Of acknowledging the truth.

'What? Before you found this out?' Gemma did that face that I'd seen a lot of young people do at work when something I said reminded them that I wasn't just a sensible old adult with a keen eye for a deadline but a fully feeling human who needed appreciation, thoughtfulness and love.

I nodded. I supposed it was a day for honesty. 'I wanted to leave after my birthday. But then I realised things were a bit tricky between you and Ben and I just didn't think it was a good time for the whole family to be in chaos. If your marriage fell apart, there needed to be a stable base somewhere for Dottie and Nell. And I know you perhaps don't have much faith in him right now, but Ben would be absolutely destroyed if you left him.'

Gemma opened her eyes wide in surprise. She paused for a moment. 'You really love Ben, don't you?'

'I do. I never understood before I had him that ferocious, maternal love. I used to look at women at work getting all stressed about missing sports day or being a few minutes late for school pick-up and think they were ridiculous. I didn't understand that primeval urge to never let your kids down, that constant desire to make things right for them even when they've got families of their own.'

'Hence not telling him how self-centred and stupid his wife is?'

'There was one other reason.' I wasn't sure I could push the words out without ripping a plaster off a wound that had yet to heal. 'This is kind of a selfish one. I've always railed against the notion that anyone should be responsible for somebody else's happiness once they are adults. But maternal love doesn't appear to care much for principles. I've no idea whether I'll make old bones and I want to know that when I'm gone, Ben has got someone there for him. Someone he can rely on. Not in a weird, needy way that stops him searching for his own car keys, but someone he can be a team with, to ride the unexpected shit that life throws up. I hoped that would be you.'

Gemma stifled a sob. 'It will be me. I do love him. I've taken a wrong turn. But there's nothing like realising what you could lose to make you appreciate what you've got.'

I sat back. 'Let's not talk about it again. Block this other man's number. Block his email. Don't look at what he's doing on Facebook. Go and pour every ounce of contrition into setting your marriage back on its feet. I'm going to forget I ever knew about it and I'll try really hard not to be the mother-in-law monitor. Now off you go, I need some time to watch my own life combust.'

Gemma hugged me, a proper grateful, heartfelt embrace. 'Thank you.'

'Could you do me a favour though? Could you not mention the whole Mal thing to Ben yet? He really should hear it from us.'

She nodded. 'It's probably the least I can do.'

I hoped Ben never ever found out what I had done. I stamped on the tiny weasel of a thought that I was doing to Ben exactly what Teresa had done to me. But I was doing it for all the right reasons. Without Gemma, he'd become a workaholic, even less sociable than he was now. I couldn't let him be that lonely middle-aged man, seeing his girls one weekend in two, living off lasagne and waiting for Monday. I just had to keep my nerve.

I was showing Gemma out when Mal drew up on the drive. She exchanged a few words with him and dived into her car. He didn't look like a man who knew the game was up. I counted his paces to the front door, ten, eleven, twelve, the beats of our old life.

He stepped inside. 'Just went to get my tyre pressures checked. Long drive up north again next week.'

'That to see Zoe, is it, or a weekend away with Wendy?'

His mouth opened.

'She can have you. I've been wanting to leave you for at least the last five years.'

Unfortunately, as so often in life, getting what I wanted didn't feel quite as satisfying when it was the only option on the table rather than the big juicy cherry of choice.

STEPH

Third week of April 2019

The days leading up to Paul's funeral were a surreal combination of marinading lamb in red wine and rosemary and refusing to engage with Mal on any level.

He kept walking into the kitchen and hovering behind me in a way that made me want to swing round and use him as a repository for my favourite chopping knife. I'd pretend he wasn't there and hum quietly to myself. The song that most often came to my lips was 'The Sun Has Got His Hat On', which was probably the most inappropriate tune I could have alighted on, but life was full of surprises.

'Steph. Just talk to me. Please.'

Stir, scrape, stir. Me, the woman who always was up for a scrap, who liked the last word, who was never going down without a good old showing. I simply couldn't be bothered. I'd reached the age where I wasn't interested in why, how, who or whatever pathetic apology, excuse or – knowing Mal – extenuating circumstance he could come up with. He'd been playing happy families at the other end of the country for twenty-three years and there was no putting a little light gold dusting of shine on that.

I didn't think it would be within my capabilities to avoid knowing the detail. I was a woman to whom detail was everything – mainly, if I was honest, so I could store it and use it against people at a later date.

He tapped my shoulder. 'Steph. We can't just brush away thirty-eight years of marriage without setting the record straight.'

I turned round. 'I can. As soon as the funeral is over, I'm going to put the house on the market and start divorce proceedings.'

He took a step back. 'And therein lies the problem.'

I was trying not to let curiosity get the better of me, to avoid getting sucked into Mal's smart way with words, to stop him wriggling and squiggling and somehow shuffling the blame for him having a whole other life for over two decades onto me.

But although I'd learnt a lot in sixty years, killing curiosity wasn't among those nuggets of knowledge. 'Oh, do share how I am part of the problem.'

'Do you know how exhausting, how hurtful it is to be presented with a series of faits accomplis?'

'As opposed to the hurt that comes from knowing your husband has had a plan B family in case the first one didn't work out? And the exhaustion that comes with wondering every single minute of the day if your whole life was some massive lie?'

Mal put his hand up to stop me. 'Just let me speak for once.'

That was rich, coming from someone who often bulldozed over other people talking, but I decided that a quick burst of listening to my shortcomings was the swiftest way to knock the conversation on the head. 'The floor's yours.'

'I don't think you have any idea what it's like to love someone like you. You're so hell-bent on proving to the world that you don't need anyone that eventually it becomes a self-fulfilling prophecy. Between you and your mother, you decided how to manage Ben's life, how to manage yours, racing about proving to everyone that you could have it all, do it all – work, get to the top of your tree, entertain better than anyone else, plan weekends away, have everyone orbiting around you, the big shining Steph star.' He looked down. 'It was hard for me to feel I had a role. You earned your own money. You knew what was best for Ben, or acted as though you did. Anything

I said was somehow white-noise nonsense. You were always telling everyone how you wanted to be wanted, rather than needed. But I did want to be needed. I longed for someone to feel they couldn't live without me. You didn't even rely on me when you had cancer, at a time when most couples would lean on each other. You just sorted out Teresa to look after you.'

I stared at him. 'Is that the story you told yourself?'

Mal shook his head. 'It wasn't a story, Steph. It's how I felt.'

Mal indulging in his own pity party might snap the last thread tethering my anger to a civilised response. 'You couldn't scuttle into the spare room fast enough. I had no option but to find someone who didn't look like they might pass out every time they caught a glimpse of my missing eyebrows.'

'You wouldn't even let me come to the hospital with you!'

I measured out the pearl barley for the casserole. 'So why didn't you leave? Why didn't you divorce me and marry Wendy?'

'I loved you.'

Anger was a difficult emotion to hold on to when sadness and self-doubt diluted it. After all these years, I should have had an instinct for whether Mal was spinning me a line and trying to save himself or was actually doing the thing he never did: speaking from the heart. I couldn't find the words to question, to pick apart his story, to defend myself.

He slumped into a chair. 'I didn't want to marry Wendy. Ever. But there was Zoe. I couldn't abandon her. I always wanted more children.'

'What?'

'I never wanted Ben to be an only child, you know that.'

I had a hazy recollection of Mal – once – discussing whether we should have another baby when Ben was about four, but I'd recently had a promotion to travel product manager for southern Europe and recalled a brief but heated row about it not being his career that would stall just as he started to get somewhere. But I couldn't remember us talking about it once Ben started school and everything seemed so much more settled.

'You're seriously expecting me to believe that you were forced to lead a double life because you wanted more kids? Something that I don't think I was even aware of?'

'You weren't aware of it because you didn't choose to listen to anything that didn't fit with your view. I wouldn't have stayed involved with Wendy if it hadn't been for Zoe. Zoe and I had a connection straight away.' His face contorted with the pain of even considering missing out on his daughter, which sent a jolt of mirrored anguish through me. 'Zoe's really smart. Good-hearted as well. In different circumstances, you'd find a lot in common.'

So many bitchy retorts swirled around my brain. But if sixty years had taught me anything, it was that attacking someone's child was the quickest way to escalate a row. I'd let that one go. If anyone was an innocent party, it was Zoe. At a later date, I'd try and find a sliver of compassion for her, some understanding of the impact of knowing that your father never fully acknowledged you publicly, that you were a shameful secret in his life. But I was quite a long way from that generosity yet.

Somewhere in Mal's words, I sensed an undertow of truth. Truth as he saw it, rather than as I did, but a truth nevertheless. I'd never lied about who or how I was, what I wanted from life. But if Mal was to be believed, that independence that he had once found so alluring had drifted into a defiance, a determination to show that I was so strong, so capable that I didn't need to rely on him for anything. And instead of that being a gift of freedom, a release to pursue his own goals and ambitions, unfettered by a wife nagging about what time he was coming in for dinner and how lonely it was without him, we'd ended up marooned on two separate islands without a connecting bridge.

I no longer trusted myself to have an objective view, to assess the accuracy of Mal's version of history that pinned at least some of the blame on me. Maybe we had moved from an equal partnership to an unconscious neglect of each other. In the absence of a clear answer, I defaulted to my lifelong conviction that I was always right. 'I'm impressed that you can come up with any crumb of defence to justify lying your backside off to me for all these years.'

He sighed. 'I'm sorry. I really really am.'

I didn't want to believe him. I wanted to think the worst of this man who'd lied barefaced to me for so long – conferences, crises at work, weeks away – it made me sick to think about my naivety, the times I took pity on him and ironed his shirts when he was pushed for time, folding them into his case so he could arrive uncrinkled and smart for Wendy. I resolved not to sift through the years, examining everything and revisiting my memories of our family under this new and unwelcome light. This resolution proved easier to keep at 11 a.m. than at four in the morning when my brain flitted through recollections of Mal's absence, digging away and triumphantly unearthing unwanted treasure.

'When are you going to tell Ben? Gemma knows, but I've asked her not to say anything. He should hear that he has a half-sister from you.'

'Why did you tell her?'

It was farcical that Mal considered he had any grounds for complaint about my behaviour but I still started to defend myself. 'I was in shock. I'd just got home when she turned up and I blurted it out.' I caught myself and stopped apologising. 'I think maybe you're not focusing on the real problem here. So back to my original point. You need to tell Ben. And preferably before the funeral so I don't have to explain why you're standing with another family that we hardly know.'

'Is it a good idea for us both to go?'

I stared at him. 'You're welcome to not pay your respects to someone we've known for the last thirty-five years, but I'm going. I'm doing all the food.'

'You're not planning to make a scene at the church, are you?'

Any inclination I had to accept a smidgen of responsibility for this whole sorry debacle evaporated. 'Give me credit for not thinking the worst day of my best friend's life is all about me. Out of respect for Teresa and also for Paul, I will put my face on for everyone. Your back-up "wife" included.'

Mal grimaced. 'Don't call her that.'

In that moment, I hated Mal. And Wendy too. Between them, they'd managed to get in the way of me focusing on Paul dying. Paul, my closest male friend. My only male friend. He'd been so warm to me over the years. Never made me feel in the way, even when I phoned during dinner or turned up when Teresa wasn't at home. He always invited me in and, crucially, often asked about Ben, which made me feel that at least one adult I respected liked him. Even in the turbulent teenage years when I couldn't chop a carrot in a way that didn't have Ben stomping off to his bedroom, Paul found the positives. 'He's a confident lad, he'll do well.' His words held genuine affection. And Ben, who ran a mile whenever anything emotionally uncomfortable was on the horizon, had been very firm about wanting to come to the funeral.

'You tell Ben by tomorrow so he has time to absorb it.'

'Shall we tell him together?'

I snorted. 'No. Your shambolic life, you deal with it. I'm pretty certain that even you can't make me out to be the bad guy in this particular circumstance. I'll pick up the pieces afterwards.'

Over the next day or so, I focused on the funeral, on doing my duty and honouring Paul. Even I wasn't selfish enough to rip Teresa apart right now. I'd ignored her calls and when I'd finally answered, I restricted myself to assuring her I had the food in hand and would drop it all round the day before the service. She tried to talk to me about why she hadn't come clean about Wendy, but the tidal wave of fury blocked her words from my ears. 'You concentrate on saying goodbye to Paul. The rest can wait.'

'I wish you'd let me explain,' she said, her yearning for forgiveness, for my understanding, straining tearfully down the line. No doubt someone with a bigger, more forgiving heart could have met her halfway. But postponing the discussion was all I could offer. I, not Wendy, had been like a sister to Teresa and it was another life lesson that I would happily have left in the box: that blood – impure, unloving, resentful as it often flowed – was still thicker than water.

I resisted phoning Evie, unwilling to drag her into our row in case she ended up being the only friend I had left. But eventually, I gave in and rang. She didn't pick up. I had a horrible suspicion that Teresa had contacted her and told her not to speak to me. Of course, Evie's loyalties would lie with her. That thought joined all the other wrathful fragments of revenge and injustice careering around my head until I couldn't bear it any more. I texted. *Did you know that Mal had had an affair and a baby with Wendy?* I really hoped her response would be shock because it was news to her as well and I wasn't the stupid sap who was the last to find out.

I waited for her reply, clattering about making food, staring at my phone, willing Evie to ring or text so I could find out if she knew. Her response when it came was entirely unsatisfactory. *Teresa has filled me in on what's happened. I'll meet you at hers at 2 p.m. tomorrow afternoon when you bring the food over. I understand why you're angry and hurt but remember that Teresa loves you and is still your best friend.*

I couldn't miss the irony of the friend who'd been absent for years trying to mediate between the friends who'd carried each other through thick and thin for decades. 'Teresa's still your best friend.' It certainly didn't feel like it. But, for once, I wasn't able to get the answers when I wanted them. I went to bed early and lay tossing and turning, digging about through half-remembered conversations, trying to make sense of it all.

By the time I drew up at Teresa's house the following day, my eyes were scratchy through lack of sleep and I wasn't sure whether I was going to burst into tears or explode with rage. Evie's Mini was already in the drive and I steeled myself for a united front.

Evie opened the door and leant over to hug me. I didn't quite brush her off, but I marched past her into the kitchen, carrying the huge vat of lamb in front of me like a shield, eyes straight ahead.

Out of the corner of her mouth, Evie muttered, 'Wendy's gone out.'

I knew she was trying to be kind, to keep me calm. However, the tiny implication that I should be creeping about apologising for my existence made me feel as though the ball of fury in my chest might suddenly burst free and torch everything in its path.

Teresa leant against the worktops, the smoking remains of trust filling the atmosphere. I managed to ask how she was doing, but she didn't answer, just said, 'Thank you for doing this. Paul would have been so grateful.' At the mention of his name, she started to cry. I moved towards her and she sobbed into my shoulder. I patted her back and made soothing noises, but my body was bristling with resentment, unable to find the forgiveness needed to connect with her pain when my own was so intense.

Evie smiled at me encouragingly over Teresa's head. But I didn't feel encouraged, I felt like the village idiot that everyone waved to, chatted to loudly and slowly, then made fun of the second they were out of earshot. Evie clearly took my comforting Teresa as a sign that we could work through this, that I'd do my customary spin on the spot, storm about for a few weeks, then everything would fade back into how it was before.

As soon as I could, I led Teresa to a chair and peeled her off me, then dashed out to the car to fetch all the spare plates and glasses.

Evie made tea. I stood, fiddling about with the crockery, while Evie valiantly carried the conversation, a Herculean task given my monosyllabic replies and Teresa forcing the words out between bursts of grief. 'How's Amelia doing?' she asked.

Teresa said, 'I don't think it's sunk in yet. She's still stuck in a baby fog.'

The conversation crawled on, dragging itself around the room between Evie's grappling for something to say, Teresa's despair and my own turmoil, which was alternating between heartbreak and something that felt dangerously close to hostility.

Eventually, the words in the room wound down. 'Right, I'll leave you to it. Probably best to get going before Wendy comes back,' I said.

Teresa started crying again. 'I'm so sorry. We should have told you at the time. Evie and I just did what we thought was best. We didn't realise what the consequences would be.'

Evie stiffened.

I stared into my mug, taking a moment to replay the words in my head. 'At the time? That weekend in Norfolk? You both knew?' I swung round to Evie, who might as well have had a cartoon 'GULP' above her head. 'You as well? Was I the only one who wasn't party to the knowledge that my husband was screwing Wendy and had a daughter?'

Evie closed her eyes and took a deep breath. 'I didn't know about Zoe until Teresa told me the other day. But I suspected he'd slept with Wendy when we went to Norfolk. I heard them when I ran back to get the first-aid kit. When Isaac cut his hand.'

I stood open-mouthed. 'And you carried on sitting there, drinking wine and eating bacon butties, in the knowledge that Wendy had been having sex with Mal under my nose and neither of you thought that it would be a good idea to share that with me?'

Teresa was the first to rally. 'It's not what you think. We were trying to protect you. Ben was a young teenager and quite a handful. You'd just been promoted, I can't remember what to, but you were always flying here, there and everywhere.'

I still registered the stab that the work achievements that meant so much to me had been conversation filler to everyone else.

Teresa cleared her throat. I nearly felt guilty for forcing her to use her limited resources at a time when she was barely holding her head above water. 'Evie wasn't absolutely certain because she didn't see them, just heard Wendy in Mal's bedroom and, er, odd noises. We thought – hoped – that if they had been up to something, it was a one-off. A lapse of judgement. We only found out for definite when I had a big row with Wendy five years later. In Suffolk. By which time you and Evie weren't speaking anyway.'

Buoyed by Teresa's explanation, Evie became braver. 'And it was so long afterwards that Teresa didn't see the point in upsetting you when you and Mal seemed fine together. I know you won't believe it, Steph, but Teresa kept quiet because she wanted to protect your friendship, not lose it.'

I folded my arms. 'A good friend would have told me. For goodness' sake, Teresa, I would have been grateful to you for not making me wait all these years to find out the truth about Mal.' As the words left my mouth, a tiny worm of doubt about how appreciatively I would have received that particular bombshell wriggled inside me.

Evie stood up. 'We did what we thought was best, Steph. And maybe we didn't make the right call. But you know what? You are terrifying when you are angry. We were young and still thought that the most important thing was keeping a marriage together. Look at me, I put up with years of shit from Neil, just so I wouldn't be a single mother. You can't judge what we did then on what we know now.'

Teresa dropped her head in despair. 'The more time passed, the harder it was to deliver something so destructive out of the blue for no obvious gain. I promise I didn't know that Wendy had an ongoing relationship with Mal or that her daughter wasn't Glenn's.'

'So you did nothing. At least if you'd told me I would have been able to decide for myself. You let me live a life that didn't even exist.'

Evie took Teresa's hand. 'No, Teresa didn't let you live a life that didn't exist. Mal, your husband, did. He's the one responsible for this mess, not Teresa.'

I looked at them huddled together, Evie defiant, Teresa broken, but still undeniably there for each other. I'd always had such a high opinion of myself. Always been the woman other less capable people turned to in a crisis. Always been the popular person around whom everyone else orbited. The one people listened to and tried to please. Sixty years in, I was learning what it felt like to have to make an effort to exist in a world that was not running to my rhythm.

I grabbed my handbag. 'I'll see you at the funeral tomorrow.'

STEPH

23 April 2019

During a rather undignified exchange in which I couldn't have been accused of taking a reasonable tone, I made it clear that I would be standing with my child and Mal could stand with his other one. An offer he'd obviously eschewed as I'd stalked past him sitting on his own in a pew near the back of the church. I stood with Ben and Gemma behind Teresa and her two kids. Next to her stood Wendy and Zoe. While the vicar intoned about Paul's love and loyalty to his family, I studied Zoe's profile. She had a great big hooter like her mother's – I should have been appalled at the little burst of triumph that Ben had a neat nose like Mal, but I defied any wronged wife not to log the wins in these circumstances. However, I couldn't deny that she had the same strong jaw as Mal and an identical tuft of hair in the nape of the neck that grew upwards. How many times must I have lain next to him, stroking that exact spot on his neck? Maybe it was the church setting that was bringing out the compassion in me, but I had a sudden trickle of regret for her. Life was tough enough without knowing from the outset that you were second best. She didn't have an apologetic demeanour about her though. Maybe starting off on the back foot had given her an inner steel.

Zoe must have felt me looking at her and glanced over her shoulder. I turned my attention back to the vicar, who was inviting Teresa to come up and pay tribute to Paul.

I didn't know she'd planned to speak and felt the needle of exclusion. The inevitable consequence of flouncing out with my skirts held high. I tried to concentrate on Teresa's words. I knew what it would be costing her even in ordinary times to speak in front of everybody. Despite myself, I felt a rush of pride that Teresa's need to do the honourable thing had overcome her desire to shy away from the spotlight.

Teresa's face had always been angular, but now she looked positively gaunt. Surprisingly her voice was strong, as though she had set herself one last test in her relationship with Paul that she was determined not to fail. 'Quite simply, I loved him and he loved me. We wanted the best for each other and for our children. It was a very straightforward formula for a happy life. I will miss him every day. Go safely, my love.'

I'd always considered Paul a lovely, solid man, but essentially cautious and staid. Although I could see the benefit of having a husband with organised racks in the garage, who, on any given day, could simply walk out and find the required screwdriver, drill or replacement light bulb, I had associated Mal's dashing into a taxi, leaping on planes, urgent phone calls firefighting last-minute changes of plan with glamour and adventure. Labels, files and drawer dividers were the bedrock of a systematic but dull marriage. Folders, storage and lists might not have shouted 'spontaneous husband', but if a notepad in the kitchen bearing the words *cottage cheese*, *loo rolls* and *dental floss* was what it took to be spared the surprise of extra offspring, well, bring on the paper clips.

As the pallbearers picked up the coffin, a wave of grief washed through me, the confused and tangled emotions of Paul's death dragging with it memories of my mum and dad. And deep within that heartache was the failure of my own relationship. When Mal and I had got married, I'd never entertained the thought that we wouldn't make it. I'd embarked on our lives together as a project to manage without any understanding of the intricate dance steps required to keep the marital monolith moving forward.

A gasp of sorrow burst from me, prompting Ben to lean around Gemma and whisper, 'Are you okay?'

Gemma grabbed my hand and held it tightly. In that moment, despite everything, I wished Mal had been standing with us. As families, we'd shared so much over the years – more than I'd realised – but it felt wrong not to close the circle with us all together. Mal was still Ben's father, even if he was no longer going to be my husband. Perhaps I should come to church more often if it filled me with good and righteous thoughts.

I caught Teresa's eye and mouthed, 'Well done'. The vicar drew the service to a close with a final prayer. I smiled at Amelia and Ross, who were holding on to each other in front of me, then averted my eyes as Wendy filed out. Ben followed on behind Zoe, his face unreadable, and my heart ached for him, this boy who always found it so much easier to communicate with animals than humans. I wondered how long it was since I'd had a proper conversation with him, one that I hadn't filtered through Gemma, who seemed to have the knack of sharing information in a way that didn't make him glance around frantically looking for an escape route.

When he was a teenager, and I was trying to understand what lay behind a dark mood or a burst of fury, his reluctance to explain led to a correlating determination from me to find out. The exact opposite of Teresa, whose softly, softly approach with Ross seemed to bear more fruit. She had the patience to wait for the right moment, but that particular skill had eluded me. Wanting an answer *now* seemed to suit me better. At the time, I'd put it down to Ross being less stubborn, rather than any special knack on Teresa's part. Now, however, I wished that instead of dogged insistence I'd just been kind, allowed him to find his way without me snapping at his heels, always encouraging him to push himself, to dismiss any disappointment, to move on.

I caught Ben observing me sometimes when I was talking to Nell, trying to boost her confidence in the face of Dottie's desire to have a crack at everything, regardless of whether she had any aptitude for it or not. I couldn't ever remember saying to Ben that it was okay to feel upset when life didn't go his way. I didn't want to consider that I'd told him to 'get over it' or defaulted to 'life isn't fair'. Whereas with Nell and Dottie, I was always telling them, 'You take a moment to feel really sorry for yourself. That's a horrible thing to happen. And then we'll have a cuddle and see if you feel better.' Thank goodness I'd had a chance to try out what I'd learnt from my mistakes with Ben on my grandchildren.

I watched as Wendy and Zoe walked past Mal. They didn't stop to talk to him. And that age-old reflex of facilitating his place in our triangle was stronger than my anger. 'Come with us.' I just managed to hold in the comment 'if your other family don't want you'. Mal acknowledged my generosity with a grateful nod, and Gemma, who was doing a grand job of treading a neutral path, walked on a little with him, chatting pleasantries about the service.

I turned to Ben. 'Are you all right, love? You've had a lot to take in. Don't feel that you have to take my side or that you can't acknowledge Zoe and Wendy.'

Though actually the idea of them trundling out to dinner together and finding each other fascinating made me want to retract that statement as soon as it left my mouth.

'It's a bit weird, Mum. I mean, I suppose she's my half-sister. That takes some getting used to after being an only child.'

I wanted to stop right there, in front of the gravestones, and beg him not to start taking Dottie and Nell to meet their Auntie Zoe, not to shift his allegiance away from me, not to find their family unit so much easier than ours. I couldn't bear it if he felt liberated by having the choice to be part of a family rather than suffering the expectation that comes from being born into one.

But I didn't say that. I stood in front of him, as though we were the only two people there, and said, 'None of this is of your making. Whatever you do, however you handle it – and handle it you will – is absolutely fine by me.' I smothered the voice in my head that was shouting, 'But please don't ever come and tell me that you're having a Merry bloody Christmas with them.' Tears were threatening to pour out of me, which was the quickest way to lose an audience with Ben. 'Just know, love, that we didn't always get it right, maybe didn't often get it right, but I love you very much. And so does Dad.'

That was all I could manage. To my surprise, his face crumpled and I pushed back the impulse to say, 'Don't cry, not here.' I didn't think I'd seen Ben cry since he was about fifteen and Sweepy, our cat, was run over.

I pulled him to one side, while he rubbed frantically at his face, trying to regain control. 'Everyone's crying today, love. And you're perfectly entitled to feel sorry for yourself. It's been a real shock to you.' I hugged him and, for a moment, I felt him give the burden of being an adult to me.

He leant back so he could make eye contact. 'Are you going to be okay? Is Dad going to go and live with her?'

'I don't know what Dad's plans are. But I'll be fine.' Standing in a churchyard lying through my teeth didn't feel like the best location to avoid a thunderbolt.

Before we could say any more, Evie came up with Isaac and introduced his wife, Rosa, who was pregnant. They all shook hands, the conversation moving on to how old Isaac and Ben were when they last saw each other. I had a burst of pride at seeing my son rise to the occasion, gracious and charming to Rosa and warm to Isaac. The realisation was bittersweet that those weekends away with the boys bodyboarding, skimming stones and looking for frogspawn – until recently a haven in an age of innocence – had actually been the start of the disintegration of my marriage.

I'd agreed with Teresa that after the church service I'd head to hers to prepare everything, so while the others made their way to the graveside, I drove away, bursting into tears as soon as I made it to the car.

When everyone else came in, cheeks red from the cold and crying, I felt as though I had at last added value to the day, as I ladled scoops of lamb into bowls. Evie ran around handing them out, while I kept the side-eye on where Wendy and Zoe were. Mal leant against the sitting-room wall. I studied him, almost through a stranger's eyes. Memories of him playing Swingball in the garden with Ben, wearing a Christmas hat, reading the newspaper over breakfast flooded in. Ordinary moments of an ordinary family life, that I forgot to appreciate in the rush to get to the next holiday, the next work trip, the next step for Ben on the academic cattle truck towards success. I didn't want ordinary then. I turned my nose up at the humdrum, the mundane as the preserve of unambitious, uninspiring people. But it was astonishing how appealing that seemed now. Mal looked every one of his sixty-three years. I did wonder what it would take for us all to be contented. Mal had the motorbikes, the Porsche, the big house with automatic gates, an office with his name on the door, not one but two families jostling for his attention, and he still had the air of a man that life had short-changed.

Teresa approached me. 'Thank you for doing all of this. I don't know how I would have managed without you. You've been such a good friend to me over the years. And I know you don't want to talk about it, but I'm so sorry.'

I wasn't at the forgiveness stage, I wasn't sure that I ever could be, but our long friendship certainly had enough goodwill and ballast to see us stumble through the funeral of the first loss in our generation. 'I loved Paul, you know that.'

I held my arms out to her, and we hugged and cried, shuddering, powerful sobs for all we'd lost, for everything that we had yet to face, for the shitty unfairness of the world and, yes, even at the age of sixty, for not being able to run to my mum and give her the problem.

As we pulled apart, Teresa's Aunt Maud shuffled up. 'Did you make this?' she asked, booming across the room and waving her empty bowl.

'No, Steph did,' she said, indicating me standing next to her.

I sent up a silent prayer that she hadn't cracked a tooth on a rogue peppercorn.

'Well, your husband is a very lucky man. Absolutely delicious.'

Out of the corner of my eye, I saw Wendy glance over to me. With an extreme effort of will, I managed not to say, 'Such a shame that he didn't appreciate that.'

STEPH

24 April 2019

Mal and I kicked off the day after Paul's funeral with a fat row. The fact that he was still questioning whether we needed to get divorced – 'Are you sure we can't get past this?' – made me so angry I felt as though a vital blood vessel might explode. But when he started to argue about selling the house to fit his timescale – 'I think we should wait until November when that bond matures. It'll free up some cash for us both' – I lost it completely.

'And how do you propose we live till then? Shall we have separate shelves in the fridge so I don't eat your ham? You've had twenty-three years to plan for this. Even you, with your shocking stupidity, must have known you were sitting on a time bomb. So forgive me if I don't want to wait seven months to start living again. Feel free to go and live with Wendy if I'm getting on your nerves, or rent somewhere. If you're worried about having to live in a shoebox, get a big mortgage and pay some of it off when you get the money from the bond.'

Mal sat at the kitchen table, steepling his fingers. 'I'm only trying to think about what will give us both the best chance of having enough capital to buy a decent house.'

'Love your concern, but way too late. You're the one who measures success by a code on the gate and an automatic garage door. I'm quite happy with a little house as long as it's got a garden.' I had the advantage of having had the wake-up call that health, not wealth, was the golden ticket.

Less than a month ago, I'd been idly checking out little cottages in Whitstable, just up the road from Evie, fantasising about a courtyard garden and a sea view. I was planning an elegant exit from my old life, an exit in which Mal and I would agree that our marriage had run its course, without anybody feeling that they had lost. I'd expected there to be some sorrow, the regret that goes with a feeling of nostalgia for the intensity of love that once existed and that, over time, has drained away. Instead – despite the unexpected bonus that I could shift the guilt onto Mal – I was livid that my hand had been forced before I was ready.

Mal took himself off for a swim at the posh hotel in town where he was a member, muttering about my childishness. I wished my life could be fixed with a few lengths of flashy crawl and a chai latte.

The only way to gain momentum was to make a bold change. I was just looking up the numbers for local estate agents when the doorbell rang. I hoped it was too soon for Teresa to be out and about and I wasn't really in the mood for Evie. I'd smiled dutifully at the funeral yesterday, but I was a long way from forgiving her for telling Teresa but not me what she'd witnessed in Norfolk.

I was scowling as I flung the door open. But it wasn't Evie or Teresa. It was Zoe. She didn't speak at first, just stood there watchful and wary, as though she was braced for a tirade.

'Can I help you?' My voice was more gentle than if Wendy had been standing there. I couldn't help thinking of Ben if the boot was on the other foot. I gave no sign of knowing who she was.

She frowned but stood her ground. 'I'm Zoe, Wendy's daughter? Would it be possible for me to come in for a minute, please?'

'I know who you are.'

I stood back to let her in.

We went through to the kitchen. 'Have a seat.'

She sat, but I stood on the opposite side of the table, needing the barrier between us, afraid of what else I might find out, what unforeseen light might shine into a recess of my life and unearth some other skeleton jiggling about.

We studied each other. 'You've got balls coming here, I'll give you that. What can I do for you?'

She looked at me with eyes that were a different colour from Mal's but had that same distinctive upwards slant. 'I'm sorry you're in this situation. And Ben too.'

I didn't want her pity. 'You didn't make it happen. That's down to your mother and Mal.'

'I can't defend what they did.'

'No one can. Anyway, I imagine you're not here to beg my forgiveness. What was it exactly that you wanted from me?'

'I'd like to talk to you about what's happened.'

'I've got stuff to do, so unless it's something I can definitely help with…' I couldn't quite inject the level of hostility into my voice that I would have expected. There was something about her that reminded me of my younger self, plunging gutsily into situations without having a clear view of what I hoped to achieve.

She pushed her chair back. 'I don't really get on with my mum. She kind of blackmailed Mal into being in a relationship with her. He didn't really want to be. I was never allowed to talk about him in front of anyone.' She looked like she might burst into tears. 'Once, when I was about three, I told Nan that my dad was called Mal and Mum slapped my legs and called me a liar.'

I felt a noisy breath of air leave my mouth. I couldn't help feeling sorry for this resilient young woman in front of me. 'But surely your grandparents suspected something?'

'They both died when I was very little. I just about remember Nan, but she was old-school. Apparently it was a big deal that Mum hadn't stuck her marriage out for longer, so everything was brushed under the carpet. Mum let them think I was Glenn's.'

'Teresa must have known.'

I wasn't sure I wanted to hear the answer, but it was my one chance to find out the unbiased truth.

She shook her head. 'I don't think you understand what it's like to live in a family where nothing gets talked about. Every time I asked anything, Mum would say, "Curiosity killed the cat" or change the subject. I wasn't a hundred per cent sure Mal was my dad until I was eighteen and we had a proper heart-to-heart without Mum hovering about. I was terrified that she might bring some weirdo out of the closet and introduce him as my dad instead.'

I wanted to reach out to this woman, to tell her that I was sorry for my husband's useless behaviour, for being such a poor excuse for a father and human being in general. And her mother too, but I wasn't going to carry the can for her as well. I restricted myself to, 'I don't know how he strung her along for all those years. That's a long time to pretend to love someone.'

'He didn't really pretend. Any fool could see he just about tolerated her. Did what he had to do.'

We both looked down at the floor when she said that. I doubted that I was the only one desperate to block the image of Mal and Wendy having sex from her mind.

Zoe took a deep breath and carried on. 'She threatened to stop him seeing me if he didn't play ball. Either that or tell you about me. As soon as I turned eighteen, he told me the truth and didn't have anything to do with her. Just me. I begged her not to tell you, but over the last few years, she's become so bitter about wasting her life on a man she couldn't make love her, I knew it would come out eventually.'

I felt a surge of compassion. What a warped view of relationships she must have. Swiftly followed by a stab of maternal jealousy as I understood that it wasn't Wendy who'd taken Mal from me, but his daughter. I couldn't remember him being so committed to Ben when he was little. Or ever, in fact. I was trying to process the unwelcome knowledge that far from being second best, Zoe was the all-powerful magnet in the family politics arena. 'I'm not sure what you need from me, Zoe. I wish you weren't involved in all of this, but I also wish I wasn't either.'

She dropped her head. 'I'm here because I don't want you to force Dad – Mal – to choose.'

'I'm not forcing him to do anything.' It caused a physical pain in my heart to hear her refer to Mal as 'Dad'. Not only because she deserved so much better than a man who slotted her into the crevices left over after work and his 'real' family, but also because I could hear in her words how much she loved him, how frightened she was of Ben and me having the power to insist he severed the relationship.

'I'm scared you'll only have him back if he stops all contact with me. Mum is already threatening not to speak to me again because she thinks I've taken his side, and I don't want to lose both my parents.'

My head was aching with the complexity of life if you didn't get the whole marriage/children thing right first time. I massaged my forehead. 'You're a bright girl. You're emotionally intelligent too.' I didn't say out loud, 'I'm not quite sure where that came from,' but she was probably smart enough to get my drift. 'I'm going to be honest with you, Zoe, if anything jeopardises Mal's relationship with Ben, I'm going to come out all guns blazing. But I'm never going to take Mal back. I don't even want him, I'm just really sorry it ended this way, in such a mess for everybody. Especially you, actually. Everyone deserves a parent who puts them first. And here's some advice, which you probably don't want, but one of the blessings of being old is that you can bestow unasked for wisdom on unwilling listeners: as you go through life, make sure you reserve just enough of yourself to survive; don't let your happiness ever depend completely on someone else.'

Zoe's eyes narrowed. She nodded slightly as she assessed the veracity of my words. 'That kind of rules out the fairy-tale ending.'

'You might be lucky, you might get one of those, but on the off-chance that you don't, you'll always know that you can survive anything. I think that's a good starting point. It's served me well.'

Despite everything, I really did wish this young woman all the best. She was unlucky to have ended up with a dad who'd kept her hidden away. Conversely, he was incredibly fortunate to have ended up with the daughter who loved him anyway.

'And you can take or leave this, but you've had the disadvantage of having to fight for your dad's love, because he already had another family elsewhere. Don't carry that over into the rest of your life. Don't feel you have to make yourself somehow worthy of someone's love or interest. Sod that. I know from Teresa you're really clever and driven. Make sure you channel that into carving out the life you want, rather than waste your energy on trying to be enough for someone to love you.'

I let the words hang there, waiting to see whether she'd bat my advice away or allow it to settle, to be carried off and dissected at a later date.

The struggle between self-protection and willingness to learn mottled her face. I hoped she was far enough beyond the arrogant edge of youth to accept that the most useful words often came from the least likely sources.

She stood up and shook my hand. 'Thank you for seeing me. And for being so honest.'

I showed her out, feeling oddly responsible for her. 'Take care.' I meant it.

TERESA

7 May 2019

Marriage has so many routines to it. The person who gets out of bed first. Who makes the pot of tea. Who picks up the newspaper and pulls out the middle section to share. Every deviation from that routine feels insulting and violent.

In the weeks following Paul's death, I realised the things I associated with being married – planning holidays, discussing whether or not we could afford a new kitchen, what to do at the weekend – were just a tiny part of the picture. It was the lack of day-to-day details that floored me – having to rinse the last few whiskers from the sink whenever I followed Paul into the bathroom, the sounds of his inefficient opening of the fridge for milk, then butter, then orange juice, the tuneless whistle as he polished his shoes for work.

The temptation to stay in bed, to let myself drift into a dark and deep sleep from which I'd wake heavy-headed and lethargic, was almost overwhelming. I lay there wondering whether my mind would ever work in an agile way again or would forever plod around, despondent. I couldn't envisage a time when I'd have the momentum to return to work, the capacity to listen to someone else's aches and pains, their stories of children, husbands (awful or otherwise), ageing parents.

Evie texted every morning. Sometimes just *Thinking of you. Give me a ring when you're ready* and other times, especially when I'd forgotten to roll out a half-cheerful response, *I'd like to pop over on Thursday. When would suit you?* I shrank at the idea of having to pull myself together enough to face her – I found it more tiring to be around people who knew me well, who wouldn't just take my word for it that I was managing 'fine'. I wasn't ready for advice about the necessity of getting out and about, of perhaps seeking out some counselling, of making sure I went for a walk in the fresh air every day. All well meant, all sensible strategies, but so far out of my reach when struggling to unscrew a stiff lid on a jar of coffee made me burst into tears.

Since the funeral a couple of weeks ago, I'd spoken to Steph several times but hadn't had either the strength or the skill to reach her. She said all the right things, was kind and soothing – 'It's such early days, you're bound to feel totally lost' – but there was a distance about her. Steph's standards for loyalty were high, in a way that charismatic people who made friends easily could afford. I'd spent most of my thirties and forties astonished about how many invitations she was trying to dodge – 'Oh that flaming woman from Ben's karate class keeps ringing to arrange a coffee with me.' 'Why do people think I want to go with them to the opening of a spa? Do I look like someone who wants their backside wrapping in seaweed?'

I struggled to scrabble up the energy to make amends. Through the fog of grief, I recognised the importance of not losing another person close to me but couldn't think clearly enough to plan a strategy. I'd never been on the wrong side of Steph before, never felt the full force of her fury and, in my widowed and weakened state, I wasn't sure I could survive the articulate vitriol I'd seen directed at people who'd let her down. I got the sense that she was protecting us both: when I'd muttered a half-hearted apology – not because I didn't fully mean it but because I was nervous of poking the bear – I'd received a brisk rebuttal: 'Teresa, this isn't the right time for either of us to get into this. You've got too much of your own shit going on.'

I couldn't formulate the words to explain that she was one of the few people who could guide me through this, the person who would know how to tread the balance between letting me howl out my sadness – 'Of course you're going to cry, you've just lost your husband' – and moving me forwards in her no-nonsense way – 'Teresa, you've still got a lot to live for. It's not the future you'd planned, but you've got Ross, Amelia and Violet.'

It was a turn-up for the books that the baby girl whom I'd judged to be the obstacle to Amelia's future, whom I'd regarded resentfully as the barrier to my own freedom, was acting like a pint-sized snowplough to push us forwards, oblivious to our loss, focused only on her needs and wants. At a time when I could barely make a choice between marmalade or peanut butter, it was like bursting onto a mountain summit at dawn when Violet treated me to one of her first smiles. There was nothing like being needed by someone whose problems I could actually solve to convince me good times would come again. My insomnia was a blessing in disguise for Amelia – I was grateful for the company of Violet sucking away on a bottle at 4 a.m. before melting into sleep, and Amelia was only too thankful to hand her over. I couldn't believe I'd been in favour of Amelia having a termination.

With Steph's birthday fast approaching, I couldn't bear to write a card thanking her for all she'd done without knowing whether we were still friends. In the end, Evie forced me to gather up my courage. 'What do we know about Steph when she's backed into a corner?'

'That she won't give up without a fight?'

'Exactly that. I think we also know that for all her wonderful qualities saying sorry isn't her most prominent personality trait.'

I smiled in recognition at that. It was probably because, unlike me, who apologised when strangers slopped their coffee on me on the train, she'd had less practice than the rest of us. Steph usually believed she was right, though occasionally she apologised when she was bored with discussing something and just wanted to change the subject.

'But to be fair, we were the ones who let her down. I suspect the only reason she isn't giving me both barrels is because Paul's died.'

'So the question is, how could we get her to forgive us? I know how her mind works. She will imagine herself at war, with Mal and Wendy on one side, with us as the supporting troops facilitating the whole messed-up family dynamics.'

'Is she in contact with you at all?' I asked.

'A few terse texts. I'm not getting the "I'd be grateful if you'd help me showcase the house for the estate agent" vibes. Given that I've barely seen her in years, it's surprising how much I miss her,' Evie said.

I fiddled with the belt on my dressing gown. 'I could've helped you smooth things over with her back then.'

'I don't think she wanted you to get in the middle, did she? I got the impression she'd asked you not to discuss it.'

'Can you imagine Steph saying that? She's always been "knowledge is power".' My eyes filled. 'For once, I felt as though I could be at the centre of the group, instead of always standing on the sidelines. Also, I wasn't in a rush for you to talk to each other because I didn't want you to mention what went on in Norfolk.'

I hung my head as I remembered what I'd told Evie, that if she wanted to get in contact with Steph, she should probably leave it for a few months, give her space to miss the friendship. And then, as time passed, and Evie broached the topic again, I offered up other excuses. 'She's very stressed at work at the moment.' 'Ben's really causing a lot of problems.' Eventually, she'd stopped asking.

'I didn't think for one minute you'd never speak again. But once the weeks became months, I was paralysed. You'd both assumed the other didn't want to know and I felt so responsible. And terrified that you'd both hate me.'

Evie looked puzzled. 'I took it for granted that Steph wasn't bothered, that friends like me were, for her, two a penny.'

'I think she's missed you every day of her life.'

Evie studied her fingernails. This friend of mine, who had a wonderful ability to see both sides, was wired up to think the best of people. Even rude shop assistants – 'You never know what's going on in their lives. Let's accept they're having a bad day.'

She was quiet for a long time, her eyes darting about as though she was weighing everything up.

'In the end, Teresa, it wasn't your responsibility to sort this out. If she'd been a bit less stubborn and I'd been a bit braver, we could've bypassed you. It's not as though we were twelve and needed a go-between. We were adults and should have sorted ourselves out.'

I really started to sob then. 'I don't actually deserve a friend as forgiving as you.'

Evie gave me a big hug. 'Look how kind you were to me when I left Neil. You and Paul. If it hadn't been for you two, I wouldn't have survived. For a start, I'd never have been able to assemble that bloody wardrobe.'

Which made me cry even more, both for her generosity and my lovely husband brandishing his Allen key.

She stood up. 'We can sit here discussing the rights and wrongs of a decision we made years ago or we can do our best to make amends. Get dressed, let's do what we can.'

I got out to punch in the gate code to Steph's house with my heart hammering. Amelia's advice was ringing in my ears: 'Steph loves you. Look how she turned up for Dad's funeral and did all the food, even though Auntie Wendy and Zoe were there. Surely you're not going to start falling out now you're pensioners!'

As Evie marched up to the door, I trailed behind her, my poor sore heart struggling to steel itself for any more adversity.

Evie grabbed my hand. 'She'd be a fool to lose you as a friend.' She rang the bell.

Steph came to the door, her face neutral.

'We've come on a peace mission.' Evie sounded much braver than I felt. I guessed she'd already confronted the smoking remains of her life when she left Neil and discovered her courage, whereas I was still closing every curtain in the house and jumping at the sound of the radiators cooling down.

I couldn't help it. I dissolved right there and then on the doorstep. As a strategy it was all I had.

Steph sighed. 'Come on in.'

It was the tidiest I'd ever seen her house. Despite Mal's insistence on a minimalist décor, rather than the rainbow retreat Steph favoured, there were usually permanent piles of clutter – papers, Steph's scarves, packets of flower seeds and gardening gloves – scattered about.

She saw my surprise. 'Embracing my inner Kondo a little late in life. It's quite therapeutic actually. Let's sit in the kitchen. I feel like I'm being ganged up on by a pair of Jehovah's Witnesses. I assume you want coffee?' she said, filling up the water tank on her machine.

I hadn't yet been demoted to the instant coffee Mal favoured.

She set it going, then turned round. 'You're making me nervous. You've obviously decided what you want to say. I'm all ears.'

I pulled myself together. 'Evie is being very generous in shouldering some of the blame. By the time we knew for certain about Wendy and Mal, you hadn't spoken to Evie for five years anyway. Whether or not it was the right call, I took the decision that I didn't want to be responsible for wrecking your marriage, when you seemed perfectly happy.'

Steph didn't interrupt with her view on the situation, which made me more nervous than ever.

I babbled on. 'Wendy let us believe Zoe's dad was Glenn but that he didn't want contact with her. If I'd known that Mal was her father, I might have seen it differently.' My voice cracked. 'You and Evie were the best friends I've ever had, probably the only really close friends I've had in my life, and I just couldn't face losing you. So I did nothing. If I'm really honest, I thought that Mal was a bit of a player, would probably be unfaithful with someone else and you'd find out about a different affair without me having to admit what I knew. As the years wore on, I pretended to myself that it had never happened.'

Steph still didn't speak.

I blundered on. 'I'm not justifying what I did, but I do think Ben benefited from having his dad while he was growing up.'

Evie did a big intake of breath next to me. I remembered too late that I was supposed to accept that we'd both been completely out of order.

'I mean, he has got a good relationship with Mal.' I realised how that sounded. 'And with you, of course.' This was why I never did confrontation. I was the ultimate people-pleaser. Anything else paralysed me.

I watched as Steph fought with herself. So many times, I'd seen her fly back at Mal, barely taking a second to process what he was saying before she dived in with her counter-argument. If it hadn't felt as though our friendship was hanging by a thread, I would've teased her.

I braced myself, hoping that our long history would mean Steph would go gently with me. The thought that she might take the opportunity to tell me some serious home truths to assuage her own pain made me want to flee out of her front door. 'For what it's worth, I know you will feel horribly betrayed, but the motivation behind it was never malicious.' I was choking up but I had to finish. 'You've been like a sister to me – much more than Wendy ever has – and I know you're hurt at the moment, and it's not much consolation that I never intended that, but when the dust has settled, I hope you'll consider being like a sister to me again.'

Evie passed me a great wodge of kitchen roll. 'It's true what she says, Steph. We never wanted to upset you. Speaking personally,

I was too much of a coward to tell you and then too chicken to stand up to Neil and continue our friendship when you called him out on being a bully. But I'm not a coward now. I wish desperately that we hadn't had all those years apart. I would find it tragic if we lost sight of what matters again.'

Steph's voice came out all tight and quivering. I wasn't sure if it was anger or an effort not to cry. 'And in your opinion, what does matter?'

Evie was quick off the mark. 'I think it matters *why* people tell the truth. There's this universal acceptance that telling the truth is always the right thing. And, of course, usually it is. But, equally, sometimes we withhold the truth precisely because sharing it would *hurt* the people we love. I didn't say anything about Mal and Wendy because I didn't know then whether being honest would do more harm than good.'

There was a challenge in Evie's voice. I wasn't entirely sure what she was getting at.

Steph glanced down. She wore her feelings so openly, I could almost see her brain picking its way through all the threads like a shuttle on a loom. 'Exactly as I've done with Gemma and Ben.'

Evie threw her hands up as though Steph had proved her point. 'Yes. You haven't lied to Ben to keep him out of the loop or to deceive him, you've done it to protect him. And other times you've been brutally honest when people didn't want to hear it, but there was no spite behind it.' Evie ran her fingers through her hair, making it stand on end. 'When you confronted Neil with the truth of him being a bully, you didn't do that to hurt me, to ruin my life, did you? You were trying to stick up for me.' Evie did her lovely half-smile. 'I realised that a little late in the day.'

Steph stood quietly for a moment, then her shoulders relaxed. 'I think we're too old for this "he said, she said" toing and froing. We're sixty. On the grounds that I'm probably not going to live long enough to make any more friends that I'm going to keep for thirty-five years, I'm going to apply the rule of one major fuck-up allowed every three decades of friendship. So you're allowed another one when we're eighty-five. How does that sound?'

Only Steph could have come up with a face-saving rule like that, but I loved her for her ingenuity.

'Shall we kiss and make up?' she asked.

She opened her arms to me and I melted into her, so relieved to be forgiven that I didn't do my usual holding back.

She whispered in my ear, 'I do love you.'

And then she was hugging Evie, and telling her that she'd only let us off because she'd be selling the house soon and she needed our help.

Evie was laughing and saying, 'I am the expert at packing the car for the dump.'

And there, in the smouldering remains of my life, flickered the first tiny ember of hope.

STEPH

Three years later

I was feeling the pressure of having forced everyone out of their comfort zone. Teresa had looked horrified when I produced the tickets to the Sing Out the Summer Festival with such a flourish, as though she would much rather have had a gift box of pâtés with a selection of farmhouse chutneys than a weekend in a tepee trying to recapture our youth. Or, as she said, 'The youth I never had.' I loved her for putting on a brave face, while no doubt mentally pencilling in a colleague to uncrack her back the second we returned.

Evie was a bit more enthusiastic. 'Wow, a tepee! I've never slept in one of those before.'

I extolled the virtues of the camp beds, the electricity, the luxury showers and decent toilets. However, no matter how much I banged on about us all needing a bit of adventure, I had the sense of trying to revive a bag of rocket past its sell-by date. The truth was, since I'd moved to Whitstable, just a couple of streets away from Evie, with Teresa coming to stay most weekends, we'd become a bit lazy about doing anything other than walking Noel and Gladys on the beach and having dinner together.

I'd said as much to Gemma, who'd nudged Ben and said, 'We'll come with you and bring the girls if they don't want to go, won't we?'

Ben had laughed. 'You're on your own with that one. I'm not a man cut out for camping and communal loos.' He'd leant in and kissed her on the cheek. 'Nothing less than a four-poster bed and rose petals on the pillow for you.'

She'd batted him away, but there was an ease, a lightness between them that relieved my guilt about everything I hadn't told him. In all but my deepest moments of self-doubt, I assuaged my conscience by reminding myself that a mother's duty was to protect her child, whatever form that took.

As the festival drew closer, I did manage to drum up some of the excitement I'd hoped for. There was a flurry of who was going to take what, and although we teased her for rocking the grandma-on-the-loose look, Evie's shopping bag on wheels seemed the perfect solution for trolleying in all our booze. 'Don't you knock it. It's brilliant for carting around all my photography gear. You'll be queuing up for a massage at Teresa's clinic when we get back after hauling your rucksack around, never mind the "can't live without" fridge.'

I'd loftily declared that we were way too old to be drinking warm white wine and had invested in a camping fridge especially for the occasion. The one detail I'd overlooked was that we would be parking miles away from the entrance and that we would be caught in a slow-moving crocodile of people half our age who had obviously nailed this festival-going malarkey in the decades since we'd last been to one. We staggered along under the weight of our extra blankets in case it was chilly at night. I kept tripping over the gardening trolley that I was using to carry my fridge. Meanwhile, the youngsters pushed wheelbarrows piled high with sleeping mats, camping chairs and wellies without breaking a sweat.

However, far more devastating than not being the coolest hippies on the ageing block was the fact that there'd been a ban on glass bottles. Short of drinking six bottles of champagne or dragging our stash a mile and a half back to the car, there was only one thing for it. I turned to Evie. 'Try and smuggle it through anyway. They're not checking everybody. If they stop you, we'll just have to take it back.'

Evie pulled a face. 'I can't do that. They might bar me from the whole festival.'

I nudged her. 'Go on, you can do it.'

'I can't. You're talking to the woman who can't even put her empty coffee cup in someone's wheelie bin when I come up from the beach.'

It was an undeniable truth that our strongest traits had become more pronounced, although, to be fair, without Paul, Teresa's tendencies towards coupon clipping and 'I'd better bring my umbrella just in case' had diminished.

My desire to get my own way, however, had not. 'We are hardly likely to start smashing bottles over people's heads.'

Teresa surprised me by saying, 'Steph, let's hide behind those cars over here, and divide up the booze so if one of us gets stopped, we don't lose it all. Evie, you keep a place in the queue.'

Evie still looked doubtful. It became a matter of principle to prove to her that sixty-four-year-old me could still break out the naughty. 'Not dead yet' was reverberating around my brain, as though sneaking a supply of Moët past the guys who were probably doing the job for a free backstage pass would somehow return me to a state of rebellious youth.

Teresa and I nipped behind a car and shared out the bottles. I shoved the camping fridge at Evie. 'Here. You take this and follow me through, but not right behind me. Teresa, you join that queue and pretend you're not with us.'

I waited until a gorgeous girl in purple tie-dye leggings and long curly blonde hair snaking down her back was stopped. While the guy pulled a bottle of wine out of her backpack and she smiled and flirted, trying to argue her case, I scuttled on past, trying not to clank. Middle age was a nightmare for knees but a blessing for invisibility. I waited two hundred metres further on, as chuffed with myself as I used to be when I snatched the contract for a popular hotel from under a competitor's nose. I didn't dare look round to see where Teresa was. And then suddenly she was rattling towards me, her face glowing with pleasure. 'Woohoo! Cheers!'

We found our way to our tepee and chose the beds.

Evie suddenly stood stock still in the middle of the tent. 'I've just had a memory about when we went to Norfolk.'

'Oh my God, is this going to show me in a terrible light?' I asked.

Evie laughed. 'Not at all. If anything, it vindicates you.'

'Oh brilliant, that doesn't happen very often. Usually people are dragging up all sorts of stuff I'd forgotten about to make me feel bad.'

She plonked down onto the camp bed. 'Sorting out who is going to sleep where made me remember driving to Norfolk, being so stressed, because I knew that Neil would be really unhappy if we didn't have the best room. I can't believe I put up with him for so long. I wish I'd been brave enough to recognise it at the time, but you did me a huge favour in calling him out on his behaviour.'

There was a beat of silence. One of the new-found skills that I was still fine-tuning was being gracious. I nearly managed it. 'I wish you pair had done likewise!' But ninety-seven per cent of my comment was good-natured. We were all trying to accept that we make different choices as we get older, simply because we know more. I wanted to believe that they were wiser choices, but sometimes I thought they were just different, not better, just from a more long-lived perspective.

Teresa always shuffled awkwardly whenever I referred to Wendy and Mal.

'I'm only joking. Let's just enjoy the weekend. This is the most carefree we've been in years.'

I meant it as a way to smooth the conversation over, to stop Teresa worrying about whether I had totally forgiven her. But as the words left my mouth, I realised they were true. We were at a stage of our lives when we were young and healthy enough to do whatever we wanted, apart from taking up the hurdles as a hobby. Old enough to have a bit of money behind us that we didn't have to make our own wine. Lucky enough to have each other as friends. Friends that we'd known over so many years that presenting an image of how we'd like to be perceived, rather than who we actually were, was out of the question.

It was astonishing how quickly Evie and I had slotted back into the rhythm of a friendship even though we'd such a long break from each other, as though the foundations and walls had been standing sturdy all these years, patiently waiting for the roof to be replaced.

But Teresa was the one that had surprised me the most. Since Paul died, it was almost as though now she had lost the person she loved the most, she was free to take more risks, because the worst had already happened. She'd debated forever about setting up her own physio practice, but Paul, who was very financially cautious, had talked her out of it once Amelia was born. Within twelve months of his death, she had rented a little place near town, which had gained a momentum all of its own – 'Typical me, just getting started when I should be retiring. Hopefully, I'll be able to hand over to Amelia by the time I'm ready.' It was a source of great pride to her that Amelia was managing to study part-time for a degree in physiotherapy.

As the weekend wore on, we all had a sense that we'd both lived and learnt a lot – that life was tough, that people let you down, but that there was always joy to be had. As Teresa sat on a scrubby patch of grass tucking into a tofu burger with ginger kombucha sauce, she laughed. 'Paul wouldn't recognise me if he could see me now. He was always "Where's the meat?"' A flicker of sadness passed over her face as the memory washed in and away again. Her expression brightened. 'I've never really been that interested in seeing live bands, but James Bay was brilliant. I'd never heard of him before. I loved it when he sang all that stuff about people being themselves in a relationship.'

'Be honest, your first proper festival has turned out much better than you expected.'

She nodded. 'It has. It's fantastic. I wouldn't ever have come to a festival if Paul was still alive. We thought they'd be full of druggies.'

'I'm pretty sure a few little spliffs will have made it past the sniffer dogs. Maybe we can do a cheeky purchase?'

Teresa's mouth dropped open. 'I'm not going to start taking drugs at sixty-seven!'

Her outrage made me laugh hysterically. 'I was having you on. Just testing to see where your boundaries are. I mean, we've had the naked man blunder past the tent playing a bagpipe, Evie's got properly attached to those fairy wings – they suit you – we've drunk cider while listening to a giraffe reading us poetry, you've gone all hippy-dippy with the tie-dye top and the glitter transfers…'

Teresa put her fingers up to the sparkly butterflies on her cheeks and smiled.

'Maybe we'll pluck up courage to go topless in the women's bar,' Evie said.

'No, there I draw the line. There's no way I'm swinging these baguettes wild and loose,' I replied. 'With age comes serious scaffolding.'

Teresa shrugged. 'It's probably quite liberating. Good practice for getting your kit out for a new man.'

Evie and I stared at her. 'Have you met someone?'

'No, of course not. I haven't ruled it out though. One day. Is that awful of me to say that? I feel guilty for even thinking it. But I loved being part of a couple. I'd like to think that I could be again. And take with me the things I've discovered about myself now, not just be the person I was with Paul.'

I admired her optimism. I'd briefly flicked through a few dating sites at the men brandishing pythons, posing in their cycling Lycras and profiles that opened with 'I like wrestling and can drive a car, though I don't own one any more because my wife took it…' and decided that Gladys and I were a fine team and fate would have to show up in a tiara and sequins for me to be tempted back into having to consider someone else on a permanent basis. 'I don't really miss having a husband at all, though I wouldn't say no to reaping the benefits of a jolly divorcé who's been housetrained by someone else.' As I said it, I realised that I didn't even think about Mal much any more, just a few twinges of regret on high days and holidays when as much as I fought against it, I couldn't dispel the idea that we should all be together.

Evie popped the cork on the champagne, trying to smother the noise in case the glass-bottle police were lurking outside our tent. We raised our plastic mugs in a toast. 'To us. To friendship. To finding men… if we want them!'

And with that, we headed off to see Kool & The Gang, confident that this was one gig when we'd be able to out-sing the twenty-year-olds. We took our chairs to stake our pitch, but I'd told the other two I wasn't going to tolerate any sitting down. 'We're dancing from the second they come on!'

They didn't let me down. Apart from a slight resistance in my hips and a reluctant gratitude to the memory foam insoles in my trainers, it could have been one of our weekends away when the boys were young and I'd made everyone get up and dance after dinner.

As I looked around me, all the people my age were singing away, the years rolling back, with smiles flickering across their faces as the songs we'd sung as young mums swept us back to times when we didn't know what life held for us but we had blind faith it would be good.

There was a group of lads next to us, younger than Ben, who knew all the words and every last drumbeat of music. Evie, who'd taken to drinking organic cider with quite some gusto on the grounds that she was convinced no additives would mean no hangover, wagged her finger at them. 'Hey, this is our music. Hands off it. How do you even know all the words?'

One of the lads with floppy dark curly hair and enough swagger that he'd have definitely been on my radar forty years ago said, 'My mum's favourite band. I was brought up on it. It wasn't a birthday in our house if you didn't have "Celebrate!" and "Get Down On It!" blaring out.'

Evie patted him on the arm. 'Your mum has got very good taste.'

The boy laughed and gave her a wink that suggested although she was way out of his age range, he could appreciate the potential. With her cropped hair and striking eyes, Evie could still turn heads. I chased away the mood-lowering thought that she'd wasted all that vibrant beauty and youth on a bloke who wanted an obedient wife as a backdrop to showcase his brilliance. This evening was not a time for dwelling on things we could not change. Instead we all giggled like schoolgirls at a disco and competed with the boys for dancing enthusiasm. Even Teresa was getting sucked in, working the sexy hips like a professional.

'What took you so long? You're a great dancer.'

She did an extra little jig. 'Got pigeonholed early on as the shy one, the daughter who didn't like drawing attention to herself.' She stopped, clearly not wanting to complete the comparison and mention Wendy.

'I'm not going to whizz off on my broom and start frying up toad teeth if you say her name. I expect you to have a relationship with her. She's your sister.' I paused. 'Bad luck.'

Teresa laughed with relief. 'That's why we are so fortunate to choose our friends.'

And right there, right then, with 'Ladies Night' making it feel as though everyone in the whole field was just loving life, that for a few hours we were being the most joyful people we knew how to be, I wouldn't have changed a thing. Maybe we'd find new husbands. Maybe we'd sell up and buy a big house together, starting on the whisky at 4 p.m. and flirting with gardeners half our age. Maybe we'd take it in turns to cook Sunday lunch and promise to tell each other when we had whiskers growing out of our chins. But these women. What rare jewels nestling in the rubble of life. We'd made mistakes, we'd frayed our friendships, we'd dented and damaged the trust between us. But we'd made it through. We'd clung on to that rare bond that starts in a fortuitous crossing of paths and grows through shared experience and indefinable chemistry.

Adventures lay ahead.

A LETTER FROM KERRY

Dear Reader,

I want to say a huge thank you for choosing to read *Other People's Marriages.* If you did enjoy it, and want to keep up to date with all my latest releases, just sign up at the following link. Your email address will never be shared and you can unsubscribe at any time.

www.bookouture.com/kerry-fisher

The little seed of an idea for this book was triggered by my daughter, my youngest child, going to university last year. After twenty years of having children at home, I – and many of my friends – were looking backwards at how motherhood had defined us for much of the last two decades, and forwards, at how our lives might change from now on. There was a certain sense of nostalgia for how easily we could solve our children's problems when they were little, alongside regret for the things we had hoped to do but didn't – I always think this is beautifully summed up by ABBA's 'Slipping Through My Fingers'. But, undeniably, there was also a level of excitement about what we might do or discover about ourselves now we didn't have the day-to-day responsibility of children.

Added into that mix was watching my daughter fly the nest with the confidence of youth that 'it will all turn out all right'. That spontaneity, that flexibility to change plans at the last minute, to live in the moment, to dismiss the need to know where you'll be eating/staying/sleeping as mere detail. It set me thinking about how we often become less adventurous, more risk-averse as we get older. In our twenties, my friends and I travelled around Europe with rucksacks the size of a handbag, slept on beaches, railway stations and in the homes of random strangers we met on trains (I know – madness!). I flew directly from a wedding in Ireland to Australia as though I was hopping on a bus to the supermarket. Fast-forward thirty years and we're all leaving home 'in plenty of time' to catch a train to London and buying our tickets in advance. I wanted to examine how that happens, how feisty young women become so much more cautious as they get older – whether it's through responsibility, lack of freedom, reliance on a husband or a gradual erosion of confidence. And how, sometimes, unexpected events can give us a renewed sense of adventure when we realise we can survive so much more than we thought.

I also wanted to look at how life veering away from its expected path can be a catalyst for a total re-evaluation of who and what matters. Whether it's divorce, illness, death or any of the many life events that can blindside us, I was keen to explore how positive things can come from these catastrophic experiences. A few years ago, my son had cancer (I write about this in my non-fiction memoir, *Take My Hand*) and I drew on my memories of this time when I was writing about Steph's dented certainty about life. She'd had the proof that bad luck could be hers. In these moments, friendships and relationships are put under the spotlight in a way that they aren't usually and it's not always the people you expect who step up to help. When the immediate crisis has passed, there is a reckoning as you can no longer escape the knowledge of who has your back and who doesn't – as happened with Steph and Mal.

Finally, I wanted to pay tribute to friendship between women, especially those friends with whom there is an indefinable chemistry that elevates them to 'friends of the heart'. How chance encounters with strangers at toddler groups, the school gates or work evolve from 'people you like' to those deep and unconditional friendships is still a mystery to me, but when it happens, it is one of life's true treasures – however long you've been apart, the months and years fade away as soon as you are together again.

For the first time, I have taken artistic licence with dates. I've set the final festival in 2022 in the world I hope will exist by then, when we will all be free to meet, gather and hug as much as we want to. Forgive me, but it was simply too depressing to end the book with the three friends sitting about forlornly with their masks on. One of the great advantages of fiction is being able to write a happy ending, but I sincerely hope we get one in real life too.

I say this every time, but one of the biggest privileges of my job is receiving messages from people who've enjoyed my books. Sometimes, my novels have prompted readers to share their own very personal stories with me. The unflinching honesty of some of these messages that you entrust me with is humbling. Thank you.

I hope you loved *Other People's Marriages* and would be very grateful if you could write a review if you did. I'd love to hear what you think, and it makes a real difference to helping new readers to discover one of my books for the first time.

I love hearing from my readers – you can get in touch on my Facebook page, through Twitter, or my website. Whenever I hear from readers, I am reminded why I love my job – your messages bring sunshine whatever the weather.

Thank you so much for reading,
Kerry Fisher

kerryfisherauthor

@KerryFSwayne

www.kerryfisherauthor.com

ACKNOWLEDGEMENTS

I feel quite humbled by how lucky I've been to work with such an incredible team of people at Bookouture. I say this every time, but it never gets old – it is an absolute privilege to work with people for whom you have the utmost respect. Ever since I wrote *The Woman I Was Before*, I'm nervous about saying I am #blessed, but I really am! My editor, Jenny Geras, is brilliant at understanding what I want to write and pinpointing what needs to happen to make sure I get there. Special thanks to Alexandra Holmes (the fount of knowledge on all things grammatical) and the production team for making sure my books are in the best possible shape. And to Kim, Noelle and Sarah for working so hard to bring the books to the attention of as many readers as possible.

I'm always incredibly grateful to my agent, Clare Wallace. Cheerleader, problem-solver and brainstormer extraordinaire. Lucky me. Thanks also to the rights team at Darley Anderson – Mary, Kristina, Georgia and Chloe – who are brilliant at getting my books out into the wider world.

Like many of us, I've been working from home more than usual. This has presented some challenges – two adult children, my husband and I all competing for Wi-Fi, as well as the peace and space to think! Thank you for muddling through with me. If we had to be in lockdown, I'm so glad it was with you three. Strangely, I even feel a bit bereft not to have the constant refrain of 'What's for dinner?' and 'Where's the meat?' punctuating my writing life (though I did manage to appropriate the latter question to recycle into this story). I have to say a special thank you to Steve for being a brilliant husband (and not at all like Mal) when it was our turn to put the 'for better, for worse' to the test. Writing this book has had the unexpected bonus of making me appreciate that all over again. I hope that goes some way to compensating for all the times I shout down the stairs for tea.

Thank you to Emma Edgar for generously sharing her knowledge about heart attacks and cardiac arrest – and for stopping me confusing the two. Also to Marika Gustafsson for fact-checking my chapter about Finnish ice-swimming – I was so lucky to count her among my readers! Sarah MacIntyre was a treasure for keeping me on the straight and narrow about possible roles in the travel business. Thanks also to the Norfolk Wildlife Trust for checking my birdwatching chapter.

Finally – a huge thank you to the bloggers and readers who buy, review and recommend my books – and especially anyone who takes the time to contact me personally. Those messages make my day.

Made in United States
North Haven, CT
02 April 2024